SECOND

CARLA

A novel
by
Mark Barry

Carla Second Edition
Published by Green Wizard 2013

First published in 2012 by Green Wizard
Green Wizard, Southwell, Nottinghamshire
Greenwizard62@blogspot.com

Cover design by Dark Dawn Creations

ISBN-13: 978-1492159445
ISBN-10: 1492159441

Dedicated to

Jim Thompson
RIP

Acknowledgements

Thanks are due to my editor, Mary Ann Bernal, whose tireless shifts with the red pen and reading glass were a credit to her profession. The book may not be radically different to the first edition, but it is definitely aesthetically neater, repetitions have been erased and it is a much tidier read.

This is a book that can fit into a handbag, a purse or a jacket pocket, and it is the first book Green Wizard has created, which fits that criteria. One more thing about Mary "MAB" Ann Bernal. I feel like a better writer after her machinations with the crimson eraser. Thank you, Mary Ann

Dark Dawn Creations created the cover from my preliminary draft. It is designed to be a seventies paperback book, an NEL or a Pan, and there are few covers like it in Independent Literature.

The cover model is a good friend of mine, Laura Jackson, who has Carla's colouring to a tee, though I met her six months AFTER I wrote the book. Recognition is due to the genial Kirsty Weedon for her involvement in developing the cover design.

I am grateful for the readers who took the time to review the first edition and made the initial six months of the book such a fun time.

I would also like to acknowledge Ngaire Elder who markets this book as if it were her own and who has always been a great fan.

From Me, Carla, John, and all the characters - we hope this book graces your bookshelves with appropriate decorum.

Novels by Mark Barry

Carla
Hollywood Shakedown
Kid Atomic
The Illustrated Woman
The Ritual
Ultra Violence
Violent Disorder

Green Wizard Anthology

Reality Bites

Frontispiece

Hello, everyone.

My name is Jonathan Dexter.
You can call me John.
Johnny, if we get to like each other.

I am forty two years old.

Some people, including one or two genuinely clever psychiatrists, consider me totally insane.

Following an all-inclusive three-year stay at an exclusive psychiatric resort, I moved to the prosperous middle England town of Wheatley Fields.

There I met Carla, a beautiful twenty year old student studying Wildlife Conservation and working behind a bar to pay her tuition fees.

In the short time we spent together, the two of us formed a relationship. It was one of the best experiences of my whole life.

Sadly, it all went wrong.

Very, very wrong, indeed.

This is our story.

Chapter I: Little Fluffy Clouds

Eight pubs in Wheatley Fields and sadly for me, the pub nearest my flat isn't the best of them. I wish it were. Nothing like a friendly pub just outside your house. You don't even have to put a coat on to visit. You could trot over in your slippers if you were so inclined.

This pub is substandard. Rank beer, unwelcoming regulars, an omniscient smell of urine just above the level of perception, as if the cleaner regularly waters the carpet with her own piss. The unwelcoming bit I'm okay with. Never been much of a mixer and you'll see why over the course of the book, so I don't care whether people are all over me like a rash or whether they shun me like a leper. Other Incomers have not been so lucky.

A huge cathedral with three steeples dominates the town, called as you might expect, The Three Steeples. As a rule, in order to get a social life in the town, you have to have been born within sight of those impressive towers. General exceptions to this tend to be anyone with money, celebrity (sport, arts), a status job (Architect, Solicitor, Estate Agent), or looks. If you can bring any of those attributes to the party, your popularity is assured. Indeed, if you're handsome, rich and have a status job, they'll be queuing up in the supermarket to shake your hand by the cold shelf. I moderated that sentence, by the way, in case any of you readers are of a sensitive disposition. If you don't tick those boxes, you'd best enjoy your own company because you are going to be spending an awful long time on your own.

Time has frozen in this pub. There is a man who has used the same stool (nearest the ale taps) since Edward Heath. Woe betides anyone who takes his seat. The Wheatley Fields Tennis Club meet there. Not even its own members like the Wheatley Fields Tennis Club. A pair of old boys turn up at 7pm on Wednesday nights. Regular as clockwork. They drink three pints, hardly say a word to each other, and leave promptly at 9pm.

They've been doing this for twenty-seven years. Try to engage them in conversation. Go on. I dare you.

I'll tell you the name of the pub, and you can travel up and have a pint. Attempt a friendly social greeting and see what happens. I tried one night shortly after my discharge. Their response wasn't for the squeamish. I think I visited the pub twice after that. Just for a couple of early evening Thor's Hammers and the odd golden bag of honey roast peanuts. I crossed the threshold no more than five or six times. Nowhere near enough to make a dent in the social ether. In reality, it was not surprising that I didn't make an instant social impression: I'm not handsome. I don't have a job (but I have money), and I'd just been freed from a three years all inclusive sojourn at a mental hospital six miles outside Charlestown.

Even the staff didn't acknowledge me, and they're paid to do that, so giving up the ghost, I tried another pub, and another, and another, before I settled on The Saddler's Arms.

You see, I like my beer. I also like to get out of my flat. I spend far too much time on my own as it is. Six years of incarceration (with a short break) can do that to a man. Either you love your own four walls or they remind you of gaol. I'm the latter. Besides, I'm doing my bit to preserve the culture. The pub is a British institution and not enough people bother in today's day and age. Not since the fag ban, pints priced like Scandinavia, the duty escalator and the advent of Me.com. No wonder pubs shut at the rate of one a day.

Visiting the pub is something I enjoy. I like it. I've always done it, and I think - luckless incarcerations notwithstanding - that I shall always do it. Of course, had those people in the pub closest to my flat been more welcoming and inviting, I might never have reached The Saddler's Arms, and I might never have met Carla.

I saw her for the first time in late January 2012. I'd been in the community for about six weeks by the time we met, and I had been adjusting well. Three years' worth of intense psychotherapy and an unrelenting regime of brutal medication had helped my discharge case. Some of the medication had been experimental. Some of it you'll hear about in the papers one day. One treatment I was prescribed makes ECT look like cuddle therapy.

My father had supplied me with a flat in the town, just like he did the last twice; a brace of unfortunate misadventures in Abingdon and Harrogate. The authorities at the hospital had signed my release docket and wrapped my clothes in the metaphorical brown paper bag. The Exit Committee told me they didn't wish to see me again, and they slapped me on the back. My Community

Psychiatric Nurse, Charlotte Brubaker-Wilmslow, visited me weekly and so far, she had been delighted with my progress. My Psychiatrist Link Worker, the magnificent Doctor Plunkett, had also visited twice, and we'd enjoyed two long conversations.

Therefore, when I walked into The Saddler's Arms that night, I felt calm and relaxed, and the prognosis was rosy.

And there she was.

Yes.

There she was.

The Saddler's Arms is an old Coachman's stopping point on the way to Charlestown, one of three old coach houses in the town, the other being The Barrels Inn on the Oxblood Road and The Saladin Hotel on the High Street itself. Open since 1734 (the year that King George II led the British into battle at Dettingen in Bavaria; incidentally, the last time a British King did something so reckless and noble); the pub has an unmistakable ambience, decent beer, and it is always warm. For three hundred years, it had stood on the corner of Steeple Street and Eastway. Soaked in atmosphere, heritage, horses, leather, smoky fires, tradition and proper ale, The Saddler's had the reputation of being the best pub in the town. I had been told by one of my few acquaintances that each month, the landlord purchases one barrel of a special Hereford Scrumpy, which is something of a destroyer of heads.

One pint and you're chilled.

Two pints and you're animated.

Three, you're on your back looking for the face of Jesus in the cracks in the ceiling.

On that first night, I was keen to try a couple of pints, but by the time I set eyes on her, I had lost interest in drinking, smoking, eating, or thinking.

She hit me hard, dear reader. I cannot remember being hit so hard by a woman. And I had something of a history of being hit hard.

This was different. As she poured beer for an elderly gentleman in a ratty cloth cap, the foaming head seeping over both sides of his jug, I felt my emotions accelerate from nought to a hundred and twenty in ten seconds. Raven black hair, abundant and lustrous, brimming with life, shoulder length, tousled fashionably, that density, that mass, the gift of the young. Something naturally fresh about her. Unpolluted, wholesome and unprocessed. A balanced face; mathematically proportional; a flawless equation. Each component in its right place, each x, each y, each bracket, and each symbol squared, precisely as it is supposed to be. She wore a milk chocolate coloured vest, which showed off her lightly tanned arms and shoulders; fatless, muscled arms, an absence of bingo wings, fibulation, ridges and scars (which you wouldn't expect from a girl this age, admittedly). Visible, crimson-red bra straps. A big watch circumnavigated her wrist with a plastic strap, fashionably kitsch. Denim skirt with random bleach splatters and fashionably frayed hem. A pair of white flip-flop style sandals, which displayed her ivory-shaded feet perfectly. My unconscious iceberg was already picturing long nights on the sofa stroking those feet. Absorbing brown eyes the colour of horse chestnuts.

(Man, those eyes.)

It had happened.

It had come back.

I had gone from a state of pleasant, unconcerned ambivalence to manic obsession in two minutes flat.

Fucking hell.

Shocked, I went outside. Stood opposite the leper colony of smokers underneath their heated canopy. Pretended to tie my shoelaces. Sat down in the darkness on a plastic chair underneath overhanging bushes dripping with raindrops.

This was a dangerous situation for me. I remembered all the feelings inside me as I sat. Recollected their power and experienced their intensity.

It was insane.

My feelings were mad.

I knew it.

Already, it felt like I had known her for ten years and we had been married for eight of them.

I suppose what I should have done was contact Doctor Plunkett.

In hindsight, that was exactly what I should have done.

Do I regret not contacting him? His mobile number is in my contacts. I could have texted him, and he would have rescued me like a shot. He would have dragged me from The Saddler's as if I was a hostage in some far-off Embassy, and he was a trooper in the SAS. My New Balance would hardly have touched the floor.

He would have saved me, I know.

You see, I shouldn't have those feelings about girls like Carla.

They're not healthy for me. They're too intense, too furious, and they overwhelm me like quicksand. I've had those feelings before, many times, and they never work.

I'm hyperemotional. I suffer from something grotesque. I know that.

Something untold inside me. Something they have to work at to uncover. Something buried, a rancid, foetid plague pit in my subconscious. I should have walked and never, ever, ever, gone back into The Saddler's Arms.

I held the mobile phone in my hand. I scrolled down to Doctor Plunkett's number, and I hovered over the green phone symbol.

(Save me!)

I shouldn't be in the same time zone as women like Carla.

("Can I be so bold, John, as to make a suggestion?" Doctor Plunkett had said, two weeks ago.

"Fire away, doc," I had replied jovially as I was wont to do with my mentor.

"You need to be going on dates with women to whom you are scarcely attracted. Can you understand that?"

"Is that right?" I said, knowing each therapist I'd ever encountered had suggested much the same thing. "I see where you're coming from."

"You don't have the best track record with women to whom you are attracted."

"That's true," I replied.

"Keep it friendly. Keep it low key. Try to keep your feelings under tight control."

"I think I will, doc," I replied. "Don't need any more fuss in my life, do I?" I said, passive and accommodating as they teach you to be at the mental hospital.)

And I meant it. Truly. I meant it.

Until that night, when I saw Carla serving beer behind the bar of The Saddler's Arms.

I should have walked away. But I didn't. Man, I just couldn't do it. I had never felt anything like the feelings I had for Carla, and what is the point in living without feeling like that?

Alive. I felt alive.

If you don't feel alive, you must be dead.

It's logic. You're just an Existence Machine.

You're just an Oxygen Recycler. A shambling, unfeeling, *zuvembie.*

I looked up into the night sky and saw a half-moon illuminating the town.

It shone next to three or four wispy clouds, seemingly travelling in two directions simultaneously, a motion parallax.

I focused on Doctor Plunkett's mobile phone number. Stared at the gate to the road outside, the road home. The road to safety.

Inevitably, I looked at the doorway back to the pub.

There was only one option for me.

There had only ever been one option.

I walked back inside. Found a bar stool. She came over. I couldn't even look at her without blinking.

Oh, her essence.

"What can I get for you?" She said, all wind-dried, coal black tresses, potent brown eyes, cherry cherry lips and a beatific look spawned deep in the innocent cosmos.

I told her, tongue-tied.

She sounds just like the girl from Orb's *Little Fluffy Clouds*, that airhead timbre, that lacquered, burnished, breathless kiss of a voice.

(Leave the pub, go home and hide. Start drinking up the Haywain with all the old boys and the beardy weirdies. Not here. Not with her. My mental state...my innards...my balance...I want to leavebutcannotmoveIwanttostayhereforeverIcannotmove.)

"That's delicious beer. I like that one. I won't be a minute," she said, a voice coated in all the ointments, which have ever existed, millions of years of oils and unguents and...

I thanked her. My stomach did a triple axle and a forward roll.

Next to me, the regulars in - what I came to know as - the Pop Side, were playing a game in which they had to guess the year of a particularly tacky Number One hit.

A curly-haired fellow, thick set, chubby, in a lime-green shirt, cords, and Wellies seemed to be deliberately getting answers wrong, a kind of surreal comedy sketch. His accent was top notch English Hunting set, a loud confident voice style I recognised from my upbringing. A woman who might have been Welsh guffawed at everything he said. The Pop Side enclosed a raucous, yet relaxed atmosphere: A safe familiar place where they all knew each other, with all the living room intimacy that generated. I didn't know any of the music, and I didn't care, because I was watching Carla work. I didn't make it obvious - I picked up today's newspaper from the rack and peered over the top - and when she returned, she offered me a look.

That glance.

I don't think that anyone had ever been so pleased to see me.

I paid and took a sip of the drink. As I did so, the comedian chortling and tipsy, propped himself at the bar next to me. I could smell his aftershave, but I didn't recognise it. He leaned on the bar with both hands and gestured to Carla.

That was how I knew her name. He called her Carla.

"Pint of Baboon and a glass of your very best medium dry white please, Carla," he ordered, chortling away.

Carla.

He glanced at me. "Did you hear that?" He said, proud of himself. "Soft Cell, I said. How can it be Soft Cell in the nineties? Arseholes! He was bloody brown bread at that point, the dirty puff! And they all *believed* me! Soft Cell. The nineties..." he shook his head one more time and said with a sigh. "Oh, I'm mental, me. Absolutely fucking mental."

I grinned at him.

"Me, too," I said, under my breath.

Chapter 2: The Insanity Industry

Insane isn't a word you'll hear in the treatment room of your friendly neighbourhood psychotherapist. I have to be careful with my choice of words. For some reason, professionals working in the Insanity Industry don't like using the word and because of that, they've invented a thousand alternative ways of describing it. Many more politically correct ways exist to describe my mental condition, but to me, none fits as snugly.

Insane. When you think about it, it's my mental condition, thank you muchly, and I can describe it exactly how I want to. These proclamations come from a psychiatric manual coming soon called the *Diagnostic and Statistics Manual* (Version Five).

Four previous versions are available. It is likely to come on the market at over a thousand pages long, including indices and appendices. Psychiatrists treat the DSM series like fire-and-brimstone preachers treat the Bible. It contains every diagnostic mental condition known to the insanity industry. Aetiology. Symptoms. Comparisons. Relationships. Possible treatments. If you visit a psychiatrist, or someone of that ilk, they will possess this portentous tome. Don't be surprised if you see them looking sneakily down into their opened top drawer when your self-descriptions threaten to baffle them.

You won't find the word insane inside, more's the pity. It has such a ring to it.

By the way, much of the time I come across as quite jovial. That's one of the advantages of being insane - the multiplicity. I have to tell you that the majority of the time, my lack of sanity is a pain in the arse. Imprisoned and/or incarcerated by court order. Probed and dissected by an array of mental health gurus and psychiatric practitioners. The drugs they give you. The treatments. Ever had ECT? Electro-convulsive therapy? AKA Shock treatment. I've endured that three times, on three different recommendations at three different points of my life. Bonce shock experts drug you to the gills and pass an electric current/pulse across your temples. Voltage anything from 100 to 450. Psychiatrists can't get enough ECT yet because of *Cuckoo's Nest*; it has a shocking reputation if you'll pardon the pun. Undeservedly so, according to head shrinkers of my acquaintance. It is a magnificent cure for depression - possibly the best - yet no one has any idea how it works.

Hah! I'll tell you how it works for nothing - people pretend not to be depressed any more to avoid being shocked.

"Please, doc. Please. Don't shock me. I'll do anything. Look - I'm doing a Happy Dance. Cured, I'm cured. Just don't..."

No. Nothing jovial about ECT, nor some of the drugs they use - psychopharmacological cocktails that rip you inside out and send you bonkers. Even more so in my case.

Bonkers. Now *there's* a word you won't hear your Community Mental Health Worker use. Of all the tools at the Industry's disposal, the most miserable of all is psychotherapy. The groups. The endless talks. The endless questions. The endless exposition.

"Hi. I am John Dexter, and I am insane."

You know the opening epigram I used? In the frontispiece? Each session started like that after a while. It became my calling card. I must have told my life story to fifty professionals. I feel like a bloody Narcissist. Self-absorbers who live on Me.com would love a year in one of the country's hundred and eighty-three secluded mental institutions: Talk about themselves to their hearts content and be rewarded for it. One big Me Me Me session in those places. No wonder then, when confronted with yet another hour of pointless conversation with someone who is paid to listen, and who couldn't give a shit whether I lived or died, that I adopt a superficially jovial tone.

Some biographical detail.

(It's important, but if you want to get back to the narrative because you're a bit busy for some essential exposition, type in **Annoyed by the antics of the regulars** and you'll be back to the story.)

Okay. I come from a rich and successful family. Dot com and engineering money. Intermarriage with top civil servants. Media money. Tons of it. Cash flows like water in our clan, and you'd scarcely notice. Except me, of course. I'm the degenerate. I'm the black sheep. I'm the one they don't talk about or if they do talk about me, they talk about me in whispers. I'm the one who exists in the shadows. The one who lives in the hinterland between gossip and dark rumour as if I don't fundamentally exist. The dark one. The mad one. The mad ghost. The tragic failure.

(And we held out such great hope for John!)

Dark Matter.

All families have one and, unfortunately, I'm the one in the Dexter tribe. My relatives are all as sober as a clergyman's day out. Not a prescribed anti-depressant between them. Healthy as a family of Swedish athletes.

It's bloody unfair, it really is.

Obvious reasons why I'm insane are rarer than hen's teeth. I wasn't beaten. I wasn't abused. Mum didn't lock me in a cellar at the age of ten like hoary old Edmund Kemper III. I didn't get a bang on the head playing football. My mother didn't smoke. The family has no history of LSD use. Hippies don't exist in the family tree, nor speed-freak beatniks, sedated romantics, opiated Pre-Raphaelites or morphine-crazed literary tyros.

My grandparents are even saner than my parents. Their parents also.

A Ponzi scheme of sanity.

I'm told of a strange great uncle on my father's side who spoke to owls in the night as the moon beamed down into rustling trees, but he's now acclaimed as something of a brilliant naturalist.

No. There is no obvious reason why I am insane.

Of course, there IS my mother.

All that gubbins with my mother, bless her.

All that unfortunateness I'd best tell you about, but most of my therapeutic interventionists tell me that my interaction with mother is just not enough to explain my condition. It is a necessary, but not sufficient explanation, they say, in that wonderful academic phrase.

My father is a successful man.

He is the multi-millionaire software magnate, Peter Dexter. If you are in banking circles, you would have heard of him, and if you are in a particular arm of banking, you might even revere him. He made your life a lot easier back in the early days of computing. I don't understand what he did, but his software revolutionised the tri-cornered relationship between time zones, money and people. It made him millions and the money rolls in because of royalties. He's genial, urbane. Do you remember Stewart Grainger in all those old movies? *King Solomon's Mines*? *The Student Prince*? That's him. Tall, grey, a pinched nose. Immaculately turned out. You never see him in shorts on the beach. In the years I've known him, I've never seen him lose his temper. Man, he exemplifies that type of aristocratic English reserve that seems so old-fashioned. You can imagine him on the battlements sipping brandy in the First Afghan War while fifteen thousand Pathans hurtled down the Khyber Pass, his only action being to twirl his moustache. He never hit us. He never chastised us, despite testing my father's patience to melting point on many, many occasions.

It cost him a fortune to keep me in hospital. At least five grand a week. Close to three quarters of a million pounds it cost him to punish me for my sins. More expense for him on the outside. I won't be able to get a job, not after the last two times (my last boss was off sick for a year), so I'll have to live on dole money, but there's no way that my father would ever let one of his offspring live on dole money so I'll get an allowance.

Forty two and getting pocket money from my dad.

Dates will queue around the block.

My father thinks I drove my mother into the arms of another man because she could not love me enough. (My stepmother always tells people that. It's so disempowering.)

You see, my dad wanted ten kids, but why would someone like me want all that competition? Therefore, he thinks I bled my mother dry of emotion, of love, of care, of existence, until she reached the point of no return.

Met an oil man at a party in Holland Park, a Brazilian tycoon named Carlos. Ran off to Venezuela. Thus, breaking my dad's heart (as much as my father's heart is capable of breaking) and leaving me feeling even more worthless, unwanted and empty.

Do you know I've not seen my mother, Gloria, since I was thirteen? Mum sees my brother twice a year, but she won't see me. I don't even get a cheap Christmas card. I don't know how I feel about that now, you know - time is a healer and other clichés - but boy, I was devastated at the time. I look back at her departure and realise it was my own fault.

My father was right. I never left her alone for a single second, you know.

I gave it to her big time. Provoked her to the point of screaming. She would strike me, and I would look at her with tears in my eyes and scream at her that she didn't love me, will never love me, and had never loved me and after, we would cuddle and cry together on her bed, and when we did, I was contented in those sumptuous feasts of intimacy.

Something like that would happen two, three times a week and in the end, it got to her. I burned her out. Burned her right out.

After, I didn't leave my room for months and my father had to send me to a Brighton crammer so I wouldn't fall behind in my education. He sent me to boarding school, but I hated the whole experience and I won't discuss it with you unless I have to. Hated, hated, hated it.

I'd shut every single one of the bastard places down, I would. I'll have to stop writing now because I'm getting all Bruce Banner thinking about it, and I must go away, calm down and recite my personal development mantras and carry out my restorative breathing exercises…

…

…

…

…

Okay, back. Sorry about that.

Naturally, what happened between mum and me was never going to happen between my stepmother, Francine, a Parisian banker my father met while working in Frankfurt. I tried to repeat the same behaviour, I must admit, but she was having none of it from minute one. Francine spotted me coming like a gazelle spots a hungry lion on the veldt and thus, she went to ground.

She hates me, I'm certain. I don't blame her. Her hatred of me doesn't hurt. It doesn't ignite my episodes. She's been consistent all the way through so I can deal with it. I hate myself. Why should I hate someone for hating me? It's not dissonant in any way. It's not a reaction formation. It's bloody perfectly understandable.

I am now *persona non grata* in the family. Particularly with my brother. Jesus, I love my younger brother, but boy, does he take some shit from me because he just cannot like me enough, he cannot respect me enough, he cannot think enough of me. I'll blast him, and I'll blast him. The last time, at that birthday party, he didn't accept my grovelling sorrow, and I haven't spoken to my brother in three years and three months. And four days, but who's counting? My stepsister, Sylvia, feels sorry for me. I understand that. I'd rather have her pity than love because it's safer that way for all of us. She visits me on occasion in a fit of piety and compassion. I'll give my brother-in-law one thing - he's always polite when we meet. I guess that's her influence. On the other hand, maybe it's because he's a Vicar.

I awe my nieces and nephews because I am so perceptibly strange to them. I am a creature of whispered notoriety in their eyes.

They saw what I did that night. They think I'm an Oh, My God Weirdo and Stuff. *Satan is his NBFF.*

I'm not bothered. I don't have much to do with kids and never have done. Don't understand them and don't particularly care for them, if

I'm being honest with you, dear reader, so they don't appear in the narrative much. I tell you all this because the story of Carla and I, for want of a better starting point, began at a party at my father's house in Hertfordshire three years and three months ago, a party in honour of my father's seventy eighth birthday. The only reason father invited me to the party at all, was because he loves me as I am his eldest son. The first born. I wasn't going to go that weekend because gatherings like that are generally over the top for me, that kind of family thing. I feel, you know, ten, and I always end up remorseful, sore, feeling like death and feeling as worthless as a chocolate penny without its shiny wrapper. It's just not worth it, but father wants his family with him, and I always feel obliged, so I give in. I'm the only single member of the family, and I feel awkward. I would hire an escort, but things go wrong in that situation and the world would know she was an escort, and I'd feel even worse. (I hired an escort for an important works event. That ended most dreadfully. Most dreadfully, indeed.)

I'm not going to go into the precise story of my father's party because it's painful and after all this time, I can't fully remember what happened. That's the adaptive function of memory. It fades over time allowing us to continue with our lives. Trauma fades into unconsciousness and God grants us oblivion.

I can genuinely only remember a few details.

Three hundred people attended, including every significant member of our family, and it was the most important party in our family history.

Three hundred people.

It's a big house. Tudor foundations, part of one of the Duke of Norfolk's estates in King Henry VIII's time, at the time of the Dissolution of the Monasteries and the institution of the Church of England. It's set in five hundred acres. You can wander in the gardens for a day and not retrace your steps.

You see, there was this girl called Nina. No one knows who invited her, no one knows why she was at the party, but boy, did she help it go with a bang. She was the hottest, just the hottest. She made a beeline for me. She shouldn't have done that because just when I was getting excited, she made a beeline for someone else, right at the stroke of midnight.

The Masked Ball. The Masque of the Red Death. Ducks lining up in a row.

She spent three hours with me. Three hours at my own father's birthday party. Three hours, I was like a normal person. A partner sipping gin and tonic. Kiddies in the play areas outside kicking balls about on the croquet lawn. Sitting down to dinner together. She was stunning. Absolutely stunning. We danced to the string quartet and the way she felt to me…

…her perfume…

…her lips…

…

…

…whispered in my ear…

…perfume…

…shoes…

(marriage, babies, at lastatlastatlastatlast)

…seventy eighth birthday…

…fitting…

…kiddies playing on the monkey climber…giggling nieces and nephews…a son…a delightful daughter…

…we shall produce such exquisite daughters…

…

…

The string quartet played Stravinsky, and I was in heaven as her head rested on my chest.

Unfortunately for me, if not for Nina, someone she knew turned up at ten to twelve and by twelve thirty, she was kissing him by the maze as if I had never ever existed.

That guy she was kissing comes from one of the oldest families in Britain. They say his ancestors were at court when Henry II suggested the murder of Becket.

1187. Historians speculate that the regent didn't actually order Becket killed, but three knights misunderstood precisely what Henry said and thus, in a show of reckless fealty, slayed him on the altar at Canterbury Cathedral. The guy she was kissing - rugged, dark, handsome - was connected distantly to the most important event in British history. Maybe even in the history of the Western World.

The Norman Conquest. Without that, nothing that happened worldwide in the last millennia would ever have happened. Honest. Look it up in your history books. The Normans added wanderlust to the Saxon-Celtic genetic. They created the administration. Money. Influence. Political power. Handsome boy's family had the lot.

(cunt)

I'd like to tell you what happened next, but I don't remember it well.

Of course, I remember the aftermath.

I remember my father's seventy eighth birthday party ending abruptly. I remember bouncers - bouncers! - dragging me away from...I remember...no, I don't remember...

...remember the blood.

...dripping from my chin.

I can taste it.

I remember the screaming.

I remember...

I remember...

Off to Cedar Forest for the second time.

Anyway...don't you just hate biographies!

Narcissism Central, what!

I spoke to Carla quite a bit that first night. Annoyed by the antics of the regulars in the Pop Side, I quietly and without fuss, moved into The Snug (which became my Carla base). I noticed how friendly she was straight away.

I didn't push it. I didn't overstay my welcome and I didn't monopolise her time, but I spoke to her, and she reciprocated. I learned important things about her. She told me that she worked weekends at The Saddler's, and she liked the job. I discovered that she was a student at the Agricultural College studying wildlife conservation (second year). She said the college was the best, and she considered herself lucky to get in.

That was an In. The wildlife conservation thing.

I love the Earth and so does Carla.

(What an In)

(Lucky man)

If I had my time over, as well as staying sane, I would forget physics. It has never done me any favours. I'd have done something with nature. I'd have done botany or something. I love reading about it. The rain forests, the ecosystems, the Gaia hypothesis, apocalypse theories. I give Greenpeace a hundred pounds per month, and (unfortunate incarcerations notwithstanding) I would have signed up for the South Atlantic missions to stop Japanese whaling. Sadly, I can't do anything like that because of my history and Greenpeace pursue references with some alacrity. You can understand why. Those journeys are long. Long journeys in confined spaces. Mixed gender groups.

You know the best thing about that night.

She asked what I did! So many people couldn't give a monkey's. She reciprocated! She went quid pro quo on the conversation. She was politely curious, just like the old days.

You ask something. They listen. They respond.

They ask something back. You listen. And you respond.

This told me more than anything else that Carla was quality.

I told her I was something to do with horses and turned the attention back to her. I remember Carla as being the most beautiful girl who ever lived, but that might not have been the case, objectively, love being blind and all that, but I can tell you without fear of contradiction that she was the loveliest person I had ever met, and I could tell that from minute one.

On the walk home after I met Carla that first night, a bellyful of Scrumpy and rain in the air, I felt strangely disconnected as if the walk home was being undertaken by someone else, and I was watching down on him from above. Tall, awkward, gangly, friends (when I had them) used to say I looked a bit like that famous rower who won Olympic Gold. You know the one I mean. The younger one.

I'm six foot four, and girls are supposed to fancy tall men, but when I looked down on the figure walking home, I wasn't enamoured. I looked closely. His mush was ill fitting, asymmetrical. Bits missing. Nothing the right size: Eyes too small, nose too big, ears not quite balanced. The rest of his body was the same sort of mess. Elongated fingers. A shoulder hunching to the left. Big feet. Walks with a slight splay. The odds of this forty two year old man in a tracksuit walking up North Gate actually attracting the girl he had fallen in love with?

Pretty long odds.

That night, I treated myself to a luxurious night in my own bed. Most of the time, I sleep on the sofa, particularly when it's cold. I can't be bothered to make the journey down the corridor. I laid down in bed that night and slept like a top. It took a while to catch off as I considered all the Carla possibilities as the afterimage of her immersive brown eyes hovered like fireflies in my field of vision.

Chapter 3: Rainstorm

For the next three days, it rained on Wheatley Fields. It rained the type of rain that soaks through clothes in seconds. It hadn't rained like this here for twenty years, and in the middle of the weirdest, warmest winter in two hundred years, it seemed incongruous. Seventy two hours of black rain fell in heavy sheets and winds howled straight from the Urals. Cars aquaplaned through the pounding floods, sending waves onto the pavements. Streams poured into the grates. A skyscape of purest gunmetal grey stretched in an unbroken mass.

I was desperate to go back to the pub to see if Carla was on shift, but I literally couldn't get out of the house. I tried the second day, but I didn't even make a hundred yards. Besides, the intensity of the emotions I experienced wasn't recommended for me, and I was glad I couldn't immediately act on my impulses. I tried to forget her…told myself it was like a serious cold, and it would go away if I worked on it.

But none of it worked. I went to bed that first night thinking about her, and it took me hours to get to sleep. I had to take Temazepam and a Tramadol, as well as my anti-psychotic, just to hasten the journey into darkness.

I woke up thinking about her. Her Little Fluffy Clouds voice in my ears. I tried to bet on the computer, on racehorses, with limited success. The heavens had opened all over the country. Several race meetings were abandoned due to severe waterlogging. Even when they raced on the All Weather, I lost money because I couldn't concentrate. All three days. Instead of focusing on the performance of my horses, I spent most of my time looking on the Internet for examples of older men and younger women getting spliced and living happily ever after.

I found plenty. Celebrities, politicians.

The French in particular. It didn't seem a taboo there.

Not like over here.

In Blighty, fancy a twenty year old girl and in the eyes of the population you were one step away from Nonceville, Arizona.

I read about etiquette.

The French Equation.

Halve your age.
Add seven years.
That's an acceptable age for a girlfriend.
I'm forty two. Half that. Makes twenty one.
Add seven.
Makes me too old for Carla.
Damn.

I re-read Oliver Reed's autobiography. Well, the later bit. The wild man actor famously married a sixteen year old girl. He even asked her father's permission. She was happy with him, and she was at his side when he died. Irritated and confused, I alternated between reading about this stuff and turning it off. For three days and nights, I was beset by an internal monologue, which was straight out of a Mills and Boons romance novel. I cursed myself for a fool, paced up and down, beset by images of domestic bliss between Carla and me. Miracle upon miracles, I fancied that she was in love with me also, love at first sight. I pictured the big house. A decent car. She wouldn't have to work. I'd do all that for her. Maybe it was time to stop drinking and gambling. I'd tell her all this. Spend our nights watching TV on the sofa, hugging and cuddling. I'd listen carefully to tales of her day. I'd be the strong silent type. We'd always eat together. We'd go away for weekends. The Lake District. Paris. Sun-drenched Spain. Three holidays a year. Walk arm-in-arm along the promenade overlooking the Med. Watch the sun melt into the sea in the distance, the sound of gulls and the Mediterranean breeze on the shore our only companions. Eat fresh shellfish in some island grotto built into the rocks near where Perseus slew Medusa, the salt between our toes, holding hands forever...

...all this gruesome stuff.
I couldn't stop thinking about us.
It was madness, and I knew it.
It was back.

I tried to focus on the horses, but it all seemed so irrelevant. In three days, I lost five hundred pounds. At the end of the second day, I rationalised the shocking performance of my horses. I saw it as a sign: Unlucky at cards. Lucky in love.

On each of those three nights, I stared out of the window thinking about Carla for hours. I watched the rain tumble down, the resonant vibrations on the pavement below, the poet in his garret awaiting the return of his long lost love. I felt simultaneously lighter than air and heavier than lead.

Happier than I'd ever been and suicidal, despairing.

Love is a bit like madness, isn't it? Don't worry. I'm not going to get all Love Is on you. Love is like the corner of a thick rug. Love is like a raindrop on the windowpane. Love is like...well...you've seen the cartoons.

But it is. Madness.

I went a bit mad when I met Carla.

A little bit insane.

Emotional Unstable Disorder or, if you are an American reader, *Borderline Personality Disorder.*

This is what the shrinks say about me most often. My diagnosis. My shifting psychological profile. I am supposed to have an aggressive, accelerated version of the disorder shared by just one-half of one-half of one percent of the population. Plus a mild and intermittent psychotic state. A fugue.

It can be cured.

In fact, they believed I was cured.

Being honest, this EUD/BPD is just part of it. Hardly any sufferers get themselves locked up in the booby hatch because of their illness. The ones that do are generally women - eight times more women than men are diagnosed with EUD/BPD. This makes me unusual, a unique case. Something else must be going on. Psychiatrists from the US, Germany, France and Australia have interviewed me, and I've been a case study for at least seven professional research teams. Doctor Plunkett gave me a co-morbid dual diagnosis of EUD/BPD and...something else I'll tell you about later.

You'll like that one - hardly anyone has ever heard of it.

You might never have heard of a personality disorder.

Am I jumping ahead of myself? Picture it as some mechanical problem in the mind, the way you think about the world. To be diagnosed as I was, a psychologist will look for inflexible and pervasive symptoms, which have been present for an extended period. You can trace the symptoms back to adolescence or at least early adulthood, and the symptoms continue to cause significant distress or negative consequences in different aspects of the person's life. Symptoms are seen in at least two of the following areas: Thoughts, Emotions (appropriateness, intensity, and range of emotional functioning), Interpersonal Functioning and Impulse Control. Fundamentally speaking, it's number two for me. I have incredible difficulty controlling my emotions.

Particularly (and as I get older, exclusively), when I get involved with women. I've emboldened it in the text above. When my emotions are engaged as they were with Carla, things happen. My emotions go into meltdown, a rapid chain reaction that all goes...well...seriously wrong, seriously fast.

You'd be surprised how fast things can go from idyllic to nightmare. It surprises me. Big time.

Horrible things happen.

And afterwards, I have to go away for a rest.

Chapter 4: Handy BPD Criteria Checklist

In DSM IV, there are nine fundamental criteria for BPD. You have to be diagnosed by a psychiatrist. You cannot be drunk or on drugs while doing BPD things. They must happen naturally.

And remember, it must be extreme behaviour.

To be diagnosed with BPD, you need five of the following nine conditions.

1. **Frantic efforts to avoid real or imagined abandonment.**

Oh, man, do I have this or what! I cling like a Velcro strap. You can't get rid of me. I do this because of pathological insecurity. If my partner leaves my sight for any period, as little as ten minutes, I forget about them. What they look like. Who they are. What they mean to me. This one is the rocket fuel. This is the one that inspires lift off. I hate being left alone by someone I love. And as you will see, and as you may have suspected, I can fall in love with a woman in about ten minutes.

When love strikes, I can't even let my woman go to the Ladies alone.

Skip forward to Part II and have a look at how I handle the Carla e-mail issue.

It's funny. You won't believe it.

2. **A pattern of unstable / intense interpersonal relationships characterised by alternating extremes of idealisation and devaluation.**

Psychologists call this Splitting. You've probably seen this in action, and if you're a woman, you may have experienced this. One minute you are the reincarnation of Queen Sophia Romanov, the most beatific woman who ever lived after Mother Teresa and the very next minute - the VERY NEXT - you're a slag.

You're a whore.

A strumpet whore.

Lower than a dancer wearing a top hat hula hula-ing under a snake's belly.

I hate you. I hate you.

Black and white thinking.

Saint or a whore.

(This is sometimes known amongst older psychiatrists as the Mary Magdalene Complex.)

Cost me two long-term girlfriends, this. The only two.

And at least thirty women whom I've known for less than three months.

I even split a woman on the first date

I mean - how? How can you split a woman within three hours? Sober. Her brother, one of my best mates and who introduced us, hates me now. All my relationships with people I love - family, friends and partners - are warzones and disaster areas. Even when things are going well and we're enjoying a Mojito on the landing of some resort with the sun in our eyes and the wind in our hair, our magnificent summer clothes, our sense of attraction for each other, you can never lower your guard because one false word…

…one false word…

…and you *definitely* can't go to the Ladies alone…

I've destroyed weddings, parties, works dos, get-togethers, reunions. You name it, I've upset the applecart.

3. **Identity disturbance or marked and persistent unstable self-image or sense of self.**

Check. No idea who I am. I am tabula rasa. The number of times I've adopted the opinions and perceptions of the woman I am with! Oh, man, I *become* you.

Can't make my mind up about anything. Have no opinions apart from yours and carry on with a spectacular sense of nothing in my mind apart from being with you. I have the weakest sense of self of anyone I have ever encountered. I am a straw man, a made-up thing, a doppelganger of you, an ephemeral spirit, and I will do and say anything to ingratiate myself with you just so you will never leave me.

And of course, the more I do this, the more I ensure that you will leave me. I am aware of modern female psychology. All the bad boy thing. All the grass is greener thing.

4. **Impulsivity in at least two areas that are potentially self-damaging, such as spending, sex, substance abuse, reckless driving or binge eating.**

I can't control myself at all. I just can't. Emotions. Out of control, and what is an impulse but a released emotion! You'll see examples of this throughout the narrative. Try and spot them.

5. **Recurrent suicidal behaviour, gestures or threats, or self-mutilating behaviour.**

Yep. All of them. I not only try to kill myself regularly, I even act it out to stop women leaving me. Isn't that shit, huh. What they don't tell you in the books is how extreme you have to be to be diagnosed by the headshrinkers. I have threatened to throw myself off the back window of a moving double-decker bus because the girl I was with wouldn't hold hands with me.

On the second date. Holding hands, huh. My, I'm a regular Jack the Ripper.

Holding hands. No one can believe it when I tell them this. I got halfway out the back window before the driver pulled me back in. I was seventeen and the girl, who was just playing hard to get and quite fancied me, burst into tears, and her brother battered me at the park the next day. Kicked the shit out of me and left me bleeding. I didn't fight back because, hey, I deserved it. Didn't enhance my reputation much. On top of the other stuff, it was fortuitous that I was at Uni, and I didn't have to go back to St Albans. (If you're reading this, you lived in St Albans, and you know who I am, I'm sorry. I can't help it. I'm crazy. Believe me, I've suffered for my sins. I've been a proper Jesuit.)

6: **Affective instability due to a marked reactivity of mood, such as intense episodic dysphoria and anxiety, which usually lasts between a few hours and several days.**

Nope. Don't have this one. I'm not all that moody. I'm split between being Mr. Sensible or Mr. BAD. Split down the middle. Yes, sir. The ultimate Jekyll and Hyde character. I nearly called the book Doctor Jekyll and Mister Hyde 2012. What do you think? Nah. Not brilliant is it?

7. **Chronic feeling of emptiness.**

Check. You'll see this throughout the book.

8. **Inappropriate. intense anger and / or difficulty controlling anger. This includes frequent displays of temper, constant anger and recurrent physical fights.**

I won't spoil the fun, but this is numero uno for me.

Check the section coming shortly on Intermittent Explosive Disorder, which has been known as *Pathological Rage Disorder* and/or *Explosive Personality Disorder.* Librarians get this. Those guys who hold it all in. It's all over the book. I'm a feisty character as Doctor Plunkett keeps telling me.

As does Kevin Flint, my usual Probation Officer.

9. **Transient, stress related paranoid ideation and/or severe dissociative symptoms.**

Hmmmmmm...don't know about this one. I'll get back to you on it.

So.

How many have you got?

I have seven, possibly eight.

Documented, sober, recorded, adjusted and certified.

Seven.

That reminds me...

Chapter 5: Barefoot in Memorial Park

I bumped into Carla a week later in the street, outside the chocolate shop. Well, that's not quite true. I didn't bump into her, and I'm not sure she saw me, but it felt like we'd met outside the pub for the first time and to me, that was an important stage in the development of our relationship. I'd only spoken to her a few times or so. Even they were the most succinct and informal conversations, so when I saw her outside the chocolate shop with her two friends, it didn't seem appropriate to approach her and say hello. But it didn't seem as *disconnected* as that, so I scrutinized her a little from a safe distance. She was wearing an army jacket and jeans that day, with an Inuit hat with the two floppy ears, with those dangly ropes reaching halfway down her coat. She looked fantastic. Her two friends were male. One tall and Italian-looking in a blue tracksuit top. The other medium-sized and quite bulky in a parka. He had a gold earring in his left ear, which seemed incongruous. They were eating chocolate while discussing something.

To avoid accusations of stalking, I pretended to text from my vantage point in the cavernous alley next to Tracey's Tresses. Three winding ginnels puncture the High Street, each leading to a variety of boutiques and emporia, and it wouldn't seem unusual for a person to be texting at the entrance. In fact, several people - a couple, a pair of elderly ladies in hats and thick tights, a schoolchild - walked past me without a second look. Carla couldn't see me, but I could see her. When she walked over the road into the market place, I took a quiet stroll to the alley nearest the Chinese takeaway, eyes firmly focused on my device, a studious look apparent. I stood next to a giant grey recycling bin, scratched my head, and looked concerned, but I was watching her.

How she giggled. How she ate. How she related. I looked for signs that she was romantically involved with one or both of the two young men she was talking with. I looked for the meaningful glance, the outstayed-welcome stare, the hand on the forearm, the ear touching, all that. Aspects flashed in every gesture she made. I felt like I knew, even at such an early stage, and she was friendly and touchy and genuinely happy so those gestures would be part of her everyday interactions.

How could I tell? I was never competent at assessing this stuff.

When they sat down opposite the Square's clock, I moved up the road toward the Art Shop and beyond. She didn't see me, and if she did, in reality, she didn't acknowledge me. I could have avoided all this by going over and saying a brief sociable hello, but I was too nervous. Watching from a distance seemed more appropriate, somehow. I stood in the doorway of the old library, which had been turned into a modern Church. I could see her, and I could watch.

I was hypnotised by her.

I saw my next-door neighbour, Heather, come out of the convenience store and wave to me. I waved back. The last person I wanted to see was Heather, and I tensed. Luckily, she was with someone, otherwise, she would have come over and had a chat, and that would have ruined my observation.

I wanted to know Carla from a distance. I wanted to know where she lived. I know I shouldn't. I know that's wrong.

I know what you're thinking about me.

I know the word you're using, but you're wrong. I'm not like that. I was just curious, so when she got up and started to walk back down the High Street, I followed her. One of the young men - the bulky one - went another direction, and it was just Carla and the Italian walking back toward North Gate, my manor. They turned left, past Dorothy's and The Saladin. They walked over the zebra crossing and into The Three Steeples Church. I followed discreetly, about two hundred yards or so behind, staring into my Blackberry. I nearly bumped into two elderly shoppers outside the new pharmacy, and they gave me filthy looks. I apologised profusely, but I wasn't sorry - I was on a mission, and casualties happen, collateral damage. It was important to me that Carla didn't see me, and she didn't.

The two of them walked through the churchyard, the green incredibly lush, possibly due to the incredible floods of two weeks previously; the trees foreboding, the shadow of the church making the environment seemed colder than it actually was. I watched the two of them walk through the park. Carla was animated and talkative, gesticulating with her arms and hands, alternately raising them to the skies as if expressing frustration with the way things are, and hiding them in the pockets of her combat coat. The Italian walked along, occasionally tapping her on the shoulder, but I didn't get anything romantic in the scene and I didn't get jealous. However, I think I was trying to control my emotions more than anything else, and later that night as I lay on my sofa watching *Justified* on Five Star, I began to see something more in the way he related to her on that walk home.

Carla, being a woman, and connected to her externality by some diaphanous web, some sixth sense, started to look behind her more and more, and I had to swiftly stand behind a giant oak, one of several that line the boulevard-style pathways on the top end of the Memorial Gardens.

I'm sure she didn't see me. The park was empty at that time of day with the school kids back in lessons, and the dog walkers three hours away from coming out for the second time, and the vast green playing fields framed the two of them in the winter sunlight. I wished I was the Italian. Next to her.

One of my few advantages is height, and it would be touch and go whether the Italian-looking young man who had accompanied her on her journey was as tall as me. I wondered whether Carla liked tall men. That'd be a card worth playing when it came down to it.

It didn't take long for me to walk home to my flat and when I got in, I wrote down some notes in my diary, and I went to bed and acted on my Carla fantasies, and the action was so intense, it was almost like she was next to me.

I don't see anything wrong with following Carla home.

Do you? Do you think I was stalking her or something?

Today, they tell me they stalk on the Internet. On Me.com and Pony Express. The Royal Mail. Does anyone track people *on foot* anymore? Has the hard labour of *tracking* gone the way of the eight-track, the wooden barrel and the Texan bar? Something to ponder isn't it? It's all Internet based today. Whatever happened to the human touch? But no, I certainly wasn't stalking Carla. I was finding out more about her. I was unearthing information. And she didn't see me, did she? I learned plenty about her on that little meander through Wheatley Fields.

It was close to the end of January. That night, I decided on a strategy to bring Carla and I closer together.

Chapter 6: The Exploding Man

That female sixth sense. It's that antennae you have.

You know. That aerial. That radar that's built in.

That sixth sense.

You girls can spot a nutbag from a thousand paces.

Now you're not always right, admit it, but you're always on your guard. Always wary, always looking for the man in the woods, the strange shadow in the corridor, the Bogeyman in the wardrobe with your aerial of suspicion.

Over the years - and you can watch out for incidences of any of these things throughout the narrative - I've been called an Arsehole (goes without saying), an Alcoholic (it's not enough, sorry), a Psychopath (bollocks), a Schizo (has its merits, theoretically), a Split Personality (no such thing), a Borderline (not many arguments with this one), a Narcissist (how, exactly, can someone who hates himself be a Narcissist?), and a Repressed Homosexual (no comment).

With the internet, popular psychology sites, popular psychology courses and a society-wide oversupply of psychology graduates looking for something to do other than flip burgers and chase shoppers in the High Street with direct debit forms, we can all be diagnostic experts. What exactly IS the point of a psychiatrist with all the stuff available free on the Internet? Thousands of personality tests exist on the internet as we speak. Free of charge.

Stop reading this. Right now.

Flip on your internet browser and find a popular search engine of your choice. Type in something like **Borderline Personality Test** and you'll find a free test of your personality. They take about fifteen minutes, and they ask you questions loosely associated with particular personality disorders.

Usually, multiple choice. A mouse click.

Well, of course, it is in today's hyperfast society. Who can be bothered to fill in boxes full of actual words?

Now. Have you done that? What does it say? Avoidant? Histrionic? How simple was that, huh?

You are now a label.

By the way, if you're an Anti-Social, don't bother reading on.

I hate you and hope your robot arse rots in hell.

If you're a borderline, get in touch. We can help each other, I'm sure. You understand, don't you? You can empathise. You know what it's like to want something so much so fast that you can never live up to the intensity of it.

You know that emptiness. That scalded skin. That ever-present sense of nausea.

You've experienced the cutting.

You would understand that, wouldn't you? The point of the blade touching your skin, the soothing sense of it, the understanding that the knife is exactly what you deserve. The cold sharp blade is your only friend and you understand the peace that can bring, the descending euphoria.

When I was inside the last time, a doctor from New Orleans reviewed my case notes and postulated the notion that as well as BPD, I also suffered from IED.

Intermittent Explosive Disorder.

(They think of a name for the lot, shrinks.)

Take this one. You won't believe it.

Lottery Disappointment Syndrome.

I couldn't believe it when I heard it, but apparently, people become so disappointed at not winning their country's version of the Lottery that they are referred to a psychiatrist. I said that it seemed a bit silly, another job creation exercise, another opportunity to be published in the journals, but Plunkett said that over seven hundred people a year worldwide are so beset by the injustice and the hopelessness of not winning the lottery that they commit suicide. Many others self-harm. Others turn to drink and drugs.

Anyway, I digress. This doctor from New Orleans called Dupont said that I was probably suffering from BPD with IED attached. Plus an organic neurosis or two (my head really IS a bloody *shed,* isn't it).

The Unit I had been referred to by my father to keep me out of prison had only twice before treated a sufferer of IED. Naturally, when he heard, father paid to bring in a specialist, and of course, I do what I always do, which is have long conversations with the specialist, long, immersive, enjoyable ones, take all the medication they ask me to, talk in the rolling grounds to Abdul and Kenny, and Wrigley and Sable, and Boyd and Leroy, and Felicity (when she's not on her treatment), and wait for Janine to come to my room whenever she's on shift.

In other words, I conform to their recovery model and eventually, having no reason anymore to keep me under observation, they release me.

IED, according to Dupont, is characterised by instability of mood with unpredictable outbursts of severe anger and violence. Librarians are common sufferers.

Yes, Librarians. Polite, quiet people who suddenly, with no warning, and for no apparent reason, start destroying their work environments. Smashing up their family homes, their loved ones looking on in terror.

I can see that.

The horror of it. If you marry a tattooed skinhead with a history of pathological violence, you can't complain when he starts destroying your country cottage in front of you because he's had a stressful day. It's what he does. It's your fault.

With a bespectacled librarian, inoffensive and polite, with his satchel and brown raincoat, his tortoiseshell spectacles, watching him take a sledgehammer to the plasma and the stereo before turning his slit-eyed gaze to you and the kids - now that's pretty scary if you ask me.

And that's what I have, apparently. They always throw one or two variations of The Psychoses in as well.

I like the word Schizophreniform, actually. I can't work out which word I like better. Schizoid or Schizophreniform.

Schizoid or Schizophreniform.

Schizoid or Schizophreniform. Hmmmmmm. It's a tough choice and should you put a gun to my head, I couldn't give you a straight answer because my opinion changes almost by the second, abstract and fragmented, a bit like the meanings themselves. Anyway, ever since I was fifteen, when the first big thing happened at school, at the school disco, the first time people sat up and took notice at the Bogeyman in their midst, they have always thrown one of The Psychoses into the cauldron. Bless them.

Psychosis.

The difficulty in separating fantasy from reality, in essence.

Voices and that.

Voices Permitting.

I knew the diagnosis was inaccurate. I mean, I went ten years without another episode. Ten whole years before that works Christmas party, that time.

Ooops. That wasn't healthy. Won't let you in on *that* secret.

A six year gap before another...explosion...if you like, but that one ended worse than before, so I guess it builds up inside me, infinitesimally slowly, so slowly that you can't see it happening, and I don't even know it's happening, and as I said, the Ducks line up in a row and...

Fifteen. Ten. Six. Three. That's my geometric mathematical descent into madness and incarceration expressed in gap years. Of course, they are only the big episodes. The ones which get me into trouble with, er, the psychotherapeutically *penal* establishment.

I haven't even factored in the others. The Friday night ones. The Saturday night ones. The normal ones, as it were.

It's no wonder I live alone, huh. I mean, what would you do with me?

Imagine bumping into this Find-A-Date profile on the internet.

Hi!

Six foot tall, fit graduate in Physics, 42, sometime writer, from traditional, wealthy family, clean-shaven, okay looking, warm, affectionate, witty, charming, tendency to commit acts of sporadic, spectacular, and quite terrifying violence when certain specific conditions are met. WLTM anyone with a pulse. (But no tattooed feet, sorry.)

They say women like bad boys. It's not been my experience. Women are no longer attracted to me it seems and yet without boasting, my mental health and criminal records - objective, Karl Popper approved, hypothetical and testable measures of Bad Boydom - suggest that I'm one of the baddest boys on the planet.

Bad motherfucker as they say in The City.

Logically, you'd think women would be beating my door down.

They don't.

Apart from my stepsister (twice), no woman has ever visited me in the asyla I have frequented. I've never had a girlfriend visit me. As the girls I have attracted have usually been present whenever, the, er, unlucky moments have occurred, they tend to do a moonlight flit afterwards. Apologies never succeed. I've met men who've battered their partners within an inch of their lives and have tearfully apologised the next morning, and they continue to be married.

I do what I do, and no apology, no depth of apology, no apological azimuth, no relationship State of the Union address, no synchronicity of remorse, no high velocity of meaning, emotion, sincerity, no promise of redemption and retraction has ever been enough to retain a woman who has seen me in action.

That's a hundred percent. No exceptions.

That's what I don't understand, you see.

It's all a Venn diagram, of course. All the Avoidants and Narcissistics, and Schizoids and Histrionics, and Anti-Socials and Obsessive Compulsives, and Borderlines, all the DSM diagnoses touch onto each other and overlap, and I understand that, but it's the Borderlines who have the closest relationship with Intermittent Explosive Disorder which, as I have told you, is what they do when things get, as the football hooligans say, on top.

Whatever you want to call it - Post Traumatic Stress Disorder, Pathological Rage Disorder, Acting Out, IED or plain being an arsehole when you are drunk - if you suffer from it, your favourite film has just got to be *The Ninth Configuration.*

Directed by William Peter Blatty of *The Exorcist* fame, it stars Stacy Keach as a military Psychiatrist named Lieutenant Kane taking over at a medieval castle full of battlefield psychiatric cases.

Ahum. This next paragraph contains spoilers. Type in **favourite film of Exploding Men** on your e-device's search function and you'll be able to watch the film because you'll skip the paragraph.

If you've seen it, more's the better.

The previous custodians of the Castle were alternative psychiatrists, like RD Laing and DB Cooper who generally let their charges run riot, acting out their psychoses in an Oxford "clinic" because he believed that there isn't much difference between those that diagnose mental illness and those who are diagnosed with it, and that the barriers between them are illusory and preventative. Kane meets many of the patients who dress up, act out plays and dramas, but over a period, you begin to realise that not all is what it seems. We discover that Kane is ex-Special Forces who has seen horrors beyond imagination and in fact, is suffering from an extreme form of Post Traumatic Stress Disorder, and when he finds himself in a bar surrounded by a fifteen strong biker gang intent on raping and murdering a friend…

Boom. Boom.

Hubba. Hubba. Hubba.

Up until that point, the film is a bizarre, disjointed mess and most cineastes are fast asleep by the time Kane finds himself in that apocalyptic biker bar, but those who stayed awake are in for a treat, a volcanic display of PTSD and IED unequalled on cinema, which had the critics purring.

The favourite film of the Exploding Men. One hundred percent.

It's funny.

Nina. That night at my father's party. Before her, I hadn't had sex for five years. Well, that's not true actually. I had passed bodily fluids when in the Cedar Forest Recuperative Hospital but that wasn't sex. That was a bit like rape. I'm uncomfortable with the word, and it doesn't wholly describe what happened to me. If I ignore what happened in hospital, when Nina pulled away and inspired one of my outbreaks, it could be seen as a quite legitimate frustration. Desperation more like.

I've forgotten how to woo a woman it seems, and the more I forget, the more it all seems like desperate measures.

Chapter 7: Strategy

Over February and early March, I went to the pub at least six nights a week. My daily routine was invariant. Shower, breakfast, horses - in Charlestown or on Satellite TV - shower encore, change and have a walk down to The Saddler's. When Carla wasn't working, I visited. Method in my madness. I wanted to avoid any possible accusation that I was stalking Carla or that she was the only reason I visited. The locals in the town would rapidly draw that conclusion, particularly with an incomer, and I didn't want the attention. I reasoned that if I went to the pub a lot and sat in The Snug, out of the way, on the one barstool, reading The Racing Post or The Guardian, I wouldn't look out of place. I usually took Monday nights off. Often visited the City greyhound track for the Opens. She generally worked Thursdays to Sundays, the weekend shift, from eight until eleven, sometimes longer. This left her plenty of time for homework and virtually no time for a social life. She was unusual that way. It never seemed to bother her, going out. It didn't seem part of her life in the same way it did other students who lived for Saturday nights in The Benbow in the centre of the town. On the nights she was off, different bar staff entertained the regulars.

Christine, a vampy older woman who I got on quite well with, and Rebecca, who I didn't. The latter was much older, and I noticed she had her favourites - always in the Pop Side. There was Kayleigh, who came and went. Anna, with a full tattoo of a Phoenix on her back reaching from her right to her left shoulder, who covered whenever anyone was sick, and who always gave me the time of day. I liked her a lot. Also, James, who liked horseracing, but not enough to talk to me about it and Leah, little Leah, who never said anything more than hello to me. She generally manned the pumps on Monday nights, and I only ever saw her twice. I didn't take offence at her attitude - she was shy and behaved like that all the time. She was one of those slackers who liked books and animals, and who had been told by eager parents to get a bar job. She lacked any desire to interact with the drinkers and just wanted to finish her shift and go back to her bedroom. However, at three fifty a pint, it's not just about serving pints any more. You have to entertain the visitors.

Earlier, I overheard a big, arrogant bloke in the other pub holding court. Unhappy with a shy barmaid's service, he took a sip of his foaming pint of Fiddling Jester and said, "When I buy a criminally expensive pint of beer in this shithole of a boozer, I want to be treated like fucking royalty. I get enough misery from the wife! I don't need it in my pub. Sack her, Landlord. Sack her! This minute!" His golf club cronies guffawed even while the tiny wisp of a girl was standing opposite him at the time.

He assured her he was joking.

I never saw her again.

Big Keith, the Landlord, who ran the pub with an iron fist, but who spent much of his time holding court on the other side of the Pop Side bar. Drinking the profits with all the regulars who kept the pub going through the winter months. At Scandinavian prices, the average age of the drinkers hit forty or fifty, and the same people gathered nightly, about ten to fifteen of them. I guessed that this was how Big Keith made his money, so I understood why he spent much of his time entertaining them. I got a couple of nods from him, but that was about it.

However, I didn't care about that as I had other goals in mind, and it suited me to be left alone. I think, after all that time, until our friendship became common knowledge amongst her friends at least, by going to The Saddler's each night, more or less, I avoided the stalking accusation that I didn't need. Each night I visited, I drank no more than three pints, and I varied the drinks. I never, ever touched more than three pints of Thor's Hammer. A lethal concoction, but I always started with one to liven me up a little. I arrived at between seven forty five and eight fifteen on consecutive nights. I varied the times within those parameters. I varied the clothes I wore. Sometimes, I took a book. Other times, I took a paper.

Holding a long conversation with bar staff is virtually impossible in a busy pub, particularly a barmaid like Carla, in demand from all the old soaks in the Pop Side, all the woe merchants and chatterboxes, but we managed to do okay those nights. The In was wildlife, as I said.

The natural world. Carla loved it.

She could talk about that for hours, and it seemed that I had been blessed with two slices of fortune.

One. I know a lot about the natural world. One advantage of my all-inclusive psychiatric package deals, I got all the time in the world to read. If you have a passion, you can indulge it. They think reading is therapeutic, and I ordered the lot. The whole kit and caboodle.

Two. Hardly anyone in the pub ever bothered to ask Carla about her college course. She told me so. Moreover, not many of the regulars could give a shit anyway. They were the kind of people who cranked up the central heating, furnished their houses with hardwood tables, and kept the taps running when they brushed their teeth. The kind of people who believed that climate change is part of a cycle and that there is nothing we can do about it. Wildlife Conservation begins and ends with a trip to see *The Lion King* for that lot.

Therefore, although I had competition - lots of it - it was never going to be enough to hold her attention. Anyone with a brain would have done what I did. And Keith didn't like her classmates coming in to bother her, and she let them know that she didn't want to be disturbed. They could drink - and a few of them did - but Carla let it be known they couldn't sit at the bar. Big Keith wouldn't like that, and she might lose her job.

However.

Little old me...

Chapter 8: The Rejection

On one of the last nights in February, I went into the pub a little earlier than usual and as I parked my cycle on the rack outside, I saw Carla talking to a man in the smoker's area. I took a step back and pretended to fiddle with my cycle brakes while I watched. He was a big chap with dark curly hair and a wine drinker's mien, reddened and scorched. His nose was huge through overindulgence in the grog, and I guessed if I went up close, it would have been like a road map, covered in tiny veins. The man confronting her was like a farmer, a landowner, something to do with horses. A creature of the country rather than of the town. As if to confirm that, he wore a cloth cap, which looked cemented to his head, like an extra limb. He pointed at Carla with big fingers, and she pointed back. They clearly knew each other. I wondered who he was. Little family resemblance. He was much older than her. The conversation was animated, and Carla picked up three or four empty pint glasses and walked back inside. The man didn't follow her. He drank a large glass of white wine, slammed it down on the table, and fuming, walked out of the backyard and hopped into a van waiting outside the pub. A non-descript white van, more suited to a painting firm. I expected to see a Land Rover or something. He got into the passenger side and whoever was driving drove off toward Charlestown. I parked the bike and locked up, walked into the pub, which was virtually empty.

Carla greeted me gently, but with no fizzy enthusiasm. She looked distracted and tired as if the argument outside had got topside of her, as if things were said, which needed to be digested.

She served me my usual, told me she was tired, and went to the other side of the bar without saying anything more to me. She stood staring over at the door as if she were expecting someone to come in at any time. I was quite upset. Bearing in mind the wonderful night we had together on Thursday, I was disappointed, but she wouldn't be the first changeable woman I had ever met, and she certainly wouldn't be the last. As my luck would have it, as I sat down, a gang of young lads came in the other side. Some walked into The Snug and stood next to me. Big Keith helped serve. They looked like rugby geezers. To help ease the crush, I took my pint and sat down on one of the tables in The Snug.

Read my paper and kept my eye out for Carla, who was showing none of her customary fizz and enthusiasm.

The lads left for town after drinking their pints. After finishing my pint, I went back and sat upon my usual stool. Keith had gone upstairs for a lie down, leaving Carla, me and three other drinkers to the pub. She came over and refilled my glass, a little more cheerful now. She warmed to me a little - that natural pleasantness difficult to suppress - and talked about her day. It became clear the big old man outside was not the only source of her problems. Her tutor, she said, had overloaded his class with assignments, and she was struggling to work and to study. She was up late last night completing statistics. "Oh, My God, I hate stats! So boring. Why do we have to do stats? If I wanted to do maths, I'd have chosen maths. He won't stop giving us work. He thinks we're a bright year, and we can handle it, but I'm getting tired, John. I might have to give up a night in the pub."

The idea of that made my blood run cold, but I nodded sympathetically.

"I can see that. Anything I can do to help?"

"Any good with stats?" She grinned. "I don't understand any of it."

"Sure. Bring down your assignment and I'll have a look for you."

"Would you, John? Oh, that's so brilliant!"

"It's my pleasure," I said, blushing. "Happy to have a look for you."

"Are you in tomorrow?"

"Of course. Not much going on in my life."

She grinned. I saw one of the regulars tap his glass on the bar from the other side. Carla heard him, and asked him to hang on. She turned back to me. "I'll bring the assignment in tomorrow night. If you can help me, I'll be grateful." She floated to the far bar. I looked at her while she served the old gent - a man who, despite drinking in the same pub as me for all this time, had never even nodded his head in acknowledgement at my presence.

She came back over. "That'll be fantastic, John. I'll buy you a pint."

"Absolutely no need for that, Carla. It will be my pleasure. I think I'll have my last now…" I finished what was left of my beer and offered her the glass.

Lulled into a sense of security by our chat and her perky change in mood, I made a classic mistake and asked her about the argument earlier while she poured.

"Who was the man talking to you earlier?"

"Who?" She replied.

"I saw you outside as I arrived. The big bloke in the dark blue coat and the Wellies."

"Him? He's no one," she said, coldly, not looking at me, concentrating on controlling the beer leaving the pump. "The beer's fizzy tonight."

She constricted my glass with her fingers as if it was the neck of someone she detested. She pulled the pump with venom. I'd not seen her react as coldly as this ever and she suddenly looked tense, almost aggressive.

"He looked a bit of a bruiser. I've not seen him before," I ploughed avidly on, regardless, suddenly liking the sound of my own voice. "I wouldn't like to meet him on a dark night."

"Do you mind," she said. "I don't want to talk about it, John." She put the beer in front of me, took the ten pound note extended in my hand, placed it into the till aggressively and walked quickly to the other bar where she started talking to the man she served earlier.

(idiot)

(total idiot)

I felt it rather than sensed it.

The loss.

It came over me in waves, and it came fast from out in the ocean.

They say that on Boxing Day 2004, on a beach in Thailand, a young English girl saw the tide recede at an alarming rate until sand was all that remained for miles. She told her mum that a Tsunami was coming, that she had learned this in a Geography lesson at school. Her mum and dad, and two brothers, packed up their belongings instantly. They told some other people surrounding, and a few of them listened, getting off the beach and heading inland as fast and as far as they could in the available time.

All of them survived the worst Tsunami in living memory.

Unlike the people who remained behind, who were brown bread the minute the wave hit the shore. I felt a bit like those people who remained behind. The wave of loss hit me. The loss.

You've lost her.

You were so close.

(Idiot)

I sat fixed on my stool, the warm feeling about helping with the statistics assignment gone forever, loaded up an Internet Poker site on my handheld and chose a £100 tournament about to start. Sixty players and a decent prize pool.

We were six handed. QQ in the big blind first hand. Under the Gun folds. The next two fold. The dealer button raises three times the BB. The small blind stays in and I three bet. The dealer button lets the timer recede and goes all in! Carla's rejection had pulverised me and beset by the incontrovertible fact that I'd lost her forever, I go all in, despite the fact he MUST have a monster of a hand.

The best I can hope for is a reckless AK, but even before all was revealed, I knew that was a fool's wish, a hopelessly romantic notion. When the cards flop onto their backs, it's a pair of bullets, AA, and I don't improve, a hundred notes burned to a cinder in just under a minute and a half. Commiserations arrive in two different languages on the chat box, and I shut down my console and watch Carla chat to the Pop Side Massive, ignoring me as if I don't exist, as if I've never existed, as if I will never exist, *(Duck Five)* and I clenched my fist, and I can feel it…FEEL IT…the wave crashing over me *(Duck Five)* the black rain, the dancing red lightning and I imagine Carla laughing at me, laughing, laughing…

…and I guzzled my pint as fast as I can, reached over to the coat rack, put on my coat and without saying goodbye, wandered out into the night and the never ending drizzle.

Chapter 9: The Cutting

As a rule, I don't cut - not at the minute - so if you do try to contact me to discuss the issue, I'll only be able to talk about it in the historical context rather than as a contemporary experience, but that night, I came close.

At one time, I used to slice up my armpits with a sharp model maker's knife I retained from the days of building Airfix kits.

Do you remember those? The injection moulded make-them-yourself aeroplanes in a box, the constituent parts of which had to be cut out of a frame. That night, Carla's dismissal circumnavigating my head, I withdrew the knife from the top left hand drawer of my writing desk. I took off my coat and scarf, and hung them both up on hooks, neat and tidy. I stood in the centre of the living room.

Held the knife in my hand and began to imagine what I used to imagine.

Cutting myself would bleed the worthlessness out of me. It would be deserved.

The knife was what I deserved.

(Cut into me. Deeply. Cut me.)

A feeling of release and euphoria.

The internal monologue was always the same. A siren song I was powerless to resist.

Sometimes, the voices came in whispers.

(Watch me bleed.)

Other times, the voices came in angry, bitter shouts.

(You are a worthless, ugly, cunt)

(Cut me. Now.)

(Slice me. Now.)

(Peel back the skin and reveal the darkness.)

(Bleed me.)

(Release me.)

(Pain is all you deserve.)

Pain is what I deserved, and the blood is the evidence of my uselessness. When I sliced, the voices stopped, and as I watched the blood drip, I felt peace. The knife I used to cut myself with never seems to need sharpening. English made. Stuff that lasted forever. Because of that engineering brilliance, I was able to cut myself from twelve until twelve thirty-five with this same knife. I don't know why I saved the knife. While therapists had cured my addiction to self-harm, I couldn't bring myself to jettison the Airfix knife, which shone in my hand. Heavier than it looked, a scalpel's heft.

That night, I stood in the centre of the room, and the entreaties and temptations came in whispers.

The usual whispers.

One light cut would sever the epidermis and the blood would flow. Generally (but not exclusively), I was prone to cut the places where Buboes grow. My arm pits, the soft skin at the top of my thighs, the soft protective skin around my manhood. I used to slice it swiftly with expert grace, and watch the blood pour down my arms and legs.

The lightness that descended upon me as I bled was like a religious experience.

You ought to see the scars.

They're like a miniature ant road map.

A thousand cuts under my armpit, now healed.

That night, I wanted to slice a motorway from the top of my thigh all the way to the knee and watch the blood spill like hot-red milk onto the carpet.

I started cutting when mum ran off with Carlos, and I only stopped when they gave me the experimental SSRI that time. I cut most often after my episodes - the weddings, the works parties, that night. Each prefaced a nuclear cutting spike that lasted a month. I'd stay in, friendless and remorseful, in my flat, sacked, excluded, disconnected from society, invisible, as if the episode had been all a terrible dream, and I'd take off my clothes, and naked, I'd start to carve the loose flesh under my armpits and down the long, smooth, soft fleshy part of my thighs.

Long sweeping divides. I have nicked my wrists on occasion, but that was a different thing altogether.

It seemed to miss the point.

That's the final cut isn't it, the wrist one.

Longways. In the bath. Pink Floyd *Dark Side of the Moon.* Bottle of vintage champagne. Six Haloperidol and thirty Temazepam.

(A photograph of Carla.)

Everyone close to me had discovered my cutting at one time or other, but luckily, apart from the two occasions that I've needed a transfusion, where my bedroom resembled a slaughterhouse, I've never been close to death through it.

Nevertheless, that's how I'll go.

I'll cut myself all over. I'll sever the right stuff.

The correct pipes.

Release the emptiness into the atmosphere, the black hole of me, watch the worthlessness drip onto the floor along with my life and soul.

I felt like that after Carla rejected me in the bar that night. But I didn't cut because the therapists had done a top job.

I did something else instead.

Chapter 10: Crazy Heart

Instead of slicing myself up, I turned on the TV and as it happened, by sheer coincidence, *Crazy Heart* was on. You know the one with Jeff Bridges and Maggie Gylenhall? The country music one, which won an Oscar? It's a sad, sad film, and it makes me sick to watch it, but I couldn't help it and zoned out on Hammer, self-pity, loss and Prozac, I watched it all the way through. I should have turned it off, but the film functioned as a form of virtual masochism, a compulsion, and after Carla's rejection of me, I just couldn't do it.

As I usually do when I watch *Crazy Heart* (it's an addiction), I ended up in floods of tears. Like I did the first time. The first time in Cedar Forest, Doctor Plunkett asked the seven of us to watch it because it's supposed to be redemptive, like *Shawshank.*

Uplifting and life enhancing, we were told.

I remember how that turned out.

Allow me a digression: I had an acquaintance in Cedar Forest called Kenny who could not stand the idea of white women sleeping with black men. He hated it with a passion. Kenny was in his thirties, tall and of Scottish origin. He was a footballer who played Conference level before his mental illness put paid to those dreams. His hatred of interracial relations became an obsession, a clinical cathexis, and it eventually drove him mad. One night in a pub in the centre of the City, he smashed a woman drinking with a black man over her head with a pint jug and split her head open. Her boyfriend kicked him half to death in the street, and when the assessments were done, they put him in the psychiatric hospital for a year.

That was the culmination. Kenny told the Police he'd been walking the streets of the City hitting white women in relationships with black men for two years.

Turns out the Peelers had been looking for him. He'd hit women with stakes. With bats. With pipe. With a shovel. In group therapy, he told us all that his first girlfriend - whom he loved - left him for a black man and it ruined his life. Any time he saw a mixed race couple, he would be in turmoil. He described his feelings to us. He described the anger, the frustration, the spinning, the nausea, the pain, and the misery in some detail. Of course, as society changed and mixed race relationships became more common, he saw incidences of it increasingly and escape from it became impossible.

TV programmes. Films. Adverts. Newspapers. Celebrities. Everywhere he looked, black man and white woman.

Then his mother started seeing a black man. That did for what was left of his sanity. That was the start of it. That sent him over the edge. I got the impression that what he did to her was worse than hitting, but he was crying when he recounted his tale, so no one pushed it.

That was his own personal Rubicon. Masked and hooded, he started hitting women - always the women - in the street. One woman, a tall blonde walking along the road with a hooded black man, he smashed over the head with a cricket bat and ran off.

I remembered reading about this, but race wasn't mentioned by the writers. She was a trainee Solicitor. The City paper said the blow caused brain damage. Leroy, who was in group and heard it all, spent the next six months taunting Kenny at each opportunity, the usual stuff. Kenny punched him in the rose garden after a particularly brutal wind up session, and had to be sedated - I felt Leroy was equally culpable. Leroy's patter was all about Kenny's mother; the dark side, once you've had black, there's no going back, all that prison stuff. But I said nothing, because it wasn't my beef.

This digression isn't all that interesting in itself, but what was interesting to me was that he revealed that he tried to cure himself of the affliction by obsessively watching Internet Porn featuring black men sleeping with white women.

"Confronting the issue head on, like. Making it seem normal and okay rather than fucking deviant and offensive, as such. I'd try it because I was going through hell."

He told us that he would spend twenty-four hours a day reading *Tumbleblogs,* the most common source. He related a few sites to us and later, I looked up one he mentioned and a few more through links. All the BBC sites. *Black Bull, White Slut. Sluts4BBC. Darkside Explorer. Willing Bitches. Blonde4Black. Black Takeover. Cocksmith Jones. Holy Black Seed. White Girl, Black Soldja.*

All the free videos on the porn sites. All the personal blogs written by white girls who favour having sex with black men.

He watched them twenty-four hours a day.

("Sludges. That's what the lads in City call 'em. Sludges. The ones I used to slap. I don't know why they call them that," I remember him saying.)

Despite this being the thing he hated most in the world, he watched the videos twenty-four hours a day for weeks and weeks. See, he had read about a technique called Flooding used to treat phobics. On the Internet.

A therapist would teach a phobic, say, someone scared of spiders, to relax over a period of time. Deep breathing, visualisation techniques etc. The phobic would be asked to sit on a comfortable armchair, and the therapist would ask the phobic to hold out a hand. The therapist would drop a live tarantula on the palm. "Flooding" the phobic's nervous system. By demonstrating that the spider couldn't hurt the phobic, mixed with immediate overstimulation and the relaxation techniques, flooding breaks the link between object and fear of the object.

Apparently, Kenny said, the technique had been proved highly effective, and he was desperate to get rid of his obsession, which had ruined his life. Doctor Plunkett, who was supervising group, pointed out at that the point that flooding is effective, but the effect doesn't last, and Kenny agreed. "I was fine for a while. I even spoke to me mother about her relationship. I tried to understand what was going on. After a while, I didn't even need the sites, and I could walk down the City streets and not be bothered, but it got awfy, really awfy and...and...well...you know...here I am..."

Many of his most vicious attacks on women in the street happened after the flooding experiment, which just goes to show that internet psychology sites should be treated with caution. Kenny's honesty was brutal and unyielding. Leroy became angry and walked out, I remember, but Plunkett asked him to carry on, and Kenny cried. No one had ever listened to him, and he had carried the coruscating obsession inside him for years. Bottled it up. It was the first time he had spoken about it. His life had already collapsed before the flooding experiment sent him insane.

Obsessions are like that. His obsession destroyed each aspect of his life. He didn't leave his house for three years, so he didn't witness mixed race couples walking together in the street, therefore, he didn't experience the compulsion to batter the women. He'd lost jobs because, for one, he daren't leave the house, and two, when he did, he would interrogate his female work colleagues about their partners. He discovered his boss had a black partner. He got drunk and called her some heavy names. She sacked him on the spot.

Eventually, he lost his mother, brother and all his friends. He couldn't have a relationship, even an e-mail or phone sex one, even when joining dating sites, because of his insistence of asking dates about their sex history, looking for the answer to the one question he had, which meant something to him. "I mean, a woman could have shagged a thahsand blokes as long as none on em were fucking *black,* you get meh? A woman could a shagged a thahsand women and I wouldn't have given a fuck. A woman could have shagged a big-dicked horse in a farmer's field, and that wouldn't have bothered me. Just as long as she weren't *ruined.* Just as long as she weren't *spoiled.* Know what I mean. Course, I never got far enough into a relationship to find out, because the women blocked meh!"

As he spoke, outside the room, Leroy kept marching up and down, giving him the wanker sign and the Nazi salute through the Perspex window. Kenny, who didn't feel he was a racist - "while they're fucking them, they ain't fucking me!" - wasn't offended and understood Leroy's feelings. He was prepared to accept they were insane. Last I heard, through Leroy's daily e-mail to me, Kenny killed himself shortly after they released him. How Leroy knew I don't know. He was more than pleased with the news.

I digress for a reason.

In my fragile emotional state, I should have turned off *Crazy Heart,* but I decided to confront the pain head on and all the way through, Carla was in my head. It didn't work. It made me worse. It made me want to cut and slice.

Watching *Crazy Heart* was like picking at a freshly formed scab.

I remember the first time I watched the film. At Cedar Forest. I mean, I like Jeff Bridges so I was happy to watch the movie the first time in Group, and I quite like country music - at least the modern stuff. It was a mistake. Despite three Prozac and a Haloperidol the size of a toy U-Boat, I STILL had to be restrained from pulling the TV off the wall. I remember thinking at the time, just before I went crazy.

How could she do that to him?

Maggie! Maggie!

Gorgeous, exquisite, Maggie Gyllenhall.

I mean, he ditches the booze. He ditches it! He does all he possibly can to beat the demon eating him away from the inside. He comes out the other side a clean and sober soul, and sixteen months later, she STILL marries someone else.

Oh, man, oh, man.

The abject hopelessness inherent in the closing moments of that film nearly vacuumed my soul straight to hell.

It's about the ONE, isn't it?

Always the one.

Maggie is so unbelievably soulful in that film.

She weeps tears of soul.

I'd never leave the house.

(ahum)

Anyway, after that little bit of group therapy, it was suicide watch for the next week and no more redemptive and uplifting/dark urban country movies for the foreseeable future.

The next film I watched with the gang was *Iron Man*, which I quite enjoyed, and the hero got the girl, so all was right with my tender world. And that night, after Carla's rejection of me, after flooding myself with *Crazy Heart* (it doesn't work, Kenny was right) I laid on the bed, crying my eyes out, pondering what I could do to put things right. Each morning I woke up thinking of ways of topping myself, and each night I went to bed thinking of ways of topping myself, and I have done since I was fifteen.

When I was a kid, I used to wake up with the certainty that my mother was going to die that day. That's part of the reason I was so unutterably clingy. I never woke up feeling sprightly (and I never have done). That cereal ad feeling, the spring in my morning step always absent, always distant. I always woke up terrified. Now, I wake up with all the gruesome stuff. All the demented, irrational hatreds of modern life. All the loss and all the fears. I'm so glad I don't have kids. I'm so glad that when I die all this will end. I hate myself, but you can't live like that, you cannot put up with the weight of that, so you fight off the feelings, and you go to work. You go out, and you get on with your life, and the next morning you wake up and you have to fight them off one more time, and after a while, it becomes pointless. The warfare becomes too fierce.

When you reach that point, you're off to the ironmongers for a length of rope. If I could describe to you the sheer density of the worthlessness I feel, you'd have sympathy for me.

Honest, you would. Even the Anti-Socials reading this would empathise because worthlessness is the saddest of all self-perceptions and we Borderlines, man, we've got worthlessness by the bucket. The two women I have loved have left me, and both of them got married and had kids with other blokes. They're happy. I don't speak to them. Why would I? Slags. They said they loved me, right? Nah. Of course, my subsequent Therapists have reassured me that it was nothing at all to do with the way I split them, or push pulled them, or acted out, or gaslit them, or faked suicide to win their affections, or over-dramatised or displayed my pathological jealousy at the most inopportune moments.

Of course not.

The following morning brought with it a contemplation of suicide. That was my only comfort and even then, the comfort was brief.

I've tried to kill myself four times, but I guess they were just cries for help. If I absolutely wanted to kill myself, I'd take skydiving lessons, or base-jump off those immense granite cliffs in the rapidly disappearing jungles of Brazil. Take a walk to those old council blocks in the City and fly off the top. Drop like a stone. It's not hard, is it? And I would imagine, the sensation of death would be quite exhilarating. Soaring into the void, seeing the sky around you, feeling the wind in your hair and your heart race to two hundred plus beats per minute. The approaching sense of peace, and joy, and contentment even more of an exhilaration than the fall. They say you are history before you hit the ground, but I've always had a strong constitution. I'm sure the cardiac theories are just suicidist propaganda.

No. That's how you'd do it. Foolproof.

Me? I tried to hang myself with my belt in psychiatric care, but the other times were strictly ingestations. Here's the first: Girlfriend, seven months, teacher, seven years older than me, blonde, loved her, dumped me out of the blue when I was twenty four - believe me, it was a terrifying dumping, even for a Norm, even for a Non Mutant, even for someone as sane as can be, even for a stable, emotionally strong, balanced, therapised individual, this would have been a dumping to shift the concrete foundations of sanity - and I went on a bender that lasted three days.

In Whitley Bay. If you're going to commit suicide in this messy, public, humiliating way, visit a holiday resort. British holiday resorts are built for suicide. I was drinking brandy. Ten bottles over the three days and twenty five to thirty pints of cider on top. Making a nuisance of myself. On the final day, dishevelled, wide-eyed, kicked and punched, shunned by the town, unable to get drunk no matter how many pints I ingested, being watched by the Police with a travel warrant - a Fuck-Up Warrant as William calls it in seaside resorts - I took a single bottle of Vintage cognac and a balloon to my hotel room along with seventy-two Co-Codamols. In floods of tears, listening to *Echoes* by Pink Floyd on my Walkman, I took the tablets one at a time, a generously filled balloon of cognac accompanying each one. With each pill and each sip of encroaching death, I toasted my ex-girlfriend ostentatiously.

Two mornings later, instead of the pillows of Heaven, I found myself in a hospital bed in Newcastle, on a drip, stomach pumped. I don't know how that happened (strong constitution and a curious maid?), but my father got to hear about it and made sure I spent six months on an all-inclusive therapeutic holiday in a resort just outside Harrogate.

As is his wont. Just writing that down made it better.

Do you keep a journal? They encourage that, you know. The psychotherapists. They encourage that kind of captivated, immersed narcissism. I've kept one for years. Whenever I am suicidal, I write about it in the frankest, most brutal terms. It sometimes helps. I tried it that morning, but the obsessions were powerful, and all it did was make me worse.

Can you imagine a life where you never wake up feeling well?

Ever?

If you can't imagine that, I envy you. I really do.

Perhaps you ought to go and read something else. How about one of those fantasy serials? They're supposed to be excellent. *Game of Thrones. Hunger Games.* Neil Gaiman. All that. All those talking flowers and sentient cats. All those evil kings and brave knights. All those pixies and fairies at the bottom of the garden.

All that infantile unreality. All that keep away from me world stuff. All that Vampire and zombie stuff. All that stuff that doesn't exist.

Babies in the nursery. Bedtime stories.

Maybe that's what I need. In fact, I think I'll try it when I finish writing this story. Might cheer me up a bit. If it wasn't for my anti-psychotic medication and Prozac, I don't think I would have survived that day. I didn't move from the sofa, and my images of Carla were all pervading and resistant to change. I knew that I had failed, and that she would never speak to me, but I resolved on a mission to apologise at The Saddler's that night, and by lying on the sofa watching *Jezza, Bargain Homes, Slappers, Word Wizard,* all the news channels, time would fly in a maelstrom of oblivion.

I didn't bet because that would require thinking, and I didn't want to think. All I wanted to do was embrace the nothingness caused by my medication and think of what might have been.

I showered for half an hour listening to *The White Stripes.* Scraped my skin with a scouring pad until I resembled a big lobster.

I shaved my chest clean of any hair. I shaved off my stubble with a fresh disposable. I moisturised until ten years disappeared from my disjointed, modern art mush.

Defiantly, I looked in the mirror. If she was going to dump me, I'd leave a clean corpse. Almost as if time had granted my wish, it was seven thirty, and I went down to The Saddler's expecting it to be the last time ever. It was a gloomy, cold night, and I was glad my parka had a giant hood and my jeans were thick.

Carla saw me and came over before I even got to the bar. I took down my hood.

"John, I'm so glad you came tonight. I didn't think you would," she said.

"Oh?" I said, playing dumb. "Why? I always pop in for a pint at this time."

She looked a bit bemused and drew back a little. Picked up some empties from a table.

"It's just, like...last night. I was sharp with you. I just want to say I'm sorry."

Relief flooded through my entire being, and I grabbed hold of a chair to stop myself from floating toward the ceiling. "No need, Carla. In fact, it's my fault. I'm so nosy at times."

She smiled at me, a look that turned my stomach to runny chocolate. Took the glasses inside to The Snug. "Come on, I'll get your usual. And I've got a surprise for you."

I took off my parka and hung it up, sat down on my stool. The pub was almost empty, except for the regulars in the Pop Side. Big Keith wouldn't be happy with this state of affairs, but I was. That night, Carla was wearing a pink tee-shirt and blue jeans, flip-flops, her hair in a ponytail. No makeup at all. She looked like she had just left a training course delivered on a beach. She poured my pint and with one hand, reached over to a red folder.

"Do you remember last night before I got bitchy? You said you might help me. With my stats?"

"How could I forget!"

"Have a look in here," she nodded at the folder.

I opened it. Inside was a card in a pink envelope on top of an assignment sheet. Embarrassed, I stared at the card and Carla looked at me. "Aren't you going to open it?" She asked, metaphorically putting her hands on her hips.

I grinned at her, sheepishly. I was much more comfortable with stats. I opened the envelope carefully. It was a light blue Apologia card, with a teddy bear and Sorry on the front. I opened the card. It was plain, with no verse. Blue handwriting.

"Sorry for snapping. This is for the stats and thanks loads for the chats!

C the Poet xx"

Stunned, I didn't know what to say, but I had to say something. "Thanks...was no need..."

"I was such a bitch last night. You were only being caring. Anyway, I mean it. I love talking to you. You're so clever. Can you have a look at those stats for me?" She asked optimistically.

"Sure. I'll do it now," I replied.

"I'd do it with you but Keith shouts at me for chatting a lot."

"Don't worry," I said. "Have you a pen?"

She reached for a blue biro near the till and I pulled out my Berry, turned on the calculator. "You serve some customers, and I'll see what I can do with this."

"Oh, John, that's lovely."

"My pleasure," I said, melting away into nothing, as if I had never existed at all, as if I was a warm raindrop spreading onto the carpet. Unable to stand it, I took my pint and the folder to one of the tables and started to work.

I'm a graduate in Physics so this kind of statistics was meat and drink, and for the rest of the night, I settled down to work, feeling a bit silly at my histrionics last night, proud that I was able to help her, and just a little bit more in love with Carla with each formula I cracked, each calculation I inputted into my Berry and each stroke of my pen.

Later that night, I made a breakthrough of sorts, however in reality, the breakthrough was made last night as I watched *Crazy Heart*. I realised that because I had suffered so much mental anguish watching that film, God had decided to redress the balance. I went to the toilet halfway through the breakthrough moment, and I thanked him while sitting on the pot. I thanked him profusely while I suppressed the urge to cry. It was at times like that I wished I was the lantern-jawed, strong, silent kind, able to withstand whatever was thrown at me, but I'm not my father, sadly. Luckily, I didn't cry as I did at the ending of *Crazy Heart*.

The breakthrough moment? Carla came to talk to me about the statistics on her break, and when I'd shown her what I'd done, highlighted the working and tried to explain the methodology, she asked me whether I'd like to go for a walk in the park. Tomorrow.

I can't remember what I said because my senses had shut down so forgive my expositional style at this point. (What do you think, I said?) I remember what she said to me, gingerly. She had something to show me, had favour to ask me. She said she was tired of talking to me over the side of a bar. She said she'd like to talk in a different environment. Was I free tomorrow? Some fellows came in from the Bowls Club, and Keith signalled that her break was over. That was when I went to the toilet. I cannot remember whether I used the word Yes or not. Or how I used it if I did. But I remember her smiling and saying 10am by the Memorial Gardens, and I remember nodding, but that was it - the Thor's Hammer was no stronger than usual - and the next thing I know, I was home, watching some poker game with a grin as wide as the Nile at its mouth.

Chapter 11: Janine Peaches

In the Cedar Forest Hospital, there was a nurse named Janine Peaches.

Actually, I called her that because I couldn't pronounce her surname, some sort of Eastern European confection with more consonants than vowels. Her English was dark and harsh, humourless and heavy, and I certainly couldn't speak her language, whatever it was, so it suited me to visualise her as a member of the Peaches family. She was one of the nurses who worked the seven till seven shift, and she was allocated to supervise me for the three years I was incarcerated. We were allowed to watch TV in the TV lounge or our own bedrooms until 10pm. In my case, Janine came to my room to give me whatever medication was on my clipboard at any one time, usually Haloperidol, or some form of anti-depressant, or some experimental drug they suggested might change me when accompanied by the relentless therapy I was asked to undergo.

Janine was a plump woman with a stocky, robust build more suited to tug-of-war or playing scrum-half then working in an asylum, with a thatch of wiry blonde hair like an upside down scrubbing brush used to clean baths or toilets. About fifty, but I may be doing her a disservice. In her white coat, blue stockings and flats, she looked like a nurse, but I'm not sure she had any qualifications in that line. She must have done. Sometimes she wore spectacles, which magnified her blue eyes and thick black mascara. Her nose was often red as if she'd been sniffing something strong. Her best feature was her lips, which were thick, and kissable, and she always smelled fresh, an agreeable perfume or anti-perspirant. Sometimes I fancied her, other times I'd rather not even look at her, and for about six months or so, she'd come into my room, give me the tablets without speaking, watch me take them, turn my light out and leave me in the darkness with only the screams and the dreams of my neighbours to accompany my passage into night.

One night, approximately six months into my incarceration, she came into my room, sat down on the chair and we started talking. I didn't prompt this. I didn't ask her to. She just did. She had a shorter coat on this time, and I could see the top of her tights, the extra thick bit at the top, the elastic circumference that helps to keep them upright. She asked me why I was in the Cedars and I told her - well, a version of it, anyway - and she asked me about my family and my goals and when I was going to get out, and I told her all this. I asked her about much the same things and all the time, she sat crossing and uncrossing her legs. On occasion, she would lean forward and cup her chin in the palm of her hand while her elbow rested on her thigh. She would bob her shoe up and down as she spoke and I would become transfixed by her shoe because she certainly had attractive feet. She took her shoe off, and I could see she had painted nails - red? Black? - and it gave me, well, a male reaction when I watched her, and I wondered why she was doing this. In six months, she had never said a word to me. Not in six months, and now she wanted to be friends, and the way I looked at it, she was flirting with me. Maybe she wasn't. In my therapy, I'd been talking about the differences between a woman flirting and a woman just being friends and all the body language, which indicates that. Coming up towards ten, when it was time to shut the door for the night, I said to her well, it's time for bed, and she said yes, it is, yes, it is, and she shut the door while inside my room and asked me to take my pyjamas off. In the hospital, after six, they make you wear linen trouser bottoms, which are like pyjamas and I asked her why, and she said because I am telling you to and believe me, you get used to being told what to do in these places, so while I carried some serious wood, I slid my linen trousers off and sat on the bed. She walked up to me and touched my manhood, which nearly burst instantly, and without another word, she took it in her hand and knelt either side of my thighs. With one hand, she had my excited member. With the other, she lifted up her skirt. I could see her tights were crotchless, and she was wearing white panties, plain, ordinary, Pound Goblin panties, panties to clean the kitchen in, throwaway panties.

While holding my cock like a vice, she pulled her gusset to one side and with military efficiency, slid me in dry as sandpaper. I could smell her. She hadn't washed herself for a week, and she had an arcane, musky odour which you love, or you hate; you hate, and I love, and I wanted to get closer to it, but she held me back by the shoulders. I lifted up my hand to try to touch her giant breasts, but she slapped it and shook her head. I wanted to kiss those kissable cherry-red lips, but she pulled away and forced herself down on me. She didn't look at me, watching a spectral mark on the wall just behind my head, and she was getting wetter.

I wanted to please her, and I concentrated on racing results and films I love, and books I love, and wonderful days in life, and I tried to visualise an apple core. I manipulated it in my mind's eye and tried not to listen to her increasing moans. The smell from her was intense, one of the most intense smells I have ever experienced. Luckily, this was her thing, this was what got her off, this control thing, this raping thing, cocks, no intimacy and she finished off, and when she did, I took a bite of the apple, fixed in my slave position, and took one last smell of her essence and ejaculated a litre of the business.

Rather than bathe in the afterglow, she lifted up her behind like a cowboy dismounting a horse, pulled down her skirt and without a word, walked out of my room into the corridor leaving a wet patch on my thigh and this intense sex and woman smell on my quilt. I pulled my trousers up, laid down on the bed in the disinfected warmth of my cell, and slept for eight hours.

For the next three nights, Janine came to my room and wordlessly fucked me in exactly the same way. It seems she had any information she wanted from me, and over the next two and a quarter years, we never spoke in anything but the most general terms. She had a rotating shift system, which meant I only saw her every three weeks, and on two or three nights of her week on my ward, Janine did the same thing. She would come to my room with medication. Shut the door and pull back her gusset with me sitting with my back to the cell wall. The position in which we had sex never altered. I asked her whether we could do it some other way. Missionary. Doggy.

She shook her head. I offered her cunnilingus. She shook her head. *Anything* I suggested, she shook her head. Some nights she couldn't come. Other nights I couldn't. Some nights were terrible and boring. Others were intense and majestic, and both of us went off like the New Year Millennium celebrations. One memorable night, she let me touch one of her breasts. She took my hand after she had mounted me and slid it under her bra and to this day as I write this, I can sense the shape and impression of her breast and nipple on my fingers and palms. I tried to keep going as much as possible because that human connection, that brief moment of real intimacy, was better than two and a half years of the rape sex we were having, but she could sense I was enjoying touching her body much more than the other thing, and she crudely and roughly pulled my hand away, and she never let me touch her again, which made me just a little bit more insane than when I arrived.

She must have known.

She must have read my notes. I used to dream about kissing those lips. Long, dreamy, intense kisses with Janine Peaches. I'd beg her to let me kiss her, but she wouldn't hear of it, wouldn't dream of it, and one day, when I expected her to come into my room at nine thirty, sitting at full attention, Pavlov's Dog, classically conditioned to the time, nine thirty, nine thirty, the ringing of the bell. I waited, and I waited, and waited, and she didn't come; Janine didn't come, and she didn't come, and I went out into the corridor and saw another nurse, a black nurse escorting Janine's trolley. I asked her about Janine, a sense of desperation inside me as loud and as heavy as an explosion, a yawning NEED for Janine to come, and she said she didn't know. That she worked for an agency, and I nearly asked her to come and do for me what Janine did for me because I had a classically conditioned excitement condition to show for it. She didn't bat an eyelid because after all, it's a dumping ground for mentally deranged people just like me, and people masturbate in the corridors for no reason and a man walking the corridors carrying a ten o clock, if you understand my meaning, is a pretty normal sight for a psychiatric nurse, and I went back into my room, relieved myself into a wastepaper bucket and cried myself to sleep.

Next time, the same thing happened.

I was Pavlov's Dog, dribbling into my basket and Dr. Pavlov didn't bring in the food. I was in despair; because I think - something that is part of my mental health profile - I had fallen in love with Janine Peaches and her ruthless rapes of my sanity - my jailer, my wonderful jailer.

My therapy became farcical, as surreal as the Marine dressing up as Superman in *T9C,* and I stole drugs from other patients to get myself out of it, into a dream world, which wasn't as painful as this one, and I lost weight, and waking moments lasted an hour and thus, days stretched out in the distance, whereas before Janine, coming would speed it all, accelerate the physics of it.

One day, two shrinks came to see me. The hitherto mentioned Dupont from New Orleans and Hethersett from somewhere near Barnsley. They asked me a series of questions about Janine Peaches. Honestly. That's how her name sounded when they said it. Nurse Janine Peaches.

They asked me whether she had ever behaved inappropriately to me. I don't know whether it was the new medication they were administering - which gave me St Vitus Dance and knocked two octaves off sounds and reduced the speed of other's speech by a million miles an hour, but I laughed, and laughed, and laughed until tears poured down my cheeks and onto my quilt in tiny silver pools.

Janine had been fucking the entire corridor, not just me.

Locate *Am I Going Insane* by Black Sabbath on the album *Sabotage*. It's a strange album like a lot of their middle period stuff. Too many drugs and too many internal management problems, but at the end of this song, there's the sound of an insane person laughing.

Well, readers. That was just like me when Dupont and Hethersett asked that question.

Of course, I said no. I told them that she was a terrific Psychiatric nurse, one of the best ever, and I miss her. Both of them nodded and took away their white coats, goatees and clipboards and left me to another of my complete and utter psychological collapses, which took me, oh, about three months to get over.

For the last three months of my stay, Janine Peaches was replaced by a Mrs. Barnes who you'd have to be a bit deranged to have sex with because she looked like a school dinner lady. I remembered the days when schools had dinner ladies, and I'm not that mad. Soon after, they released me...and I met Nina...and soon I was back with Mrs. Barnes wishing she was Janine Peaches.

Chapter 12: The Secret Flower Garden

Overcast weather that morning with spots of rain about. The sun tried to peek through gaps, but even when it succeeded in doing so, other near-inky black nebulae overwhelmed its rays.

The council gardener drove his lawnmower back and forth across the top football pitch, and a pungent smell of freshly-cut grass filled the morning air; somehow it made me more nervous. Already, she was fifteen minutes late. I wore my Barbour hunting coat, blue jeans and some non-descript boots, and I leaned on the Memorial Arch waiting for her at the entrance to the park.

With each minute that went past, I became more despondent. It doesn't take a lot, but a girl I'm in love with not turning up for a date is up with the best of the reasons. It wasn't a surprise. I didn't expect her to turn up, but I hoped to beat the odds. I began to pace between one half of the arch and the other, the gravel noisy underneath my boot heels. I could sense the contents of my stomach beginning to liquefy.

Inevitably, the typical mental processes circulated.

She's twenty, you're over forty.

What would her friends think?

Her friends probably counselled her last night. They had probably ripped her ambitions to shreds. They had probably ridiculed her. Called her names and called ME names. Probably said I was a pervert and told her she could do a lot better than me.

I'd seen one of her friends in the pub, a pretty girl named Charlotte, and I saw her look at me with complete and utter contempt. When I had finished facing that first wave of self-hatred, I was ready to return home, and I cursed my optimism, my vainglorious plan. I stopped pacing up and down for a moment as a couple walked past me on the way to the Bowls Club, an older couple, and they wished me good morning, the old lady wearing a thick aquamarine coloured coat and a floppy crimson hat, which made her look a tiny bit like Princess Margaret used to look. I wished them the same in return.

As soon as they had passed, I went back in to my fugue, the second wave of self-hatred coming in on a black and portentous tide. Repeatedly, I went into the reasons why it would be madness for her to turn up, that it shouldn't be seen as a reflection on me in any way, that it was all just a silly thing, a silly, spontaneous thing, which was never going to work.

I leaned on the arch and bit my nail. My nails have been eviscerated over the years to the point where they hardly exist. Neither do the tip of my fingers because I am a biter, an anxious biter, and sometimes, I get so worried, I chew the fingerprints off my fingers when no nail protrusion is left to bite on. Thus, my thumbs get whitlows and blains from nails regrowing into the skin and most of the time, my thumbs are swollen and blistered.

Checked my watch.

Ten twenty.

That's it, I thought. She isn't coming. That's the end for me down The Saddler's. I'll never be able to see her. The aftermath of her rejection will be unbearable. The embarrassment. The sheer, coruscating blushing embarrassment. I'll never be able to drink in The Saddler's, even if she isn't working. Churned stomach, flushed cheeks, burning eyes and beating temples, I pictured going home, turning the heating on, undressing, naked, sitting down on the sofa, listening to music, some David Bowie, some Lou Reed, something like that, and while I rest, I'll slice chunks out of my armpit, pick the stitches out of the previous lattice -

- make it bleed, and bleed, and bleed, maybe start on my legs.

The image of cutting calmed me and even before I was aware of this happening, I found myself walking backwards up past some of the oldest oak trees in Wheatley Fields, halfway between despair and anticipation.

I heard a shout from near the Prebend opposite the arches. "John!"

It was her. Carla. Quilted jacket, red scarf, jeans and Wellington boots. She wore a royal blue woolly hat, two floppy dog-ears dangling to her shoulders from the sides. I stopped and waved, watched her skip over toward me. She carried on her natter, that incredible creamy soft middle class burnished accent that I remembered from my time in Cambridge.

"I am so sorry I'm late, John. My tutor called me and he just would not get off the phone! I feel a bit guilty because I told him I'd run out of charge."

"Was it important?" I asked, relieved.

"He thinks it's always important," she said. "But it usually never is. What he said could have waited until tomorrow," she said, scratching her nose.

I calmed down, slowly, and as I did so, I felt a different kind of nervousness, a polar opposite emotion, a wild swing from despair to elation, some kind of buzzing, and I immediately clamped down on it. Taking hidden breaths, I engaged my positive, sensible, well trained self-talk, much of it to stop me from proposing marriage.

(You might think I'm kidding. My record for this romantic gesture is three and a half hours into a first date. She looked at me as if I was crackers and dumped me on the spot.)

I listened to her natter about her tutor and her course, and constructed a gentle gaze, hoping I didn't look like a psycho of my inner self-portrait. The simian dribbler, the fecund drooler. The tilted head, the heavy-lidded eyes of the lizard. The missing tooth. The giant ears almost detached, a Lombroso-measured head twice the average, football sized. I watched her talk, never leaving her eyes, her cavernous, enormous brown eyes. If she was wearing any makeup, it was so tastefully applied that I couldn't tell. Her lashes long and perfectly balanced. Her plain, symmetrical expression, devoid of marks, clear and fresh, as if she had woken this morning, walked down into her garden and splashed herself in a crystal clear pool while mounted on a water lily. She didn't seem to notice how ugly I was and if she did, she hid it well, politeness personified. When she spoke - and I have to confess, dear reader, that I wasn't listening to all she said about college - her pink lips caressed each syllable perfectly.

As she spoke about some Open Day she had to help organise, I distinctly remember thinking that I could spend the rest of my life just staring at her, occasionally reaching over to cup her cheek, stroking her.

That voice.

Oh, man, I could listen to Carla talk. She could recite a Hovermower instruction manual from cover-to-cover, and I would never interrupt.

She seemed to dry up, and she grabbed my arm. "Let's go and have a walk down to the flower garden. I've been told the cherry blossom trees bloomed last night, and we won't have much of a window to see them," she said, and I nodded, and the two of us, hands in pockets, walked down past the changing rooms toward the destination.

"Did you know that eight years ago, a developer put in an application to build three hundred houses on all this, John?" She asked, sweeping her right arm imperiously as we walked down.

"Really?"

"Can you believe that? The council threw it out straight away, but for one reason or another, they allowed the same developer to build on a wood up near the garden centre. Lots of protests at the time, but they weren't enough to stop him. It's a tragedy, don't you think?"

"I would imagine they would argue that people have to live somewhere," I replied.

"My tutor said that four out of five people who purchased the houses on the wood that died were from outside of town. That can't be right, can it? It upsets me. Can you imagine if they ever built on this?"

We walked through a small graveyard at the bottom of the Memorial Park. No more than thirty gravestones in various states of repair. I looked at the dates. They were very old graves.

"Are they allowed to build on cemeteries like this?"

She stopped and crouched over one. "I don't know. I'll ask my tutor. Look at this one," she said, gesturing me over. I crouched down next to her and felt my knee crack. She seemed to do the crouching thing a lot easier than I did. I read the weather-beaten, faded writing on the granite stone. **Amy Cooper. 1843 - 1869. She Was Much Loved.**

"I wonder what her life must have been like? She was a real person. She must have gone to school, worked, loved, had children. Look at how young she was when she died. Just twenty six. Oh, My God, that's just six years older than me, John."

"You'll live to be a hundred, Carla," I said, grinning.

She tapped me on the arm playfully. "No way am I going to be a hundred. That's so old."

"On average, women live about eight years longer than men, all other things being equal," I replied.

She stood up. "That makes sense," she said. "Both my grandmothers are alive, and both my grandfathers passed away. Don't want to be a hundred. All that wee..." she said. "What do you think Amy did?" She said referring to the gravestone.

Truth be told, I wasn't interested in the slightest, but I could listen to her forever, and I wasn't bothered what she spoke about.

I remember that time well. If she wanted to talk about it, I wanted to listen. It was as simple as that and that never varied, never altered. If we'd have married, I am absolutely, incontrovertibly convinced that that pattern would have continued. I sometimes wonder whether I was in love with her voice. "Don't know," I said, with that desire in mind. "You tell me."

With that, Carla playfully recounted her story of Amy Cooper.

"Oh, for sure the daughter of a Merchant, I think. Very pretty..." and as we walked down to the flower garden behind the cemetery, I made sure each step was like walking on the moon, slow and measured, almost floating, as if I was an old man indeed, while she knitted her elegant story of young Amy Cooper. Her life, her loves, her ambitions, her personality, all the way to her passing. She described her clothes, her hair, her smile, like a born writer, and I knew that she was studying the wrong subject; a girl with an imagination like this should study English Literature somewhere grand, write sweeping stories, historical romances, historical transpositions, what-if histories, all the stuff people buy in lorry loads.

I made each step to the flower garden last ten seconds by some contrivance or another. Each time Carla faltered in her narrative, I prompted her to go in another direction. Each time she responded, earnestly, vivacious, in that sublime, balmy, measured, unutterably hypnotic voice of hers, with its occasional redundant, trans-Atlantic inter-connectives, its likes, and stuffs, and oh, my gods, and I feasted on it, each word exploding in fountains of gold. Cleopatra never luxuriated in her marble bathtubs full of asses milk as joyously as I relished listening to Carla.

(If you want to learn to be a listener, rather than be one of those people who wait for their turn to speak, listen to someone with a voice like Carla's. You'll be a Melanie Klein quality listener in weeks.)

Eventually, we reached a high hedge, which hadn't been trimmed in an age, its tendrils and tiny branches pulling the whole over. "I've run out of things to say about Amy," she said, somewhat flat and awkward.

"Let's go and look at some flowers. I'm looking forward to this," I replied.

"Oh, I am. I've only been here a couple of times. I've brought my camera. I was thinking of doing a project. Will you help me write it?"

"How?" I asked.

"You're clever, I can tell," she blushed. "You know things."

"I don't know much about flowers. I'm a physicist."

"Oh, no," she said shaking her head. "I can tell. You're much more than that. Will you help me? I have to write a project on wild environments under pressure in Wheatley Fields. That's how I know about the development application and stuff. We can visit the Cherry Wood and cycle up the Heritage Trail near the college."

She suddenly did that thing young girls do, that eye thing, that cat's eye thing, the one where their eyes expand to the size of the twin moons of Saturn. She put her hand on my Barboured forearm. "Please, John. I'd love it if you could help me."

What could a love-struck man say in this situation but "Of course, I will. I'll be glad to help."

"Fantastic! Thank you. Between us..." she said, struggling with the door to the gardens, I, too stupefied to help her open it, too dull witted, too stunned at the amazing turn of events, all of it, "...I think we'll create the *best* project."

The two of us might have entered the secret flower garden at that point, but I'd entered another place entirely.

We walked into the garden, with its early spring riches, its Snow Blossom, its nascent Crocus, its carpet of Bluebells, its Pink Belladonna bushes, its sweeping banks of Snowdrops, its Daffodils, Holly bushes to the north side, the fledgling mauve and lemon Primroses, the Azeleas and the Apple Blossoms.

We stood for ages underneath a row of Cherry Blossom trees, not quite in full bloom, a few days off, but we could smell them, and the fragrance of those trees allied to Carla's presence will stay with me forever, I think.

That ten minutes, that nexus, in that flower garden, with the cherry blossom just beginning to bloom, Carla talking animatedly about the beauty of nature and the sanctity of wild flowers, was without doubt, the finest ten minutes of my entire life.

Nothing had gone before.

Nothing would occur in the future.

If a God watches over us (and I doubt that), he would have stopped time, or at least suspended Carla and I in a perpetual Groundhog Ten Minutes because I was in heaven and whatever had assailed me previously had gone.

All the pain, the misery, the anger, the pathology, the flawed disturbed psychology, the tortured impulses, the desire to cut, the desire to end it, the memories (oh, those horror memories), had gone.

I was at one.

And do you know what?

I never told Carla.

I simply carried on listening to her talk. When it came to my turn, I talked about the cycle of the four winds, and we walked up toward The Three Steeples. All I can remember her saying for the rest of that day is how much she enjoyed our walk and how much she was looking forward to working on the project with me, and I could have cried.

I can see her now, walking into the town, waving at me - her floppy hat, her swinging scarf - skipping happily toward the shops where she'd arranged to meet some friends.

Chapter 13: The Just Say No Club

So why don't I just stop it, I hear you ask on the plane, the train, or in the back of the car?

Why doesn't he just stop it, Phyllis?

I don't know, Nigel. Pass the sherbert lemons.

Why don't I just stop it?

You ever see the film *Frightmare*?

1974. If you've seen it, you're in a serious minority. It's a rarity and a curio. Check out Star channel 319. I saw it when I was a kid with my mum, bless her little Venezuelan socks. We have a spoiler situation on its way so type **virgin-white sheepskin rug** into the thingy, and you'll miss this bit if you want to see the film, and I suggest you do because the last five minutes makes anything directed in the interim look like a bus trip to Predictable City.

I'm still shaking now, thirty-six years on.

Frightmare is about a mentally ill woman who commits terrible crimes and is consequently sentenced to a mental asylum. After an indefinite period, she is released because psychiatrists believe she is now so old and so well psychotherapied that she is no longer a danger to the public.

Hah!

She sets herself up in the Home Counties countryside as a tarot reader and spiritualist, with the aid of her devoted husband, and advertises her service in the London papers. Soon, clients begin to appear and equally so, those same clients begin to disappear. A psychiatrist involved with the woman's daughter suspects something is wrong and begins to investigate.

Cue total carnage.

You see, personality disorders like mine are fixed, ingrained and as difficult to shift as a red wine stain on a virgin-white sheepskin rug. At least fifty psychologists, psychiatrists, therapists, counsellors and psycho-pharmacologists have given me Counselling, Psychoanalysis, DBT, MBT, CNT, IPT, CBT, MACT, CAT and PST and all the other therapies, plus the anti-depressants, the anti-psychotics, the lithium, the anti-convulsives, all I can handle - all the Christmas tins full of chocolate sweets, all the centres, all the wrappings, with and without the parallel-talking cures.

And do you know what? It all works. It's all brilliant. It's all top hole. I love talking to these guys. They know what they're talking about. After a certain period of time, usually three years, enough time for him to forget the last dodgy thing I did, my father will call a case conference of social workers, psychologists, psychiatrists, therapists, counsellors and psychopharmacologists. He will attend. After a time, they will conclude that I am as cured as I am ever going to be inside, and they will set up the Frightmare Package. A Care In The Community intervention involving a flat (like the one I'm in now), a medication programme and a Community Psychiatric Nurse to visit to check on my progress (all of which my software magnate father pays for). You see, I'm totally okay at that point. I can go years without an episode, by which time I've developed new social networks, new work friendships and (with due remorse) re-established a version of the old ones.

I mean, what does a person with a personality disorder look like?

He looks like you.

She looks like you.

Are you on a train?

Have a look.

A hundred people crammed in like sardines? A busy journey? Out of those hundred people, up to three have an Anti-Social Personality Disorder. That's a Psychopath to you and me. Possibly more in the London commuter belt. In less politically correct days, those people used to be known as Psychopaths. Affectionless psychopaths. Robotic men and women with no emotions, no morals, and worse, no understanding of your feelings and morals.

Up to six of those will suffer my BPD condition (probably not to my extent). Shrinks diagnose women with my condition far more than they diagnose men, so if you're on a train rammed with several hen parties, it's possible six out of a hundred will be Borderlines. Anything from one to three will be Histrionic. One might be Schizoid.

Luckily for the world, the explosive disorders, the IED's are pretty rare. Less than six in a thousand and even that might be an overestimate.

Man, that uniqueness feeds my narcissistic impulses like a three-course roast dinner sometimes. Speaking of which, up to ten will have a Narcissistic Personality Disorder.

Are you on **Me.Com?**

The social network, which carries all before it? Come on, admit it. You are. Well, some new research suggests that one in ten of you might be a Narcissist serious enough to need therapy.

(Not that I'm suggesting that you are the narcissist, dear friend. Oh, no. It's that bloke sitting next to you!)

Felicity, my mate from inside Cedar Forest, showed me her friends list. She asked me my opinion on a friend of hers, a sometime acquaintance, she knew from a job in the days when her suicidal ideations and self-harming were something she could cope with. His photo array contained sixteen photographs. With sixteen photographs, a typical Me.com user might have photographs of the kids, an album cover, a favourite comic amongst them, quirky and surreal photographs of a much beloved pet.

Not this guy.

Felicity's Me-friend had sixteen photographs of himself in various poses, mostly close up - a fly's eye of loving self-images. A man so in love with his image that nothing else exists. A man so pathologically egocentric that he made a marble collage of himself on his computer.

You know the weird thing? No teenage girl is going to be putting a poster of me on the wall, I grant you that, but this guy? He looked like a half-sucked pear drop.

I made sure she de-friended him. I mean, it's not beneficial for her to know someone like that, is it? She's such a frail little thing.

So. Personality disordered people. They look like you. No mad staring eyes. No spider-web tattoos inked around the eyes. No Kyocera knives secreted in back pockets. No drooling, no crazed chortles in the darkness.

They look just like you do.

And so do I.

In the three years at Cedar Forest, I hadn't exploded, overdramatised, threatened suicide, faked suicide, split, push-pulled, acted out, clung, gaslit, or otherwise made a complete prick of myself because I didn't care enough about anyone to do those things. And no one gave a damn about me in there. Hence, the hospital was a Borderline-neutral environment. If I had formed a relationship inside - I've never indulged: however, some do, and it's often quite touching to watch - I might have done all those things because...because...I do those things, unfortunately for me. After three years of toeing the line, of going to therapy, of taking my meds, of being pleasant to all and sundry and brushing my teeth in the morning, what else can the mental health profession do but discharge me. They can't keep me inside forever.

The beds are needed.

Awful lot of crazy people in the world.

Chapter 14: e-mail Protocol

Carla had told me that she wasn't working at The Saddler's that night, and she was planning to catch up with an assessed essay. She hadn't told me the topic. She asked me whether I was on any social networks, and I said no. She seemed disappointed, but I told her I was on e-mail, and I gave her my business card. She took it, put it in her purse, and said she would drop me an e-mail later.

(Can't be doing with social networking. What's the point? It's people I crave, not two-dimensional copies of people! Don't try and find me on Me.com, Network, or Contact Book, or anything like that. You're wasting your time. I'm on Pony Express, and you have to know me to get that address!)

At home, I counted down the minutes until she did, being unable to write, constantly interrupting my mental process to see whether she had sent the mail, constantly logging in and out of my Pony Express e-mail account, in and out, typing in my password each time (Blackhole62. That's my password. Or it was until I wrote this…), and I must have logged in a hundred times in five hours. In and out, in and out, staring at the screen, obsessively logging in and out. At one point, I got down on my knees and prayed to a God that I don't believe in for her to send me the mail because I needed her to do so with my whole being, and not being with her in some ethereal sense was already far too painful for me to withstand.

Her absence was already causing obsessive cognitive chains. Compulsions. Hyper-negative, damaging, self-talk.

I started to do that thing I do with a compass point.

I jab the soft connecting bit behind the elbow with a compass point to draw blood.

If I'm feeling gruesome, I'll play that game where I try and get as close as possible to the vein. (Have a look. Right now. Quite a few veins inside. A little patchwork. They come to life after a bicep curl session at the gym. It's standard junky territory. (There is a significant arterial channel underneath, but I've never checked this out. My bubo pits have taken the significant damage, but I guess I should mention it anyway.)

See if I can burst it. See if I can make it pop. It was a relief when, about seven forty five, I logged in and found it.

An email.

Subject box: Hi! Address: **sweetcarla92@network.com.**

Man: Was THAT a relief!

My nervous system, sympathetic and parasympathetic, my interconnecting neuronal brain networks, my ephemeral, Descartian psyche, my tortured consciousness, and my controlling, sinister unconscious had been immediately satisfied by that single mail.

This isn't right, is it? I knew it wasn't right. This isn't the way people behave.

This is, in a nutshell, why I've spent a quarter of my life under the supervision of the Insanity Industry.

Normal people do not suspend their entire life to wait for an e-mail.

For the rest of the night, I sat eating Oatcakes and Fatbuster yoghurt while playing on my computer, and Carla and I e-mailed each other all night. Jokey mails, serious mails about the project, one-line mails, paragraph mails. Two wonderful mails especially - each one of them I treasure, even to this day. Even now, when I get the chance, I open the little yellow Carla folder on occasion, and go through all the mails she sent to me.

The first of the two thanked me for the time walking through the wild parts of Wheatley Fields. She asked me to accompany her on the weekend for a walk up the Heritage Trail to Bloodworth and Follow Fields. She suggested cycling the fourteen miles. She said we could have a picnic by the old mill halfway down if I wanted. What I especially liked about that mail was the implicit tone that she was somehow troubling me with the request!

As if she was asking me for a favour. Oh, man, I nearly choked on my yoghurt at that point.

I considered the invitational e-mail and wrote back to her after about fifteen minutes. A measured and calculated gap. I didn't want her to think that all I was doing was waiting for her e-mails, reading her e-mails, and replying to her e-mails even though that was exactly what I was doing. I composed the reply, a cheeky two liner telling her I was already looking forward to it, and that I indeed, did have a cycle, and would love a bike ride in the sunshine. I began to stab a rotting apple core on my desk with the aforementioned compass point to pass the time.

The second e-mail was about a lad on her course who was hassling her. You can imagine what the mail said because she wrote quite a long one, and it's a typical story of boy meets girl, girl rejects boy because she doesn't fancy him, and boy not taking no for an answer, and by the end of the tale, I was Bruce Banner. I could see the veins on my arms begin to turn into cable, and if I had any mirrors in my house, I'm sure I would have been turning a shade of lime green.

I can't remember precisely how I replied to the mail - I've not saved it - but it wasn't what you might think.

(Go on, I know what you think of me.)

I've been in hospital with people who would go straight to the dormitory and kick seven bells out of the lad before the e-mail reply had crossed cyberspace. I've known people who would blame her for his behaviour (I've even done a bit of that myself on occasion, in the middle of the borderline cycle, in the middle of the forming of the lines of quacking ducks). I've also known people who would dismiss her concerns and tell her to get on with it.

Me? I just listened to her. Listened to what she had to say. I empathised and told her she was strong enough to deal with it, and that he would eventually go away. My reply was something like that anyway, and she seemed happy with it. I'm sure it wasn't one of those e-mails, which required any action from me, like getting in my car, driving up to the college, finding the young lad, and hammering the fingers of his right hand with a lump hammer one-by-one until he agreed to leave her alone. If it did come across like that, she never mentioned it, and after a time, indeed, his hassling did fade away as it does with most folk.

(The crazy ones are a bit more persistent.)

At about midnight, she wrote me a final e-mail, saying she was in her pyjamas, and she was ready for bed. She thanked me one final time and said nighty night with two kisses. I e-mailed her back and said exactly what she did.

Nighty night xx.

I've never said nighty night in my entire life.

(And what about those kisses? Interpret that for me. Nighty nightxx What did those two kisses mean? What would it have meant if she gave me one kiss. Or three kisses. Was I a friend? A potential lover? An acquaintance? Would it have made any difference if she hadn't have kissed me at all in that e-mail? I am clueless. That night, I sat up till 3am working out what she meant by those two kisses.

Tell me, dear social networking reader. Define for me your x strategy? What do you mean by it? Who gets one kiss? Zero snogs? Who gets two smackers?

Do you ever give three little puckered beauties?

What an extravagance that must be. xxx

What's the difference anyway?

What's the symbolism? How does it connect to real life? Is there a vector? A Venn diagram? Or do you just throw kisses to your friends, male, female, animal, mineral. One kiss, two kisses, three kisses. I have absolutely no idea what it means, and I'm glad I don't do the Me.com thing. It would drive me mad.)

To anyone. I'm not even sure I've ever written the words down.

Nighty night.

Nighty night. No, they're not familiar to me, but now, I can't forget them, and I happily wrote them down and pressed return on my laptop and the wonderful, wonderful day with Carla was over.

You see, I admit my Borderline tendencies.

You know, that e-mail psychosis.

At least when you meet me, you can run a mile or humiliate me horribly with a magnificently grotesque putdown. All that will do is confirm my sense of uselessness, of emptiness, of worthlessness (which was your intention anyway, admit it, to make me feel shit about myself), but at least it won't eventually spark an explosion of pathological violence in the immediate environment spectacular enough to make the TV news.

Seventy-five percent of Borderline diagnoses go to women, by the way. If you're a bloke reading this, imagine a woman writes it and the protagonist's target is a barman called Carl. That is more likely to happen, statistically and medically speaking. If you're a bloke, they're more likely to diagnose you with Anti-Social Personality, but that isn't I. Not at all.

Oh, the remorse. The remorse. Can't begin to describe to you how strong the remorse is.

And it's real. I'm not copying it off someone else, like psychopaths do. Psychopathic anti-socials are remorseless in the true sense. They can personally lay off ten-thousand workers in a chocolate factory to boost the balance sheet for the sole purpose of personal enrichment, and they won't even stop to think about the individual damage they've done.

Here's a super Anti-Social story for you.

A story about a Psychopath.

I heard this from a therapist four years ago, and it describes to an absolute tee the Anti-Social personality.

A handsome young man in his mid-twenties joined a firm of data archivists. It's a respectable job with sociable people, and generally, it all works. At the Christmas party, he managed to find his way into his boss's knickers in a store cupboard. So far, so corporately festive. The boss was extremely popular amongst her staff. She manages eighty people, and her work is her life. It is her sustenance, finance, and identity. She shouldn't have shagged the lad, but she's single, married to her job, temporarily lonely, and he's a bit of alright, and that night she dropped her guard after half a bottle of vodka and George Michael's Greatest Hits.

Unknown to her, the young man filmed the sexual exchange on the in-house close circuit TV, and the next day picked up the tape, transferred it to DVD.

Time passed. The young man became popular with his workmates and eventually became a big part of the team, and the boss got on with her life. The company organised a free thank you trip to Blackpool, a coach trip and they all booked on, including the boss and the handsome young man. Eventually, about sixty people got on a luxury coach for the day out. Halfway up the motorway, the young man asked the coach driver if there was an in-coach DVD player. The driver said yes.

"Put this on," he replied, handing the driver a DVD. "It'll be a right nobble," he said.

The driver did so. The coach started to watch. Slowly, the entire bus realised that what they were watching on the DVD was the grainy footage of their beloved manager being rogered from behind over stacks of A4 paper by said handsome young man.

The driver turned it off quickly, and the previously convivial and excited atmosphere turned frigid. The manager was in floods of tears, and at least six other young men were vigorously threatening the handsome young man.

"What?" He said, being pushed up to a window by his throat

"Why are you getting so angry? It's just a joke, mate...*I'm just having a laugh...*"

Horrible story that, isn't it.

I'll bet you three things.

One, the next morning he went to work to be sacked without a care in the world.

Two, he'll have found another job in a week, and three, he'll do something similar and not care a fig about it.

I'll take any stake, and I'll take any price.

You see, Anti-Socials are wired differently to everyday people. They have no conscience, no empathy, no real understanding of the emotions when they have their, er, little jokes. They're robots who, as a psychiatrist told me, are capable of replicating human emotions perfectly without actually experiencing them.

Borderlines like me?

Way too much emotion.

Chapter 15: Cherry

The inconsiderate neighbours above me were playing their dance music when I awoke on the sofa, fully clothed, pounding, ugly, bass heavy dance music, my ceiling bending under the sheer amplitude of it, but this time, rather than the other times, I didn't care. I was hopelessly in love, and I laid there on top of my bed, and looked forward to opening up the PC to see her morning message. When that moment arrived the next day, I decided to delay my gratification and instead of opening up my mail account straight away, I skipped into the shower and washed myself down. Freshened up.

I wondered what she would say. I wondered how many kisses she would append her message with. Would there be Smilies? Would there be x's or those Smiley lips?

No. It was too early for that. Nevertheless I wanted with all my heart to open a message, which contained Smiley lips at the end, I knew that wasn't going to happen. It was early, and our relationship - such as it was - was only just beginning. I began to breathe slowly. Turned the shower temperature down and felt the cold jets spatter on my forehead, giving me brain freeze.

When I was in Cedar Forest, they let you shower as often as you wanted, and I was always taking one. I love showers. Apart from taking repeated doses of the now banned painkiller Co-Proxamol, a spectacular dose of two particular experimental anti-psychotics (the name of which I will keep to myself), and a smidgeon of Attivan, (wow), I never feel better than being in a shower.

I don't need to explain why.

Do I? No. I didn't think so.

After, I changed into an Adidas tracksuit and tennis shoes. Carla and I had not arranged to meet today because she was at college, and in the evening she would be down at The Saddler's pouring pints. I'd pop down about nine when the early evening rush was over. I'd sit quietly in The Snug. I wouldn't hassle her. I'd take my laptop and carry on writing, or I'd take a book.

At that time, I was re-reading *An American Dream* by Norman Mailer.

Have you read that book?

It's a belter, yet it was absolutely pilloried by critics when it first appeared in nineteen sixty five. Absolutely destroyed. One critic described it as the worst novel he had ever read. Jesus. (Please don't say that about me, will you. You know how upset I get!)

Anyway, type in **mystifying lapse of taste** into your electronic thingy and you'll skip the spoilers I'm going to splash all over the next paragraph. The book concerns a war hero (Rojack) who marries an heiress in post-war New York. She's the daughter of a big player in American construction. The two of them have a terrible, bitter, violent marriage. Elements of undiagnosed PTSD are involved - and undiagnosed BPD - in both of them - but the protagonists love each other in that destructive, in-out, push-pull, love-hate kind of way, until finally, it all ends, and the heiress dumps her husband in the cruellest, cruellest way of all. In a fit of madness, Rojack kills her. Immediately afterward, he sleeps with her German maid, who he accidentally catches masturbating, the author clearly speculating on the relationship between sex and death - quite successfully in my view. He decides to throw his murdered wife from the penthouse window, to give the impression of suicide. The Police take him in, and they know he's guilty of murder, but they can't hold him until the results of the post-mortem. While he's in the station, he bumps into Cherry, a stunning, but jaded Southern torch singer who a sneering NYPD detective informs him, has a taste for black men, including a famous black singer with his own TV show. Kenny would have loved this storyline!

Rojack falls instantly in love with her (see why I like this book?) and the feeling is reciprocated.

Despite being threatened by numerous hard-core gangland figures, including her on-off black boyfriend, the two form a relationship in the shadow of the murder investigation and post-mortem on his ex-wife - the strongest, most powerful part of the book. Mailer's description of Cherry is astonishing - her corruption, her beauty, her ruined persona, her dignity, her flawed edifice as a woman - and I must have read those passages six or seven times. Heartbreakingly, in the end, the enraged and cuckolded singer beats Cherry to death with his bare hands in a Harlem tenement while his ex-wife's brutal father dangles Rojack from a twenty-storey roof. It's a classic noir pastiche, incredibly sad and empty, soulless and yet intensely emotional, and the best book I've read this year. I read loads of books in hospital, but how this one after forty-two years escaped me, I will never know.

I planned to sit and read that in The Snug and see how Carla compares and contrasts with Cherry. It's going to be mostly contrast, I know. At least I hope so.

(I've tried my best to describe Carla to you - and Nina - but I can't match what Mailer did with Cherry. I wish I could, but this is Norman Mailer we're talking about here. Buy the book. You won't regret it.)

Cherry would kill me, no question. My loved ones would be free of me. I wouldn't survive falling in love with Cherry.

Chapter 16: Kisses and Cuddles

Planning the rest of my day when I heard a knock on the door, and I recognised the knock straight away. It was Heather, my neighbour. The knock seemed quite urgent. I mentioned Heather earlier. Nosy Heather patrolling the communal area of the flats where I live like some curious Praetorian Guard. I don't mind her in small doses, but I do know that other people avoid her as much as possible, and you can see people looking out the window to see whether she is about before they go out to their cars. She generally adds half an hour to a polite person's trip. "Heather. Come in," I said to her, and she needed no second invitation. She was wearing a v-necked golf jumper, the pattern of which showed a mystifying lapse of taste.

"Saw you yesterday, you old bugger."

"I beg your pardon," I replied.

"Saw you on the park." Heather's greying blonde hair, a thick mess of it, was in a pony tail under a tennis visor, and she wore a shapeless pink jogging combo.

I've seen her on a hot summer's day on the communal sunbeds wearing a gold bikini which would shame a porn star - and don't forget, she's sixty plus. It isn't pretty. I feel like going out to tell her to put it all away because she's making people hate her even more, but she wouldn't listen if I did, being one of those bizarre women who think that even though Father Time has waved his catastrophic wand, it's spell has missed her, and she is thus, forever young and attractive. One of my other neighbours, a drunken cook who left three weeks ago to live with a cleaner in Charlestown, said he'd rather have sex with a rotating pencil sharpener. She's a sight in mid-summer.

"Oh," I replied. "And what was I doing?"

"You were with a young girl, you sly old dog."

"That's a friend of mine," I replied, a little annoyed, but not much. "From the college."

"You looked a lot closer than friends to me..." she grinned.

"Well, I can assure you, she's just a friend," I said firmly. We stood in my corridor, the door open. If you came to see me, I'd invite you in and make a pot of Darjeeling tea and bring out the fig rolls and the digestives, but I've done that before with Heather and it wiped out most of my day and inspired some murderous impulses, which took two days to fade away.

"Can I come in for a cuppa?" She asked, peering around each of my shoulders as if looking to see if anyone was in.

"Sorry, Heather. I'm just off, out to the shops," I lied. "…the launderette."

She moved a bit closer to me. I smelled nutmeg and some bizarre linctus. I even sensed some garlic on her breath, which I didn't want to experience before I sat down to enjoy my breakfast. "Are you going to meet that girl?"

"No, I'm not," I said, my head feeling tight, as if someone had tied a retracting metal band around it. I vowed to ignore the door next time and wished I'd done so this time.

"It was acceptable in my day you know, to squire a young lady. When I was young, I was engaged to a fifty year old potato merchant. I was only nineteen and no one batted an eyelid."

Regrettably curious, I asked what happened to the relationship.

"Oh, he fell off his tractor and got crushed under one of the wheels, bless him. Me life would have been so different. Particularly if I'd have married him before he had his accident…" she teased, and I moved towards the door, simultaneously closing the space between us and opening it at the same time, hoping she would walk backwards out.

"Sorry to hear that, Heather. Listen, I've got a busy day…"

"You need a woman to look after you, Johnny. Living here all on your own at your age isn't healthy."

"No one will have me, Heather," I said, jollily.

"I saw this girl, and she likes you. You never know…" she said, walking to the door reluctantly. "You could be married this year."

"I'll be sure to invite you, Heather," I replied, grabbing hold of the door frame. "In fact, you can be one of the maids of honour."

She poked her head in between the door and the jamb. "Bride chooses those. You'll have to introduce me."

I shut the door and waved. I went to the PC and opened up my e-mail account and felt myself start to despair; no message from Carla.

Damn.

Oh, no.

No message. I checked the junk folder.

I logged off and logged in.

No message.

Oh, nonononononononononono

(Bitch)

Oh, no.

I sat down. Logged in and logged out another twenty times. Racing tips, gallops reports from Max Thomson Jones. Detailed form messages from the brilliant Mr. Potts previewing the day's cards. Nag Me alerts for greyhounds and horses I'd been following. A reminder that my Goldconnectedhearts subscription was about to run out (waste of time that was!); a get well soon card from someone I had never heard of. A request for funds from a Venezuelan poet and his gay persecuted friend. Viagra junk mail. A note from my mate, Leroy, from inside the hospital, which I would read later. Lots of advert stuff. No matter how many times I logged in and logged out, twenty, thirty, forty times: No messages from Carla. I checked the time. It was ten fifteen. She must have been in lectures for an hour and a quarter. I felt relieved and sat back. She might not have been near a PC yet. Phew. Panic over. The world circumnavigates the sun and the wind blows.

Deep breaths, Johnny.

Deep, deep breaths.

My self-talk was going insane, and a huge dialogue developed.

(Write to her.)

(But she said she'd write to me.)

(Wish her a good morning. Go on. Take control.)

(No. I can't.)

(She'll be pleased. She'll like you.)

(No. That's what she said. She'll write to me. She'll think I'm a stalker.)

(It's the modern world.)

(If I do, how many kisses do I put on?)

(What?)

(With how many kisses do I append the morning message?)

(Are you crackers?)

(It's a code. I could ruin it all. If I don't append, she might think I'm not interested. If I append with one x, she might think that's not enough. If I append with TWO xx's, she might think that's over the top!)

(Okay, you've beat me. You're right. Wait for her to e-mail you.)

And like all self-talk, it makes you feel crap afterward, and I knew that Carla not writing a good morning message was potentially (oh, no, oh, no) the first duck in the row, and then the VERY minute I remembered that DUCK thing, I logged on and logged off and when I logged on, there it was, a morning hello from Carla.

I saved the message in a special folder.

"Hi, Johnny. Loved yesterday. In lectures. Boring, boring lol. Are you coming in the pub tonight? We can plan Sunday. Laters, Cxx"

The relief spread over me as if someone had injected me with an ounce of purest morphine. I laid on the sofa and started to shake. I could have cried. I could have cried with relief.

I could have sobbed.

I got back up and replied. "Hi, C, J here. Look forward to talking tonight. I'll see you at nine. Don't fall asleep! Jxx," a neutral enough message, and I sent it off and turned off my PC and went back in the shower because a sheen of sweat spread underneath my tracksuit top which, had you scraped it with a spatula, would have gone some way to filling the reservoirs in the absence of any rainfall.

Later, I could swear Carla peeked at me in a way that suggested she wanted a relationship, not just a friendship. She wanted me. I could have sworn it. The pub was busy, busier than usual, and even The Snug was packed with all the usual Wheatley Fields suspects, the young students, the retired couples, the suits and the workers, and I suspected the darts team was in because the Pop Side was rammed, and the atmosphere buzzed. Carla served alone, big Keith on his night off, and she did it brilliantly, pouring the real ale, chatting to the old boys (who like me, were clearly smitten), as if she enjoyed being warm as a person, rather than it being something she was being paid to do, like so many others.

I was sitting reading *An American Dream* and sipping a pint of Thor's Hammer, looking up at her and just as she was serving Gwyneth, the slim Welsh woman with the page boy haircut who I quite fancied before Carla appeared, I saw her look over, and it was a look that I'd not seen previously. A more intimate look.

I'm not saying that she wanted to marry me or anything (however, I'd have married her on the spot, to be perfectly honest with you), but she had a definite grin, a I'm Happy To See You smile, and then it was gone, and she chatted away to Gwyneth who could throw back real ale like a camel filling its hump before a journey across the desert. That look said so many things to me. It confirmed I was in love. It said she liked me, too, but on what level, I did not know. It promised some kind of future, be it one day, one more sublime day, or a lifetime. It also made me nervous. It also made me a little scared.

You see, I've felt like this before.

I call it The Vice.

Not in terms of sex, or drugs, or rock and roll, a slightly carnal hobby. A steel vice, a heavy bastard crushing my insides slowly.

I can hear the handle clatter as it transverses positions in the inlet. A rock solid steel vice. I felt it with Nina at my father's birthday bash.

In the past, I have felt it with Deb, Candy, Candice, Caroline, Carol, Janine, Lea, Francis, Francine, Betty, Martina, Nadine, Natalie, Alice, Amy, Arabella, Annie, Alex, Penny, Marjorie, Melanie, Christina, Marisa, Marika, Florence, Bernice, Zoe, Xena, Sarah, Sara, Sonja, Sofia, Uma, Ulla, Una, Yuna and Wilhelmina, and my mother, my beloved mother, out there somewhere in Caracas, lying in the arms of Carlos, the swarthy, moustachioed Brazilian oilman, the scent of hibiscus, the canopy of bougainvillea and eucalyptus stretching as far as the eye can see.

Some of these women (and the others whose names escape me) actually liked me back. Some even loved me. All that did so, no longer speak to me because I swallowed their love whole, chewed on it and spat it out like something unwanted because The Vice crushed me and I had to escape its gruesome clutches.

With Carla that night, I could feel the first creaking turn of The Vice as well as the intense lung-bursting elation that accompanied my growing undying love for her

Listen.

There isn't a woman in the world who can love me enough.

Yet my clinginess begins at minute one. It does. I fell in love with Nina within four minutes. That's nutty! I know that! Do you think I'm stupid? I possess a first class degree in Physics. I know it's mad. I know grown men don't fall in love with women who they have a one percent chance of having a relationship with at a party, and cling to them like cactus sprigs as if the two lovebirds had been married for ten years! It's no wonder I ended up on the front page of every newspaper in the South of England and in Cedar Forest.

Yet the strange thing is, if you DO reciprocate, it doesn't work. That's the paradox. That's the problem. The law of averages means that eventually my overzealous romanticism is going to encounter a similarly overzealous romantic. It's just a question of how many rejections one can withstand before one does bump into Mrs. Right. You see, that IS the problem. Even if we meet and you fall in love with me, it isn't going to be happy ever after. Even if you are the type of insecure, obsessive woman who'll pledge undying love to knife wielding bank robbers with all your heart, all the grinning, moustachioed pimps, all the beaters, the control freaks, all the liars and frauds, and cheats, and death row merchants, all the giant Bosnians who'll kick you to death for going out with your mousey friends for a latte, all the philanderers and casanovas who never mean a word of it, not a single word of it, even if you have an awful lot of love to give, a nuclear tank sized full of wonderful, tender, all consuming love, it would never be enough for me.

My mum loved me. I burned her right out.

In. Out. In. Out. She didn't know what hit her, bless her.

(Carlos is such a fair bloke by all accounts. A gentle soul. One of the chaps. Kind to animals. Consistent.)

Even if your love was as intense as mine, I wouldn't want it anyway because eventually, given a long enough timeline, you'll dump me.

Yes, you will. Got evidence. I may as well consume your love first. Before you do it to me, I'll burn you out. I'll leave you an empty husk. My walls of Jericho are so high in the sky I'll throw you off the battlements and regret what I've done, and by that time, after a hundred, two hundred times, all the love you had for my empty wasteland of a soul has gone, all that eternal, wonderful, sincere, passionate, crystal clear love, which reached to the blue horizon and back has gone, and you've gone along with it.

You've abandoned me, you bitch. I love you. *I hate you.*

Girls out there can tell you I've done this to them in a week. Those, they hate me when they see me in the street. They gave me no second chances.

Oh, My God, to coin the lingua franca of the young, I've done this on *first dates.*

I've done this clingy romantic explosion thing on first dates set up by my friends.

I went out with my boss who fancied me a bit, and to whom I subsequently gave a royal command performance on the steps of the Corn Exchange in Cambridge at two in the morning.

Offers of marriage.

Tears. Don't leave me. All that stuff…

Poor woman was terrified.

Our first date.

My boss.

Can you imagine being me and going to work the next day?

Can you imagine the Goggle Eyes?

Goggle Eyes?

You know Goggle Eyes?

Do you?

Let me remind you, dear reader. You've been to an important party the night before, and you're now lying in your bed half-asleep, early in the morning. Cosy, and warm, and toasty. A quiet lie in, a gentle fantasy, turning over the pillow to find the cold bit, maybe wrapping your leg around the quilt, stretching your body a little. Luxuriating. Resting.

Sigh. That wonderful stretchy feeling.

Quietly, uninvited, an image sneaks up on you as full consciousness approaches, and a messenger taps you on the shoulder and goes, hey, look at this, and shows you a film of what you said last night to your husband, or what you did to your brother, or what you said to your boss, or who you tried to get off with at the works party, and your Eyes Suddenly Expand into BIG Goggles and you realise that you've been anything from a total dick, and what you did will take a month to recover from, to a potential violent criminal whose actions will probably be never forgotten by that social group, and it is likely that you've lost the lot.

That's Goggle Eyes.

Just in case you are one of those well balanced people who doesn't get into scrapes like this, specific examples, which often inspire Goggle Eyes might be snogging someone you shouldn't, giving someone who thoroughly deserves it, a piece of your mind (only they have no idea what you're talking about), fighting in an important social event given by someone you like; telling your boss that he can stick your 40k a year job up his arse, or giving your family some ancient history they didn't particularly want to hear, and which has laid happily dormant for a generation.

Have you experienced this? Goggle Eyes, huh.

(I've done all that, by the way.)

(That's how I know.)

My.

The morning after sensation.

You know this one.

This terrified sensation? I live with that each day of my life.

I need a woman who is going to love me so much it will fill the massive void in my soul. And when I find them, they overwhelm me and I reject them, sometimes causing massive damage. To me and to them. As I got older, I got fatter, and uglier, and slower witted, and duller, and more masculine, and women just got harder and nastier, calloused and bruised as they are in later life, naturally, due to the baggage and the bruises, their limited patience for the weaknesses of men.

I ended up alone. There's a sensible part of me.

A normal part of me.

People like that part of me. This is the part of me that attracts friends (or it used to before I got old) into my orbit.

It is charming, rational, logical and has a social conscience. As I sat there that night thinking about what Carla said, I wanted her to walk up to me, punch me hard, call me an old pervert and tell me to go away. Tell me that if I came into the pub one more time she'd call the Police.

Tell me that I'm so ugly she is sick whenever she sees my suppurating, ill-formed boat.

Laugh at me. Please, Carla.

Laugh at me and save yourself. You're the nicest person in the pub. At college. Maybe even in Wheatley Fields, a land of nice people.

Don't get involved with me. I come with small print.

A digression: For later in the book, I'll let you into some secrets. Some things I've learned through all the therapy engaged in during my multiple incarcerations. Not just from the Therapists, but from all the people I've met - the Leroy's, the Sables, the Felicity's et al - and lsao from all the little accidents of history that led me to those unfortunate respites. I talked earlier about all the ducks lining up in a row.

Oh, sorry. Spoilers. If you want to skip the psychological clues and/or work them out for yourself, type in **Deviant Climax** into your electronic device.

Okay? I can continue.

Anyway, ahum. The Borderline ducks lining up in a row.

Let's list a few of them in handy number points.

Here's how you can ensure I go for a three-year stay in Cedar Forest Hospital in Charlestown.

One: Give me the benefit of the doubt when I approach you. Like me. Listen to my patter, admire my grand schemes, comment on my brilliant listening technique, and notice the little thing I do with my eyelid when I sip a drink. Like me. Arrange to meet me later or say you'll dance with me, all the little insignificant contracts that form the intricate and subtle lattice of the jigsaw dance between men and women.

Duck One.

Two: Ignore the amount I'm drinking. By this point of the dance, I'm monstered because I'm enjoying myself. I can't get enough booze. The more I drink, the more I am. I've engaged your attention. I know what to say because I'm no chump, but if I hadn't taken a single sip of booze, I wouldn't have gotten to Duck One in the first place, which is that magnificent paradox in action.

Approach you? You must be crackers. With my sense of worthlessness? I can feel my manhood inflate by the gallon with each sip of Vodka I take and you are enamoured by this point with my never ending, urbane chatter. This is Duck Two.

Three: Am I sunburned? I suffer awful sunstroke, I have to tell you. Many of my borderline explosions have, historically speaking, occurred on hot days.

Duck Three.

Four: Do I look stressed? Have I alluded to work stressors? To a situation in my family life? Something that's been bugging me. Something I should have dealt with had I not historically suffered a serious omission in the Passive-Aggressive continuum.

You know what's missing, don't you? If you don't, you should have skipped this bit.

If I have mentioned any of these things - this is Duck Four.

And finally.

Five - change your mind about Duck One.

Duck Five.

(Quack. Quack. Quack. Quack. Quack).

Hah!

Fusion. The ducks line up in a row. The chain reaction begins.

The neutrons sizzle. The moment of Borderline Explosion Fusion. Ping. Woosh.

Everyone at the party is in big trouble.

You, Milady de Winter, perusing this tome on your electronic device, could save all and sundry an awful lot of grief by saying you'd rather shag a syphilitic leper in response to my approach. At least I'll just go away and embrace my sense of complete and utter worthlessness like a teddy bear, and the only damage you will have done is to confirm what I already know about myself. It's the hope you see. The hopefulness. The hopefulness infusing the optimism of our early exchanges is the petroleum of the explosion.

At least that's what Pine Ridge's Doctor Vortex said to me a few years ago in group therapy after I'd totally obliterated the top table at my oldest friend's wedding.

Anxiety Ad Break

Hey.

You out there. Reading this. Yes, you.

I'll bet you're worried about Carla now, aren't you.

She's magic, you know. Normal, friendly, happy-go-lucky. Popular as anything. Always time for a chat with an old soldier. First in the queue at the Voluntary Centre. Drops off selection boxes at the local kids hospital. A certain naïveté about her.

We all love Carla.

Whoops.

I'll bet some of you reading this are shitting bricks.

When the rush died down, Carla came over, and I knew that what I was thinking wasn't possible. I couldn't leave her behind, and I prayed that she never, ever left me. She picked up my glass. She was wearing that pair of ripped black jeans and black baseball boots. Two gold studs and her hair in a ponytail. Accessible, open eyes. No makeup except for the most subtle of pink lip glosses. A faded grey vest top. Underneath, you could see the imprint of a belly piercing. She smelled unbelievable - some top quality perfume or maybe even some Pound Goblin stuff, who knows - she could spread her own urine over herself, and she'd smell gorgeous to me - and she'd clearly showered before she came to work. You could smell the freshness.

"I'll come and talk to you on my break. We'll go outside with all the faggers. We can arrange Sunday. I'm so looking forward to it. Are you?" She asked, and it looked as if she was genuinely interested in my answer.

"Absolutely," I replied. I considered saying deffo or something like that, but she would have seen through me straight away. I was already wearing a tracksuit: Next time, she would expect to see me wearing a pair of Doctor Beats headphones and a leather bum bag.

"I am. Better go," she said. "Keith's watching me from the other side."

And with that, she took my glass, wandered into The Snug Bar, and started serving.

Chapter 17: Pavlov, his Dog

The next three days were agony. On the Thursday, Carla had a full book of lectures all the way until 7pm. The way education is now, they cram lectures into one day as much as possible, enabling the student to go out and get a job to pay the ruinous tuition fees and personal expenses. When I was a kid, that wasn't a problem, and I knew people from up North who got full grants of about £63 a week (at a time when full board lodging on Cambridge High Street was about £30) and all their tuition paid. You can't tell a young person that today because they get shirty, and I understand why. Some of these kids will leave Uni with a debt of forty grand. It's astonishing. Bizarre, even. Why bother?

I can tell you about the origin of the neutron, the Big Bang, the process of nuclear fission (and fusion - I could even carry it out, given the equipment) and the proton, and the electron, and James Chadwick, and Ernest Rutherford, and the fundamentals of Einstein's General Theory; I could tell you all about that and more, and yet I can't stay out of mental hospitals for more than a year, so what, exactly, was the point of all that learning?

What the country needs is more plumbers.

Anyway, I digress. On top of her lectures, she was booked in at The Saddler's on Thursday, Friday and Saturday night, and I couldn't go in there every night, could I?

Not on my own. I'd look like a stalker.

I couldn't give a toss whatever that lot in the Pop Side thought of me, but if I went in every single night, *she'd* think I was stalking her. I couldn't have that. My stalking adventures in the past had always ended poorly. I always got caught, being taller than average. The stalkee could spot me a mile off and often did.

In fact, they almost always spotted me. One ill-advised and idiotic stalking adventure led to a short incarceration in a hospital in Barcelona, but I won't go into that in much detail: You'll think ill of me and I'd hate that after all this time together. I could ask Heather to go with me, but that is a grotesque idea. Nothing for it. I had to miss out the Saturday night, and the contemplation of it made me feel like puking onto the carpet.

In those three days, and I love her for this, she religiously mailed me at about ten with a morning message.

Invariant kisses. Always two. Always two sumptuous kisses. I love her for her regularity because I had developed an obsessional chain about the time and the sequence.

If she significantly varied, (and on the Saturday morning, when she was going shopping into the City with her friends Katy and Natasha, she was half an hour early), I'd go into a confused and deviant fugue state, which would generally involve despair, cutting fantasies and feelings of atomic worthlessness you could bottle and use as a secret weapon.

(I couldn't help it. It's my condition. Don't you understand that? It's my deformed emotional liability, is what it is. What rational person behaves like this?)

I managed to fill my time somehow.

I spent each afternoon in Jim's betting shop in Charlestown with some new friends. It was Aintree races, the Grand National meeting. In order to salve the ruptured, leaking emptiness at my core, I bet on each race (four meetings), each dog race (two meetings), and kept two Hypnotic FOBT slot machines going at the same time.

I bet the 49's twice and left fifty Irish lottery tickets behind the counter for the next two weeks. Mischa, the bubbly girl behind the counter, lost track of my bets at one time. I'm a whirlwind when I get started. Some horses won. I won £340 with ten pounds on a winning outsider on the flat at Catterick, and some lost; £130 when a Nicholls favourite went down like the Belgrano at 8/13. I lost nearly a thousand pounds on the Hypnotics, the roulette betting terminals, which send people mad, and which have led punters to suicide.

That didn't matter, it was the gambling that counted, the activity, the process, the bustle and the hustle, not the winning, and Jim, the bookie, couldn't believe what he was seeing and neither could Big John from Wolverhampton, and Big Graham, the dogman, punters who take their time and pick their spots.

I reckon I lost about four grand in those two afternoons in the centre of Charlestown with the harassed shoppers walking past, the single parents, the teenage mothers, the unemployed Poles, the unemployed Estonians with the bottles of cider by the cycle racks outside, the kids walking home from school in their blazers and ties, and a choir singing for Save The Children on the pavement outside.

I took a break from the action and went outside with Big John to watch them sing. They were from the local comprehensive and they were smartly dressed, and they were (I would estimate) between fourteen and sixteen.

They sang marvellously; *Feed The World, Evergreen,* something by Robbie Williams, and a wonderful version of *Mack The Knife,* which must be the best song to have emerged from the United States ever.

As they sang it, you could see the kids sway with the beat, and when they'd finished, I suppressed an urge to give them a massive, disproportional round of applause. Instead, I went and found the choirmaster, a dark-haired woman with square spectacles, white-linen trousers and gold sandals, and I gave her two hundred pounds. All the cash I had on me.

She looked at me bemused and so did the choir, and I said to her, better you have it than the bookies, huh, and she nodded, confused and embarrassed.

I returned to the bookmakers and cashed a ticket for a hundred pounds, and stuck it all on a horse called **Cape Tribulation,** which won pulling a bus at 14/1, and I won £1,500, proving that God is Karma, and you reap what you sow.

I watched as Jim, a top bloke, put his head in his hands. I said to him not to worry because it was going straight into the Hypnotics anyway, which it did, over two hours, that and greyhounds at Crayford and Sunderland, but it didn't matter because I was six hours closer on both days to seeing Carla.

I cycled the eight miles back to Wheatley Fields like a man possessed, and went home and got changed into something cool and young looking, a long-sleeved black shirt I've had for ten years that my stepmother bought for me at Harvey Nichols, American-made blue jeans and Timbo boots. I couldn't do much about my mug, all disconnected and unbalanced, pulled out of place and as disproportional as some of my episodes, but I brushed my teeth and put on some Collateral Damage aftershave and before I knew it, I was in The Snug and Carla looked absolutely magnificent, and you know what?

You know what? She came over to me during her break and said: "You look well tonight. Who are you trying to impress?" And walked back to her place behind the bar, winking at me and I could have cried.

Are you a bloke?

A normal bloke would have had a hard-on, which ripped the hell out of your zip fastener, but no, not me. That didn't interest me. That's not what it was about. Can't you see it yet?

What is it I'm interested in?

Carla's hot, you know. I watched her walk behind her bar.

That first night of the three, she was wearing a green vest and a red bra. Freckles scattered across her back like cities on a Coppertoned map. Her hair was straight and down, black, not a kink or camber in it. Blue jeans gripped her legs like Velcro, a pair of flat gold sandals, black toenail polish and a little silver toe ring on the third toe of her left foot. Honestly, you couldn't handle her.

What would you do? Stop her going out?

In the City, every lad from St Martin's to The Meadowlands would be after her like bees after pollen, and they'd never let up for a single second. The collective Textile Quarter would show her an open chequebook for just one drink and a dance in La Moda, or Intrigue, or Mama Class. You'd never be able to let her out of your sight.

What's the scariest thing a girl like Carla can say to an insecure, loved-up bloke?

"Off, out with me mates on Friday night. To a club. Might stop at Kitty's house. Ta-ra."

That night would be a living hell.

Wouldn't it?

You ever seen *Boxing Helena*? I haven't - it's supposed to be a bit sick, and I've seen enough of sick in my life - so there's no need for a spoiler fast forward at this point, but as I understand it, a jealous chap chops the arms and legs off his gorgeous wife and keeps her alive in a box just for him, and you know, seeing Carla sway as she walked back to that bar, on form, confident, looking hotter than the planet Mercury on a summer's day, you can see the bloke's point, even if you don't altogether approve of his methodology!

What is it?

Come on. Tell me.

What am I interested in?

It isn't sex, I can tell you that now.

It never ends like this (however, it always begins this way). I could marry Carla and sit and stare at her all day, and every day like a drooling idiot, rocking my head backwards and forwards as I sit and listen to her voice. And at night, I'd cuddle her to sleep.

(Boy, that's red blooded, isn't it. Cuddle fantasies. The porn companies would have to fight off the membership enquiries on that site with swords and shields! I'll never be able to go to the shops if anyone I actually know reads this, not that I know many people outside St Albans, The Saddler's, my estranged family, and various mental institutions.)

Anyway, I sat outside The Saddler's on two of the three nights to avoid accusations of stalking and I only saw her on her break, which she spent with me (and several other blokes who wouldn't leave her alone, the arseholes).

And when I went home, after waving goodbye to her (and Big Keith), from the doorway, I sat and waited by my PC for her to send me a goodnight e-mail, which she did both nights, with two kisses, and for that I am truly, truly grateful.

The Saturday?

I didn't see her at all. I stayed away from The Saddler's in a fit of common sense. No one in Wheatley Fields goes to the pub on three consecutive nights: Not in today's day and age, not at three pounds fifty a pint.

People would start to talk, and I didn't want to attract the attention. I'd managed to avoid the gossips and the natter - Carla would have told me if anything untoward was being said, and because she was so friendly and liberal with her welcome, people weren't threatened by me. It was natural for men to be there when she was working, and I wasn't the only one doing it. I was sure I was the only one taking Carla for walks.

So on Friday, I told Carla a lie, informed her I was going to see a friend in Charlestown early Saturday night and she said that she was sorry about that, and she'd miss seeing me.

Not miss me, I noticed.

Miss seeing me.

Thankfully, the subtle difference in the semantics kept the lid on my emotions screwed down tight without deflating my ambitions, and I didn't overreact. Not in front of her anyway - the fact she had used the word MISS at all in connection with ME kept me awake for an hour before I could sleep that night.

Further, she asked whether she could text me and I said yes, but that made me uneasy.

Texts are much more random than e-mails, which I have noticed, tend to be ordered and which, when conforming to predictable mathematical and geometric patterns, keep the demons quiet and mewling in their cages. Unlike texts, which are random things, the electrons of the communication process bounce madly around the nucleus of the communication atom. They can come any time because of the sender's mobility, and they make my stomach churn, ensuring I spend my life in an endless, nagging, irritating fugue of anticipation.

And then there's the text tone.

I became classically conditioned to a text tone from a woman like Carla, whom I was over-involved with at an early stage.

Her name was Yvonne, and I met her on Superdate.com back before my second all-inclusive at the Cedar Forest. She worked for the Council in Economic Development, quite high up and she was fairly pretty, apart from one of her teeth being nearly brown and one of her ears being slightly bigger than the other.

Other than that, I remember she had impish green eyes, and kept herself in shape.

She loved to text.

Yvonne texted me whenever and wherever she could. Text. Text. Text. My phone at the time had a simple text tone, a hum drum, unremarkable monotone four beat ring tone - Beep Beep (two second gap) Beep Beep - and during the eight days we knew each other, that text tone never left my head, and I came to associate it purely with Yvonne.

As my feelings for her grew, oh, after about a day and a half, I'd hear my next-door neighbour's doorbell go and think it was another text from Yvonne.

Any chime would make me think of her and thus, I couldn't escape her presence. She sent me thirty-seven texts in one day. Mostly status texts.

Eight days after we met, in a fit of quite typical over-confidence and neediness, I told her I loved her in a romantic moment in a Trentside Tapas bar, and she poured a large glass of Barolo over my head, and called me a nutter. Naturally, I Bruce Bannered, destroyed the wine bar and got three months in North Camp for my remorse.

Do you take the City Post newspaper?

I made page five on that one, it is my shame to admit. This time, my father couldn't save me and the Magistrate called me an animal who needed putting down. While I waited to be sentenced, and bereft at her absence, I couldn't listen to bells without being reminded of her. Any bells at all. Doorbells. The bells on the bus. Church bells. Anyone else's text tone. Bells on the TV. All of them would make me think of HER and each time I heard a bell, I would feel like bursting into tears with the sense of loss.

And... oh - the time expansion. Each minute of my life, which during those eight days passed in a blur of speedy anticipation as I waited for another text to arrive, now expanded into infinity.

The days passed so slowly without my Yvonne's texts, and I felt like ending it. Course, after a while, I realised that I didn't love her, but it felt like it at the time - do you know what I mean? - Can you understand that? - and my Therapist, in the weeks before my imprisonment, told me to wear ear plugs, and after a time, the stimulus-response chains became unlearned as they say in that bizarre psychologist language and now, I cannot even remember the ring tone, which I feel represents something of an improvement in my mental state.

I told Carla I'd love to text, and she said that was bonus. She gave me that wink, and I watched her sway back to the bar. My stomach turned over as if it was the digestive equivalent of the Titanic.

Getting through the Saturday was tough, like a ten year old on Christmas Eve.

The emotions got the better of me in the end, and when I looked back on the day, I realised that I did all the things I used to. Some of the habits that had passed into antiquity came flooding back. I lost three thousand eight hundred pounds in Jim's, mostly at Aintree, and just as I was about to leave, the commiserations of my friends in the bookies ringing in my ears, I noticed a little grin on Jim's mush.

That didn't bother me. He's a bookmaker.

It's his job to destroy me and put me out of business, and he did a brilliant job. Over the course of the day, four horses and seven Newcastle dogs finished second - had they run that bit faster, I would have won ten grand, and it would have been little me with the cheeky grin.

Afterwards, I brought three doner kebabs on Naan, each lavishly spread with hot chilli sauce and mint yoghurt, plus six pieces of fried chicken and two bags of large chips. I cycled home with the food in my backpack and microwaved them until they were all piping hot. Without plating them up, I ate the lot with my fingers while I watched Doctor Who - the one with James Corden and the weird staircase - and followed it up with half a Community Fayre chocolate and vanilla cheesecake. Logged in and logged out of my e-mail account a hundred times and stabbed myself in the armpit with my golden compass because Carla, bless her, had sent me just the one text all day, the cruel, cruel girl, and hadn't responded to my reply. These are just the things I remember. I can't remember whether I cried in the shower. I might have done, but sometimes, my mind plays tricks, and I might have done that on another occasion. Not seeing Carla that night was horrible and in the end, I took three little pink Temazepams with half a litre of Wicked Gandalf Scrumpy and knocked myself out, unwilling to wait for Father Time to bring Sunday to me. Before I conked, I texted her one more time, told her I was ill and was going to bed, and I would see her as arranged at one o clock outside the Sea of Tranquility on our bikes. I appended the message with Jxx. Within seconds, my text tone chimed. Carla. Saying

"Hi, J. At work. Can't wait, Cxx," and I needn't have bothered with the sleeping tablets after all, but there's one thing about Temazepam tablets - they do the trick.

Chapter 18: Two Gods

This time of year, thousands and thousands of half-grown apples line the hedgerows, half eaten by birds and left to rot. It gives the place a delicious atmosphere. If it rains, unless you're unlucky, the trees and the hedges give you shelter. If it's sunny, they'll give you shade. It's almost flat, Wildflowers and fauna of all types and colours grow, protected by the mighty trees. Behind the hedgerows and trees are acres and acres of green fields, equestrian centres, gardens and arborea. Nature lovers reckon hundreds of rare butterflies live along the trail. Compared to the aerial domination of the off-white common butterflies of my youth - hundreds and thousands, billowing underneath bright blue skies, buffeted by pillows of wind, but at the same time in full control, just like the migration of the Canadian Monarchs, literally hundreds of them - I've been disappointed by their absence.

Sometimes, you might disturb a Red Admiral from its slumbers. I guess the farmers and their murderous pesticides have done for them as much as the Lords of the Manor did for the mighty oaks of the Royal Sherwood Forest, and the grey squirrels did for the native red. Hundreds of grey squirrels along the trail, but they aren't worth writing about. The trail supports a wide range of habitats because it crosses two distinct geological areas. There are the Sherwood Sandstone field to the north of Bilsthorpe, and the Keupar Marl further south from Kirklington towards Wheatley Fields. The Sherwood Sandstone is acidic and supports soils low in nutrients, yielding relatively few species. The Keupar Marl is entirely different, being characterised by species-rich meadows and woodlands. The common lizard (in the open areas surrounding Follow Field), various birds of prey including sparrow hawks and many butterflies, for example, the speckled wood.

"The Cherry Blossom can't get a foothold this year," she said. "Last week I was sunbathing on the park and this week…" she flicked the earflap of her hat… "well, you've seen it yourself. What do you put it down to?" She asked, as we walked past the first style on the way to Follow Field. Carla had texted me first thing in the morning to say her front wheel had buckled, and she wanted to walk halfway instead.

"Oh, deforestation," I replied. "The Brazilians are getting rid of a patch of rain forest the size of our country annually. By 2030, half of the Amazon rainforest will be gone. In Indonesia, ninety percent of the rain forest has been cut down. Malaysia also. The big Japanese companies have bought huge swathes of tribal land in places like Papua, New Guinea. The Indonesians have turned huge areas into wasteland in just twenty years."

"But why does this change the climate?" She asked.

"We produce the same amount of carbon dioxide, India and China in particular, but the trees that used to act as the planet's lungs, recycling and absorbing the pollutants we produce, are being cut down. Hardwoods were brilliant sponges for our pollutants. Hardly any left. Picture the Earth two thousand years ago as a non-smoker. Healthy and fit. The Romans started to cut down the forests for their ships. By the year 1000, the earth was smoking five cigarettes a day. By 1700, the Europeans had cut down eighty percent of their forests. With the Great American Deforestation just about to begin, the earth was a twenty a day smoker, coughing and gasping for breath after exertions.

By last year, after the industrial revolution, with the Indonesians, the Malaysians and the Brazilians cutting down most of their equatorial forest, the earth was now a sixty a day smoker with asthma and breathing difficulties. It affects all that we do. It's not about temperature, it's about consistency. Some of the weird weather patterns in the past five years cannot be explained by anything else. The sea is acidifying, animals are being born with genetic defects the world over, and we're running out of landfill space. It has to stop. Someone has to stop it."

"Have you ever seen those pictures of the impact of zinc poisoning on the land in Sudbury, Toronto?" She asked.

"No," I replied, interested.

She shook her head and she looked quite angry, her cheeks reddening.

"Honestly, John. I was in tears when I saw them the first time. Oh, My God, it was, like, watching the surface of the moon appear in a back garden."

"I'll have to look those up," I said.

"Do. They don't make batteries on that site, but you can pick up ten for a pound in the Charlestown Pound Goblin, so someone, somewhere is poisoning the earth. It makes me so mad, Johnny."

"Me, too. Snow blossom's out,' I said, seizing the opportunity to lighten the mood. We had reached a row of trees, each flowering a snowy white. Behind and above the row, the sun peeked through the clouds and shone a sliver of its light upon the flowers. The scene was temporarily glorious. She reached up and plucked a flower from the tree and smelled it. "Isn't it wonderful? The Earth is such an amazing home, and all we do is abuse her."

"We could be stewards, couldn't we? Stewards of the Earth. Forget the cars..."

I looked into her eyes, and she saw what I was thinking.

"Go back to horses," she replied. "Fine looking strong horses. Carts and blacksmiths."

"Manure for the roses and the potatoes..."

"You can shovel that," she said, giggling.

"Send all the planes to the Nevada desert one final time..."

"Send each other letters by ship..."

"Windpower for light..."

"Live a simple life, grow our own food, make our own clothes..."

"Sing round the piano, log fires in the evening, hymns at Christmas."

"Regrow the forests..."

"A moratorium on worldwide fishing for five years..."

She looked at me. "A mora what?"

"Stop fishing."

"I've learned something today," she said, laughing, and she did something magnificent, something splendid, something that if I live to be a hundred and twenty years old I will never forget. She put her arm in mine as we walked past the pony riding school, and I felt like a God. I felt like Zeus. If I could have frozen my life at one specific point, it would have been that one. I had no idea what the gesture meant, but I wanted her to hold my arm forever nonetheless.

We walked quietly for a bit, and she leaned her head on the upper part of my arm, making me feel like Two Gods, a Two God moment.

"You're such an attentive listener, Johnny. Here's me spoiling our walks with my ceaseless prattling and you never interrupt me. And you're so intelligent."

Suddenly bashful, I couldn't think of a thing to say, so I did a weird gesture with my chin.

"I hope I haven't embarrassed you," she said, and I felt her arm start to pull away slightly from mine, and I began to panic.

"No, not at all. It's just, just; I'm not used to people saying anything..well...positive...."

"Well, get used to it. You're such a wonderful man, and you deserve it. I love our walks. Do you?"

"Oh, indeed."

The underestimated response of the entire decade. Just walking with Carla, the touch of her gloved hand on my quilted hunting coat, the gentle pressure, the ambiguity of meaning in the gesture, the infinite promise, was a feeling as sublime as a shot of heroin. It had been three and a half years, maybe even longer, and I wasn't going to balls it up this time, no way. No grand gestures, no declarations, no jokey comments. I was older than she was. More mature, and I was going to behave like it. No need for her to find out about my past or the fever that lurks in my brain. I had become my father, mature, detached, and sensible, and I liked the feeling, the fevered, manic despair of this morning as I got ready to see her, the long five-hour wait a distant memory.

"I love the trail. I used to come with my dad, only from the other end. We used to walk here. Ten miles thereabouts, and I fell in love with it. I was born just outside Follow Field," she continued.

"Not from Wheatley Fields?"

"No. Only college." She frowned imperceptibly. We passed two giant fields full of bright yellow rapeseed, shielded by a row of oaks and beech, struggling to come to life after the winter slumber.

A man walking an Airedale came around the corner from the nursery and nodded to us as he walked past.

"My dad..." she continued. "...we were close when I was young."

"You say that as if you're no longer so."

"We don't speak any more," she said. "But that's another story."

"You can talk about it if you want."

She shook her head firmly, and in that moment I could see that Carla was made of strong stuff and that she was no one's patsy. "No, I don't think so. It will spoil a perfect day. Look, in the trees." She scampered off to the stile ahead of us. "Come quickly."

I followed, and we stood on the green stile together. "A Sparrowhawk, look," she continued.

High on an oak tree, an eagle watched something in the fields to one side. I didn't know what type it was and relied on Carla's judgement. It perched majestic. Then as if aware of us, it soared away into the sky, its loping, carefree flight a joy to watch.

"Isn't that magnificent, Johnny."

"It is," I replied, hoping she'd put her arm in mine because I was beginning to feel disconnected and lost, adrift and I could feel the buzzing beginning to start, like a distant echo in the lower part of my head. Luckily, she did so, pacifying me, a dose of a painkiller calming, and we walked on toward the second part of the trail.

We reached the gatehouse that marks the halfway point of the trail, and we had a decision to make.

It was another two and a half miles to Follow Field, and in total, it would be an eleven-mile walk. The clocks had gone forward two weeks previously, which meant plenty of light.

However, I didn't like the look of those clouds above - swirling, slow moving grey cumulus, full of Spring rains - and the wind had whipped up. I was happy to listen to Carla's tales of nature, wildlife, her friends at college and anything she wanted to talk about, and I left it up to her, but I could tell that she was thinking the same thing.

"Shall we turn back, Johnny? Or do you want to carry on."

"I'd like to carry on, actually. What do you think? Let's be devils."

"What if it rains?"

"The trees and the hedges will protect us, and besides…" I flicked one of her ear flaps. "…you've got a hat on."

"No, I think we'd best turn back, otherwise, we'll be late back. I've got an essay to do tonight. Are you okay with that?"

I was less than okay with that, and I felt a brief but intense pinprick of misery and self-pity come over me. I didn't want this day to end, and Carla was ending it, putting limits on it, fencing it off timewise and distance wise, cutting it short (you boring bastard), wanting to go home, had a disappointing day, didn't want to spend any more time than is absolutely necessary (with Mr. Dull) and she would sit in her communal kitchen, and giggle with her friends (at the boring bloke with the disjointed face), and this would be the last time we'd ever go for a walk and I could feel the tears rising from a point of sadness buried inside me and CRASHHHHHHHHH, I slammed the lid down on the madness rising...

"You're so right," I said, the biggest grin I have ever, ever manufactured. "And it's going to rain. Let's go home."

And because I'd listened and agreed, Carla smiled and put her arm in mine.

"We'd best get cracking. I've been caught on the trail in the rain and contracted a flu, which lasted a month," and the two of us started to walk back to Wheatley Fields.

One other moment I ought to tell you about.

After we'd walked back, with the low cloud gathering and the wind beginning to step on the gas, I carried on past my house and walked her all the way home from the trail to the college, which was two-and-a-half miles, and she held my arm all the way.

I idly considered asking her into my flat for coffee, but I shut the door on that notion as soon as it appeared. If it had to take five years for that to happen, it would take five years and not a day less. My self-control elated me, and I thanked Doctor Plunkett for what he had done. On the way home, we talked about many, many things, all Green. We talked about the rain forests, the acidification of the seas, the mass extinctions of plants and fauna due to the greed of man.

Wasn't all doom and gloom. I told her about an article I'd read on the regeneration of the Great American Plains, and the reintroduction of the bison from the Yellowstone rescue herd. From less than a thousand left in 1900, there are now a quarter of a million bison wandering the Kansas, Wyoming and North Dakota plains. Carpets of them existed in 1850. Incalculable amounts of bison ideally suited to the environment and each one of them serving a precise purpose, each one of them a critical point at the centre of a delicate eco-system between man, land, and beast.

Thus, as we're doing with the magnificent rain forests, we wiped them out. Irish cattle barons saw them as unnecessary competition. The US Army saw their eradication as an ideal way of starving the natives. They died because they were slow-witted and dull, like the Dodo. Women in frocks used to fire Winchesters out of train windows on the way to the West, pick them off, leaving the corpse to rot on the Plains. White men used to chase them off cliffs because their pelts were so plentiful, a market wasn't worth it. Environmentalists were trying to make amends for what the Americans did. Carla considered it an inspiring story, and I resolved to tell her my Flower of Joy story next time - that would have her weeping in the aisle. Even I cry at that story, and I don't cry often. (Oh, all right - I'm always blubbing. It's those over active pituitary glands.)

And at the end of the story, Carla kissed me.

Not a kiss on the cheek, a chaste, drying peck, not an air kiss, or a mwah mwah, or a kiss from an aunt to another aunt, but a proper kiss, sitting in the empty bus shelter outside the college. It didn't last long, the kiss, no more than five seconds, but I could taste her lips, and she put her hand on my shoulder while she did it. I don't think I'll ever forget that kiss, which, when I look back at it, could have meant anything, but I took it to mean all the best things.

"Thank you, John. I've had a fantastic day," she said, when the kiss was over, when the tactile imprint was all that remained, along with the faintest hint of her perfume and the merest trace of her moisturiser. "Can't wait to do it," she said, happy and waving as she ran over to her halls of residences, and I waved back, floating.

Do you know? I never laid a finger on her.

Never touched her.

Not even a reassuring embrace of her arm as she kissed me. I just let her do what she wanted and what she wanted to do was kiss me. I was satisfied with that. It was enough for me. More than enough, and the lingering trace of her lips on mine stayed with me for the rest of the evening and well beyond.

Chapter 19: Dino

The next night, when I went into the pub, I noticed a boy standing in the place I usually drink. I say boy, a boy relative to me, but he was more like a man in reality, and he was talking to Carla, and she was chortling along with him with that elfin, girly giggle I believed she'd reserved for me. She was so engrossed in the conversation, she didn't notice me arrive, and I furtively retreated from the doorway to The Snug and sat on nearest table in the middle bar, the rickety old hardwood table and the medieval banqueting throne, and sat down, pretended to take my coat and rucsac off, taking my time, trying to listen to all she said. I couldn't hear anything because the wall was in the way and like kids do, they communicated quietly, and I couldn't see anything because the wall was in the way (hit him), and I slowly took off my coat and sat down, fiddled obsessively with my wallet as if I was checking to see if I had enough money for a drink, or if I was checking to see whether I had a receipt for something, and all the time I could hear Carla laugh (he's a lot funnier than you, isn't he), and I'd had enough, and I walked into The Snug, and Carla, I will give her that, seemed pleased to see me and I said hello calmly, my mask tied on with nuts and bolts.

"Johnny, this is Dino. Dino, this is my friend, Johnny. We go walking together."

"Mate, alright?" Dino said, offering his hand.

(Bastard)

"I'm fine, mate." Taking it and shaking it firmly.

I'd seen him before, that day I'd followed her home. He was as least as tall as me, maybe even taller. Dressed in a red Formula One jacket and smart blue jeans. He looked half Italian, maybe even full Italian, but his voice was local. The worst thing…shit handsome. (You are SO doomed, Johnnyboy. You are so doomed), and while Carla poured my drink, the two of us stood like lemons not sure of what to say. He was no more than twenty, and he may have even been younger. Carla chatted away to both of us about how quiet the pub was, but I didn't notice, couldn't see, couldn't hear, couldn't breathe (kick his head in), and when she gave me my pint, I said I'd see her later and went to sit in the other bar, which was empty except for me. Listening to the two of them joking in The Snug was one of the worst moments of my life.

It was like being on The Rack. Being stretched upon it.

So soon after the kiss (go and kick the living crap out of him. Go on. You've been in prison, and you're rock hard. No one knows it because you wear silly square glasses, and you look like a dweeb, but you are, you are rock hard, and you'll leave him damaged), the apex, the high point - finally; finally I was growing in Carla's estimation and as it turned out (dumbarse), I wasn't growing at all.

Luckily, a rush. Ladies darts, a mob of them from the Haywain with their heavy drinking partners, and I knew that Carla would be busy from now until closing time, and twatty Dino would be standing like a plum (and you'll be sitting like a plum) waiting for her to come back and talk to him.

Carla came over to talk to me, telling me how much she enjoyed Sunday, and asked me whether I'd like to go walking with her in Columbus Park next Sabbath and I said that would be brilliant, although it was only Tuesday. I would have all that time to suffer, but I didn't ask her to go for dinner with me or for a drink. I just nodded, and she touched my hand, oh, so gently, and said I'm so glad, and she had denim shorts on with ribbed tights, and ankle boots, and a woolly jumper, and her hair was in a ponytail.

At least Dino wouldn't see her with her green vest on like I have.

She went back to the bar, and I never got the chance to speak to her that night, but Dino did and by the time it came for me to leave, I went through all the ways I could think of to murder the bastard, and to get away with it, I'd stalk him. Decapitate him. Bury his body in the Cherry Woods one night and no one would ever be the wiser, yet who would be the first person the Police speak to?

The released mental patient in the flat at the end of the road.

I was damned, dear reader. I was truly damned.

That night, when I got home, Carla sent me a goodnight message with two kisses as usual. Afterward, I stripped to my boxer shorts. Cut into my armpit with the Airfix knife and watched the blood trickle like a tributary down my obliques onto my naked thighs.

Things got worse the next night. Much worse.

I began to think that the kiss we shared outside her halls of residence was going to be the apex of it.

I was standing in The Saddler's enjoying a pint of Thor's Hammer and talking to Carla, when someone tapped me on the shoulder. Carla went off to serve someone in the bar, and I turned behind me and was surprised to see Willie Nelson.

"How do," he said. "I see you're up to your old tricks, you old cunt."

"What old tricks might they be," I replied.

"You and birds. You and birds."

His name was William Nelson, and I knew him from Cedar Forest, the first time I had ever seen anyone from inside, outside. He was short, grey, in his early sixties and wearing a non-descript beige coat, some old black shoes, and a cloth cap.

He was a nasty piece of work, and I didn't like him. He was short, and I had to bend my neck to talk to him. I think, if I remember correctly, he was an ex-work rider from a big stable in the time of Mill Reef before his demons got the better of him.

"She's just a friend, Willie."

"Course she is. I've been in them talks wi'you. I've heard." He tapped me on the shoulder with the biggest grin across his boat imaginable. It wasn't a friendly grin - it was the other type of grin, the one blackmailers and gaolers use. "Don't worry; secret's safe wi'me."

Ah! Group Therapy. Okay idea if you're in an another country and you never plan to return, but what if you bump into your fellow therapees afterwards? Some right nutters in those groups and Nelson fits snugly into the nutter category. I didn't like him in the slightest. His presence unnerved me. He was one of those people with an aura of dark electricity.

One of those auras, which inexplicably ensure you feel a little off for the rest of the day after the encounter. Something wrong with him. In Group, he never spoke and to be honest with you, I have no precise idea what he was in the Cedar Forest for. Rumours abounded among the patients that it was something to do with arson; I heard a shotgun wounding mentioned, a love rival in the stable yard, but no one would spill the beans. He was only at the

Cedar for a year, and he was considered a tourist, and after a while, I forgot him. Like your first class at school, you never forget the people who engage in Group Therapy with you. They're like blood brothers for life. They know so much about you and you know so much about them, they own you. You can never escape them. That's why Nelson felt able to tap me on my shoulder. He's my brother in misery and exposition. "I've got no secrets, but thanks. How are you doing?"

"Got myself a driving job. Horseboxes and such. I drive for Bill Tait. He looked after me. I'm here for races tomorrow. Stopping with me sister. Do you want a ticket?"

"No, thanks. Busy tomorrow."

He looked over at Carla. "She got the day off?" For some reason, Nelson found whatever he said highly amusing, and he was getting on my nerves.

"I've no idea."

"Course you ain't," he said, taking a draught of his Mischievous Rat blonde beer. "Your place or 'ers, huh!"

"You're not moving to Wheatley Fields are you?"

"Why? Would thee object?" His eyes flashed. In 1968, Willie told me he got to the semi finals of the stable lads boxing championships before losing to a jockey who had won the Champion Stakes. Even now, he looked like he could handle himself.

"It's not...beneficial...for people from...there...to meet outside. One cannot forget."

"One cannot forget, don't you know. Oh, one cannot forget. One thinks that you're not pleased to see me."

I walked away from the bar and sat down in the far corner. Nelson followed. "I'm not pleased to see you. No one knows..."

"Why should you live rahnd 'ere and not me? What's so special about you?"

"I was here first."

"My sister's lived 'ere for thirty years. I might just move into the back room. Are you going to stop me?"

"Can't you drink elsewhere?" I said.

"Can't you drink elsewhere?" He replied, imitating my voice.

I grinned nervously.

This was getting us nowhere fast. Nelson knew it as well and began to talk to me about horses and the day's racing tomorrow. I wasn't listening. I could see my life in the Fields disappearing before my eyes.

All the work I'd done.

Carla.

Nelson wasn't the type of man to keep secrets for long. Fill him with enough grog and he'd inform on his own mother. One night he'd be talking to big Keith, and Ian, and Anna, and Melon, and Gwyneth, and he'd snitch. He'd tell them all, and I'd be *personae non grata.* It wouldn't bother Nelson if they found out about him. He'd just move on to another town like the affectionless Anti-Social he is. Nevertheless, it would hole my ship below the waterline.

I looked up at the bar. Carla was serving one of the regulars, a Doncaster Rovers fan who I'd spoken to on occasion with a thick beard and long hair. She looked adorable, the little mistress of all she surveyed, her hair in a ponytail, her green vest, laces on her wrist and two long diamond-style earrings dangling onto her shoulders.

Carla, my God. If Nelson spilled the beans on me, she'd never speak to me, and I'd lose her.

I looked at the old man talking for England about things I didn't want to listen to, and I knew I couldn't let him do this. The idea of Nelson stalking me, my past in his pocket like a secret weapon, filled me with dread, and I started to panic inside. I wanted him gone. I wanted him out of my life. I wanted him out of The Saddler's, and I began to think.

Just as I started to think, in came Dino. In his black tracksuit top, jeans and Wellington boots, he looked like he'd just finished a shift marshalling a Point-To-Point.

Nelson on one side, talking, talking, uncaring whether I listened or not.

Dino on the other. He nodded at me cheerfully. Carla's greeting made my blood run cold.

In one week, since that kiss on the trail, I'd lost the lot.

I tapped Nelson on the shoulder, asked him if he wanted a pint. Of course, he said. "I'll try the Reverend Fox."

I walked up to the bar, tapped Dino on the shoulder and told him I'd get these, and as he would do, he said, "yeh, cheers." Carla seemed pleased to see her old and new boyfriends getting on. I ordered a pint of Thor's Hammer and a double chaser, and big Keith noticed the cost of the drinks approvingly from his perch on the other side of the bar. After all, we were living in a world where one traditional pub shuts every fifteen minutes as successive governments continued to re-engineer British society to match its Scandinavian ancestors: A fifteen pound round kept The Saddlers going for another hour. Dino said thanks and I went back down and spent the rest of the night alternating my gaze between Nelson and Dino and plotting a little bit. In the weeks following my first encounter with Dino, I saw him sometimes with Carla and sometimes not. It was uncanny, as if God had introduced something into my world. A Dinototem, a Dinomonitor, a Dinobug. Dino was like the eaty thing in Pacman. He was always around a corner, always there, and if I were just a tiny bit more insane than I actually was, I might have believed he was doing it deliberately.

Shopping in the Community Fayre, there he was, basket in hand, eight cans of cheap lager and two family-sized bags of peanuts. A cheery wave.

In the greetings card shop, buying a birthday card, there he was, chatting to the woman behind the counter.

On the park, walking his dog. And those times I saw him walking along with Carla, to and from the college. On the park, walking with Carla. By the swings...on the way to the Secret Garden.

(they look so *right* together)

(she must like tall men)

In the Chip Shop, in the Post Office, even in Pietro's when I stopped off for an Americano one afternoon, he was in there, waving. Carla told me that his family and the family that owns Pietro's are related, and his presence could be explained by rational means. There is one person I spoke to on my first day in the town who I have never seen since, and I know she lives here because she told me. That last time, I had to acknowledge what was happening. It would have been awkward not to do so.

"We keep bumping into each other, mate," I said.

"Mate, sure we do," he said.

I wondered what Carla told him about me.

Chapter 20: Sharn

Something weird is going on that I don't understand. In the last ten days, Carla has yet to miss an e-mail to me, a morning greeting or a night passing. She's been brilliant. Ever since that kiss on the trail. We haven't seen each other (she's been busy, I know, what with essays and working); we've been attached by some cyber-umbilical cord. She's hardly acknowledged the presence of Dino, his existence. Why hasn't she mentioned him? He's either too important or not important enough to mention to me. Of course, I haven't. Why would I mention him? It's dangerous. I'll tell you why.

a) Mentioning him gives him power. Not mentioning him means that you are unconcerned.

b) Even a question like "how's Dino" will get the alarm bells going. Why is he asking that? What does he mean by that?

So I'm in a difficult situation. I want to know the SP, but I daren't ask without risking Carla running for the exit door. I want to know whether she fancies him.

Sharna approached me in The Saddler's one night cordially. She's proper Green, Sharna. A big mop of dirty blonde hair, big thighs and an arse that could swamp the girth of a shire horse. Old school horsewoman who'd been riding since she was old enough to talk.

On each occasion I'd bumped into Sharna, she'd been cheerful with me, which is more than could be said for one or two of Carla's friends.

That night, as I sipped a Thor's Hammer, keeping an eye on the door for Nelson (who seemed to have disappeared), and Dino (who would be in later, the bastard), she sat next to me. I asked her what she was drinking and I meant it in the information, academic sense, but she said cheers, I'll have a Rat, and I laughed, and she laughed, and I saw Carla laugh, too, and I realised I'd been conned, and I paid up with a smirk.

"I hear you two are going to Columbus Park on Sunday."

"That's right."

"She's enjoying your trips, she tells me," Sharna said. "But don't tell her I told you."

"I'm enjoying them...and I won't! Cheers." We clinked glasses. Sharna leaned back on the chair and slammed the sole of her riding boot on the stool. She was one of those people who walked as if she owned the pub. No, not just the pub - the world. She seemed older than Carla and later, she confirmed she was twenty six.

"Coming up the Open Day on Friday?"

"Where?"

"The college. They're inviting the community to help with the old orchard."

Carla hadn't mentioned it. "No, I wasn't planning to."

"They're looking for some muscle. Diggers and shovellers. They plan to replant most of it, cut down some of the dying trees, a renewal exercise. Ideal to bring the community in. You look like you can handle a pickaxe, shift some earth."

"I'd like that. Friday, you say?"

"All day. Just turn up with a shovel. Carla's on the steering committee."

I wondered why she hadn't invited me.

Dino distressed me temporarily. Sharna looked at me as if she could detect the essence of what I was thinking, if not the content. A group of young lads pushed past into The Snug, loud and boisterous, ordering Rat and Bishop's Mitre, the new lager, and their presence temporarily silenced us. Big Keith, all shoulders and short-sleeved shirts, all tattoos and hairy arms, looked over from the other side. He ran The Saddler's with an iron fist and limits to the boisterousness he allowed in his boozer existed, solid ones. One of the lads noticed his look, and as if by magic, they calmed down and took Carla-poured pints back into the Lounge.

"It doesn't bother her that you're older, you know. In fact, I think she quite likes it," Sharna said.

"Really? That's bad to know. I'm conscious of it."

"You don't look your age. You look like that rowing fella."

I nodded. I wasn't offended by the comparison, nor was I pleased with it, but I realised that you could do a lot worse. She carried on.

"In the horse industry, mixed-age relationships are common as stable muck. When I was eighteen, I used to see a thirty year old bloke and my boyfriend now's a bit older than me. Five-year gap.

Been seeing him three years so it must work. I don't usually last more than six months wi'fellas, but he's a tops guy. He has that level headedness I need. I go out with guys my age, and it's just a competition."

I felt heartened by what she said as she sat sipping beer.

"I'm not sure we're in a relationship, Sharna. We're friends."

"That's how it starts, isn't it? Friends. Give it time. She's shy, but she knows her own mind. You're lucky. Put it this way. Carla is a hot piece of ass - even I fancy Carla! - and she gets chatted up all over the shop. Do you know what? I'll tell you this for another pint. You're the only fella that's got close to her this year. Honest. One lad on her course would give his eye teeth to go walking with Carla like you did, and she just isn't interested."

I wanted to ask about Dino (Please, please talk about Dino, Sharna. Please…), but she was talking as if he didn't exist, as least with a name.

She winked at me and leaned over slightly. I could feel her arm brushing mine. "You look like a decent bloke. Are you a decent bloke?" She quizzed.

"I suppose so. I've got a dark side…" I felt I had to say that, but I regretted it, but she seemed to miss it, let it wash over her.

"She's been out with some total nobs these past two years. Some utter…." She used the C word, which I didn't expect, but I knew from elements of my childhood that they breed them tough in riding stables, an environment the modern world seemed to have forgotten. "She told me you've behaved like a gent."

"Is there any other way to behave?" I said, feeling guilty and averting my eyes.

"You'd be surprised. Carla's quality, classy. Be nice to her and you've got a friend forever. You'd think that would be easy to work out, but I know one lad who got frisky with her on the first date, and she won't speak to him even now, no matter how much he apologises. And he does. He keeps on apologising. It's bolloxed him actually. He's upset, but she's having none of it."

The idea of anyone touching her made me feel a little bit seasick, and I could feel one of my ears redden. "Lad at college?"

"Nope. My brother."

"That must be awkward."

She was matter of fact about it and plucked a loose hair from her head. "Not really. It's his own fault, and he knows it. He should have known better, and he won't make that mistake with a woman like Carla. He's kicking himself now. Carla fancied him until that point, and now she hardly talks to him. I don't think she gives second chances. Anyway, you've behaved like a proper gent, and she respects that. That's important to her. I reckon she's a proper lady and deserves someone the same."

"I do, too," I said.

"I look after her. Particularly here and in the City. I don't like blokes messing with Carla, and they will do. Well, anyway, you'd know that being a bloke," she grinned. "Excuse me, Johnny, I've got to text someone. Be a sec."

She started thumb-texting on her Berry, and the dexterity of it was awe-inspiring. Carla was one of those rare girls who didn't spend all her time on the phone. I often caught the bus into town, and you see them, the banks of young girls all texting and BBMing all the way down. I hardly ever used my Berry. Sharna was one of the phone-attached, that much was obvious.

While she texted, I pondered Dino.

She'd not mentioned him at all. I was desperate to find out about Dino, but I didn't want to be direct about it. The first chance she got, Sharna would tell Carla I asked. I planned to wait for her to mention him. I wanted to crush him, actually. I wanted Sharna to tell me he's a prick, and that he's nothing to Carla. In order to extend the time Sharna had available to tell me those things, I went to the bar, winked at Carla and gave her my most natural look, and she returned it, and I ordered two more pints.

"Getting my friend drunk, are we?" She asked, grinning. "I've been warned about men like you." I replied that we were just talking, and she winked at me.

"That's what they all say. Are you around later?" She asked, and I said I was. "You can walk me home if you want," she said.

I nodded nonchalantly, and said I'd be glad to, and she told me not to go away. I paid for the pints, and I experienced a Montgolfier moment. My body, my soul, my heart, my consciousness, my spiritual being inflated; nitrogen, oxygen, hydrogen, helium and the stuff stars are made of.

I said I wouldn't leave, took the pints back to the table, and Sharna and I carried on talking. To be honest, I can't remember what we said because swallows, thrushes and finches flew around my head.

I was going to walk Carla home.

Me.

Not Dino, not Dino, me, me, me and I couldn't wait.

It was ten past nine, and I had nearly two hours to wait. Sharna, a popular girl, came and went, sat talking on her phone, texted, spoke to me, spoke to Carla and did her thing, a communicator and I didn't mind the lack of focus because all I could think about was Carla. I waited for Dino, but that night, Dino didn't arrive, a Dino-less evening for a change.

Sharna never did mention him, and yet another night passed where the tall Italian remained a mystery because there was no way I was going to ask Carla about him.

That night, a warm spring night, the clouds obscuring a half moon, the stars glittering, I walked Carla back to her halls.

Most of the time, Big Keith paid for a taxi for her, but not tonight for some reason.

I suspected she had recognised that she'd been spending a little too much time with Dino and this was an ideal opportunity for us to spend some time together.

She held my arm all the way home as we walked up past the cottages and Prebends of Steeple Street, and the merchant's houses, and magistrate's mansions of Northgate, and down past the Leisure Centre, past more traditional nineteenth century cottages, and up, in the darkness toward the college. I asked her why she didn't mention the Open Day on Friday. .She said she did! That she invited me and that I said I wasn't bothered about coming! She was slightly put out, I think. I apologised, said it slipped my mind (it was never in it as far as I was aware), and told her to enjoy it. I said I would buy her a refreshing pint in the pub, and she said she would appreciate that.

We talked about many things, and I could feel a developing intimacy between us, an encroaching closeness, which she allowed to happen. When we arrived, we kissed under the awning of a Beech tree just outside the college. Not a demanding kiss, not a forthright kiss, but a pleasant one, an old-fashioned goodnight kiss, and she held me tight, and this for me, was like drugs.

And do you know what, dear reader?

Do you know what? I didn't push it. I didn't force the issue.

I just let it happen, and Carla waved goodbye to me as she skipped across the gardens to her halls, and I waved back, put my hands in my pockets, stone cold sober, stone cold sane, and walked back to Wheatley Fields.

You're not expecting this are you?

You were expecting me to banjax this, but I'm afraid I'm going to seriously disappoint you. I acted my age.

I was the mature English gentleman so many women expected me to be in the past, only to be disappointed.

I was Hugh Grindley.

Self effacing, humble, quiet, reflective, wise, slightly fey and because this was the new me, I let her set the pace. I was prepared to let her set the pace for as long as she wanted. I'd never make the first move, I'd never strike, never do anything to hurt or embarrass her. If it came to something, it came to something. If it didn't, it didn't. The old me was gone.

Medicated and psychotherapied out by the British Insanity Industry.

Thank you, Doctor Plunkett.

Thank you, Nurse Peaches (wherever you are!).

I was cured, and the unambiguously chaste kiss under the spreading Beech tree was surely proof.

Chapter 21: Sable

Despite the optimism I felt on that walk up to the college, I knew the Dino thing wasn't over. It hung like a cloud over me. Nelson seemed to have departed, but Dino was always nearby. Lurking in The Snug. Watching her from two rows back in the lecture theatre. I didn't want to talk about him to her or her friends, but I knew I needed to know my enemy without letting anyone know that I needed to know my enemy, so as I walked home, glowing and easy, confident and urbane, a successful evening, I made cunning plans to check out his turf - the college.

Thursday I spent planning Friday, which meant I had to visit the City and pick up supplies. This took most of the day, and I had to come back in a taxi with all the stuff. I texted Carla something witty from outside the Castle, and she texted something witty back with two delicious kisses.

She wasn't working tonight, but she said she had an essay to do on the reintroduction of the wild boar to what remained of Sherwood Forest, and I said that we could message each other if she wanted. She sent me a Smiley, which I took to mean yes, and I was already looking forward to it. Sharna's pep talk had given me confidence, and although I had to deal with Dino, because, because…well, he had to be dealt with…I managed to focus on the best points and that kiss last night lingered on my lips, and I could taste her, smell her perfume and her moisturiser.

I had to be sure - and I couldn't ask anyone, so I had to see for myself.

On Thursday night, I popped into The Saddler's for just the one, to show the Pop Side that I wasn't solely beholden to love, and on my return, I planned my trip to the Open Day while I spoke to Carla on the computer for four hours, a cornucopia of PC-based kisses and winks.

We had hit a rhythm, and none of my previous insecurities and insanities applied and after I had laid out my equipment for the next day, I had a hot bath, said a fulsome goodnight (which took about twenty minutes) to Carla, and said I would see her in The Saddler's tomorrow.

In hospital, I knew a gardener called Sable.

I knew why she was inside and it isn't a story to share, so to spare her blushes, I won't tell you. She spent most of her time gardening, and I was told that she had little chance of getting out. The modern world, the speed of it, the communication, the Americanisation of it, was always going to mash her head. I always wanted out of these places and did all that I could to facilitate that, but not Sable. She was happy at Cedar Forest. Nine in the morning until nine at night in summer, she'd be out there, tending the roses and growing vegetables. She supervised all the other patients and was sensitive and tender to their needs. Even the staff who worked with her bowed to her horticultural knowledge. She could grow anything on any terrain. Plants loved her and so did the soil. She was fantastic with roses; the banks surrounding the hospital garden were covered in roses. Red, pink and mauve, a sunburst bank of lemon-yellow roses, a whole host of white roses to the north side like a carpet of summer snow.

When Sable arrived in 2001, the garden was in a sorry state, and its health and vitality was entirely down to her. They didn't give Sable therapy or drugs. They gave her a spade and let her green fingers do the rest. Some of the colours were astonishing, and when the roses were in full bloom and the sun shone, the hospital garden was one of the most picturesque places I have ever seen. I became friends with her of sorts. She didn't relate to humans much, partly because of her condition. Sable suffered a variation of Proteus Disease, a condition so rare fewer than 1,000 cases have ever been recorded.

Joseph Merrick, the Elephant Man of lore, may have suffered from Proteus.

Proteus is the continuing and asymmetrical overgrowth of body parts, commonly facial. Sadly for her, one side of Sable's skull had never stopped growing, so her forehead hung like bunches of grapes over her nose on one side. They called her the Elephant Woman on her estate in Burnley, and kids being kids, tortured her to madness. You know the other thing that sent her mad? One side of her was unspeakably ugly, and the other....well, the other was stunning, to prove that God, if He exists, has a vicious sense of humour.

If you stood next to Sable on one side, you would fall in love with her.

If you stood on the other side, you would run screaming in horror.

Imagine being Sable.

Ecotherapy was the only thing that worked at calming down her rage, and she learned to shun most humans, particularly after the thing she did that time up in Accrington. It made the papers, so go and look it up.

Type in...no...you do some research for a change.

Anyway, Sable and I spent many a long summer night together in the gardens because I fancy myself as a bit of a gardener, and we talked plants, and foodstuffs, and soils, and the best methods for growing this and the best methods for preparing that, and I became quite attached to her. When I departed, we wrote letters to each other for a year afterwards, and then I was incarcerated in Cedar Forest. Whether they stopped our correspondence or not, it ended nonetheless. I've not spoken to her for ages until last week, when I wrote to her in some depth, and I hope she gets the letter and writes back because my problems are nothing compared to hers. Despite those, she found peace in her garden, peace with her roses, in the same way that I'm finding peace with my Carla.

I didn't mention her in the letter because...well...just because.

For practical reasons and as a kind of tribute, I decided to become Sable for my mission to the college. I wanted to see Dino and Carla in their home environment, and I didn't want them to see me, nor did I want anyone else to see me. Sable would be the ideal disguise.

In Wheatley Fields, a town which lives for the surface, a person like Sable would be ostracised and kept in an attic, and even her own family would pretend she didn't exist. The town's residents would shun and ignore her. Plenty of people in the town would hate Sable. Hate her for what she is, a mirror; a warped funhouse mirror that reveals exactly who you are on the inside.

Not who she is - who YOU are. Looking closely at Sable can tell you an awful lot about yourself.

The town's residents would just walk past her in the street, too tasteful and self-righteous to gawp, and too vain and capricious to incorporate her in the life of the town.

A week of visits from Sable and she would regenerate that orchard. No question about that. She'd only have to run her fingers through the earth or hold a sapling in her hand, and a hundred concerned townies and some wildlife students would be largely redundant.

In the City, there is a fancy dress shop near the cemetery, which is the envy of other cities. It can supply an aspiring Thespian with just about anything, including Latex. I also brought a top of the range wig, which made me look a little like Cleopatra.

Like curtains, the ebony wig covered both sides of me, and with sunglasses, you would have to look closely to see that it was me.

I visited a workwear store in St Martin's and brought a pair of dark blue overalls, a pair of steel toe-capped boots, thick walking socks, three pairs of safety gloves, and a fluorescent safety waistcoat. The freshness and novelty of the work wear would not be a problem - in Wheatley Fields, it's always new, and I was prepared to bet that those who attended the Open Day would also buy new stuff. Eagle-eyed residents would be more likely to spot me if I wore grotty old gear.

I also visited the Pound Goblin and bought plasters, bandages and a pair of oversized black sunglasses - a pair Sophia Loren might have worn in Rome during one of those fifties romances. Being just a pound, their inherent disposability meant that it made no difference whether they would fit round my prosthetics, but it would add some extra security if they did.

I visited a department store and brought a 40DD plain-white brassiere, nothing fancy. Finally, I visited the High Chaparral DIY outlet near the hospital and spent an hour browsing, buying essentials. A tool belt for starters; a black and white wheelbarrow with sparkling tubular frames. A brand-new shovel, a pitchfork, several hand tools, including garden forks and plant snippers, which I planned to add to my tool belt. They promised to deliver the items the same day, and they did. Whether I'd need them or not was another matter, but it was better to be safe than sorry, and I would donate them to the college afterwards.

In the morning, I found a How To blog written by a make-up artist and special effects designer on the Internet, and I set to work rebuilding myself in Sable's image. I sat naked and listened to music as I did so, some Tangerine Dream, something to calm the seething anticipation in my breast and my coruscating acid stomach.

Within two hours, the right side had been transformed. Wow! I didn't recognise myself. I looked more like Sable than Sable did. My forehead acted as a parasol to my right eye and a lump the size of a boulder extended from my cheekbone. I was difficult to look at and would be nearly impossible to recognise from the right hand side.

To make sure, I added the sunglasses. I had to bend the right arm to fit it over part of the forehead overhang, but they fitted okay and I put them to one side, not sure about whether to use them or not. It would be an easier decision to make if it was sunny.

The wig fitted perfectly.

Do you remember Wacky Races?

I used to watch that as a kid.

Dick Dastardly and Muttley? Sure, you remember!

Anyway, in the cartoon, two cavemen with extremely long hair and two mighty clubs were always in Dick and Muttley's way, and they often won the Wacky Race. In the wig, I looked a bit like one of those cavemen. The overalls fitted perfectly as did the boots. I planned to jump in some mud along the banks at the side of the road on the walk up.

I filled the brassiere with various padding and put it on underneath a tee-shirt. My new breasts were ample, but not ostentatious. The bra and its contents felt awkward and heavy, and I couldn't wait to get it off that night. Before the town was up and about, I went furtively outside into the communal gardens and rubbed soil and earth into the mounds and into my hands, and smeared some into the overalls.

I prepared the barrow and the tools, put on my safety vest, and I was ready.

I made breakfast - a bacon and egg sandwich - and practiced Sable's Lancashire accent, just in case anyone spoke to me, which I doubted. I didn't want anyone to speak to me. I wanted to watch

Carla and Dino relate, and I wanted to assess how much of a threat he was to our happiness.

It was okay using second hand accounts - like Sharna's two nights ago - to reassure my tender ego, but it's nothing like seeing it for yourself.

Laboratory conditions as it were, as I made breakfast, I was beset with a horrible notion. What if Dino wasn't there? I was running a tremendous risk for nothing, and it made my heart stop temporarily. I was almost certain that Carla wouldn't recognise me, but what if she did? It would be all over.

I suppressed the urge to rip off my Latex disguise and go back to bed. This was MADNESS! I must be CRACKERS to do this! I decided that if Dino was absent, I would leave the barrow and tools, disappear quietly into the woods surrounding the college, and return home.

If I could see him, I'd watch him like a hawk.

I departed for the college, pushing the barrow before me. Underneath my overalls, I wore a hoodie and luckily, it was raining lightly, which gave me an excuse to put it up. Sunglasses and hoods don't usually mix, but I was frightened to take them off and decided to take the risk. My boots were stiff and heavy, but I didn't mind. I was sure that you couldn't see the latex work underneath the hood and the wig, and I wondered whether it had been necessary. As I walked down toward the leisure centre, several people passed me, and none of them looked my way, not even curiously, which could have meant anything.

The road to the college is uphill, and it lasts about a mile. It was an effort to push the barrow full of tools. A red van went past, and the driver and passenger waved - I guessed they were also going to the Open Day.

It took about twenty minutes to reach the college and by the time I arrived, I was damp and sweaty. A young girl at the gate with green plaits and purple nail varnish, took my details (delivered in my best Lancashire accent).

She made a joke about the equipment, pointed me in the direction of the Wood, and wished me well, and I waved a gloved hand, carried on pushing the new barrow.

I could see people mill up ahead on the other side of a green expanse, and I started to feel a vice-like grip on my heart.

Carla.

In addition, Dino.

I was glad to see plenty of people for the open day - about a hundred including the students. As I approached, I noticed several people look at me curiously, but - putting away my paranoia for a second - I realised that they were looking at the barrow and the tools.

A bespectacled man with long hair and a thick beard, who I guessed must be a tutor, walked up to me. "Thank God someone's used their heads," he said. "Thank you for bringing your own stuff. We've had a bumper turn out, and I don't have enough tools to share. And this barrow is going to be useful. New isn't it?"

I nodded and mumbled in assent.

"It'll get dirty, I can assure you," he said, matter-of-factly. I picked his accent as from the South West, and he didn't seem to notice my artificial disfigurement under the hood and the sunglasses. I realised that I had covered it well - no trace of embarrassment or shock as he spoke.

In my best Burnley accent delivered slowly, Sable style, I told him that I was glad to help. He told me his name was Brian and he gave me a list of instructions, most of which involved moving soil from one part of the orchard to another, and I said that would be fine. The mobility allowed me to get close to Carla and Dino, who I couldn't see yet, allowing me to assess what I needed to assess.

I gestured to the tools and mumbled that he could distribute them, and he picked up the fork and walked off, telling me I would need the shovel. I liked his matter-of-factness and his bustling approach, and if he was Carla's tutor, it was obvious she was being looked after.

The weather was that weird April mix of sunny spells and showers, and it was quite warm. I felt a sheen on my back, and I was desperate to remove a layer, but I knew I couldn't do so, especially when I saw Carla and Dino walk across the expanse to the wood. I felt my heart stop when I saw them *(You old tosser! They look so vibrant together. Let them go. Let them live.)*, and my stomach did a forward roll, nearly depositing the remains of breakfast into a freshly-dug mound of earth.

Dino dwarfed Carla. Wearing a black tracksuit top, tight blue jeans and a pair of Wellingtons, his full head of hair, dark skin and golden earring, I could see why she was laughing and joking in his company. He carried a shovel over his shoulder and Carla would touch him, put her arm around his back, and look up at him, and each time she did so, I felt nauseous and tense (kill him), and wanted to run and hide or run into him like a berserker warrior and chop his head off with my newly minted shovel, and they walked past me, right past me, close enough that I could smell her perfume and hear the tonality of her voice as she spoke, walking toward a group of young people digging a trench; her quilted anorak and jeans, her hair wrapped up in a band.

I filled up the barrow with soil and transported it to its new destination, my head down, hood and sunglasses on. I was pleased that Carla hadn't noticed me, and I knew my disguise had worked, but I knew that further testing was necessary. I needed to hear them talk together, I needed the full picture (You'll only hurt yourself. Plunkett said this is what you do, and you're supposed to be stopping it.) to work out what I needed to do, and after I deposited the first barrowload of soil, I headed over to the trench and slowly began to fill the barrow up with earth.

As I did so, I saw Carla digging and instinctively, I wanted to go over and help her. Dino, by her side, effortlessly extracted a hundred weight of soil in record time, and Carla looked at him in a way that I interpreted as adoring, but which may have been something else entirely. He was trying to impress her, I knew, and I wanted to walk up behind him and whack him over the head, but I suppressed the impulse and moved the soil back toward the new plantation (please God, don't let me see Carla kiss Dino, please God) and then back again, and so forth.

As I shovelled fresh soil into my barrow a fifth time, a man came up to me - not a student, a resident. He was carrying a hand fork. He was no more than thirty, and like me, he wore overalls. I kept myself hidden from him.

"Do I know you from the town," he asked.

I'd never seen him before. I was wearing a hood and sunglasses, and my long black hair stuck out of my wig in all directions. Who did he think I was, and why was he approaching me? I didn't need that. Not at all. Instantly, I felt awkward and tongue-tied. I shook my head, elevated my tone. "I'm from Lancashire. Just passing through."

"You drink in Haywain, don't you?" He asked, smirking amiably.

I shook my head, carried on transferring the soil.

"Yes, you do. I was chatting to you on Friday night. About growing apples. Surely you remember?"

He was confident, and cocksure, and had a certain look about him. He was attending the Open Day for a reason and that reason was obvious. I told him he must have been mistaken. I picked up the barrow and wheeled it across the mud and the grass toward the plantation. Not getting the message, the man followed me.

"Are you sure you don't remember? I'm Gerry. You'd had a bit to drink."

"It's not me," I said, in an amazingly accurate Lancashire accent. "I don't drink."

"Oh, well," he said. "Must be mistaken. Anyroad, ne'er mind that. You doing owt tonight?"

Apart from two lecturers standing next to an oak tree chatting about something, and some students in a line on their knees planting saplings, the two of us were alone by the mound. As I emptied the barrow, I decided to end the conversation. I took off my sunglasses and pulled down my hood, and showed him the Protean growths I had so lovingly prepared that morning.

"Love to go out, Gerry. I know a magnificent restaurant in the City," I said and watched his shocked face slide down into his neck, the confident cheekiness disappearing, his eyes protruding on stalks. He spluttered something and then backed off, and I quickly put my hood and glasses back on as he walked toward the college, his Open Day over before it had started, turning toward me in disbelief. He almost ran.

"Must have overdone the 40DD," I thought.

The rest of the day passed by. Carla never noticed me, in fact, no one noticed me, the hood, the sunglasses an effective deterrent against chat and conviviality. Not even Brian spoke to me. The students only had eyes for each other. The residents busied themselves industriously, and I pushed my barrow back and forth watching Carla and Dino flirt and chat in the trenches.

Sharna came by at lunch, and I stayed out of the way. I got the impression when we spoke that she was a shrewd cookie, and I didn't want to take the risk of her picking up my furtive aura.

She soon left, and I spent the afternoon watching Carla and Dino, trying to work out what he meant to her, who he was and whether he was a threat to me or not.

By the time it came for wrap up - the two of them walking and joshing across the expanse back to the college, Dino, fleetingly putting his arm around her shoulders and Carla letting him, accommodating him, the impression of inseparability in every movement, I was still no wiser.

They never kissed. I left the barrow and the tools, and walked out of the iron gates and down toward the town.

Carla worked that night, and we had a delightful time, our usual over-the-bar banter. She looked magnificent in a white vest, a blue bra (I could see the straps), no makeup, her raven hair down, a pair of blue jeans and her baseball boots. She showed me her hands - they were blistered, and I suppressed an impulse to kiss them better. A real warmth existed between us that night. Dino didn't appear, and she didn't mention him, and I didn't ask about him. Nelson didn't turn up. Big Keith was on a crawl with the other landlords and this left plenty of time for Carla and I to talk.

And talk we did.

No matter how many times other blokes from the Pop Side tried to monopolise her company, she always came back to me.

We were getting closer and closer, I could feel it.

Late in the evening, she said she couldn't walk home, which disappointed me because she had to wait for Keith who had planned a lock in for the Landlords and was paying her an extra fifty to stay on. I commented that she must be tired after the Open Day, but she said she needed the money, and she had no choice.

I remember thinking she wouldn't need any money if she married me. I could finance her entire education. Idly, while she served someone in the Pop Side, I wondered how I could suggest this.

I was serious about it, however mad it may seem to you.

After an extra pint (four instead of three), I saw Big Keith and his gang take up their spaces, and I knew that it was time to go. I said goodbye to Carla and told her not to worry about sending a goodnight message, told her to get straight to bed, and she nearly kissed me on the cheek, which would have got the tongues wagging, but she tapped me on the hand and winked, said she would see me tomorrow night and that she couldn't wait for the trip to Columbus Park.

As I walked out the pub, I remember thinking how happy I was.

Something different about this one.

None of the *sturm and drang.*

None of the ultimatums and the insanities, the grand gestures and the pathetic notions.

It felt normal.

Like how non-mutants behave.

A normal, slow developing relationship.

And I loved it.

As I walked onto Steeple Street, a van pulled up next to me with a screech. Before I had chance to react, two burly, hooded men ran out of the back of the van, grabbed me, and with force, threw me inside.

Van sped off.

Chapter 22: Farmyard Blues

They started hitting me the minute I hit the van floor, and it took them a few minutes of kicks and punches before they stopped. I've had worse, but not much worse. They wore masks and black boiler suits, and they were all men as far as I could gather. The balaclavas masked their voices so I couldn't get a handle on where they came from. The City probably. First thing they did was put a hood on my head. Shouting as they kicked and punched me. I was like one of those transparent blue conditioner balls in an empty washing machine. I felt my nose go. One guy repeatedly punched me in the ribs and kidneys. Had I not had several Hammers inside me, those punches would have hurt a lot more, but they smarted and I knew I was going to hurt the next day, assuming, of course, another day would happen for me. I had no idea who these guys were or what they would want with me.

In the months I'd been out of Cedar Forest, I had been meticulous in avoiding trouble and had towed the line, stayed under the radar. Of course, I'd pissed people off in the past - hence my overflowing online contact book of around four people - but not to this extent. I wondered whether I'd been mistaken for someone else, but I overheard one of them on his mobile use my name to whoever was on the other end of the line.

It was me they wanted, and it was me they'd got.

Three main routes exist out of Wheatley Fields if you ignore the Racecourse Road (which is often gated), and the hidden country roads only locals know about. The first goes to the City past my house, but from where I was taken outside The Saddler's, the van would have had to slow down and make at least two stops at junctions. I didn't think we'd done that.

The second goes to Charlestown via a village called Upsley, but that is bisected by a steep hill and I couldn't altogether tell whether we'd ascended to that extent. The third heads to the main road up to Doncaster, and I suspected that was our destination, a straight flat road down towards a big A road.

After a while, the men became quiet and left me in a ball on the van. I could sense their presence and their body heat. One of them was smoking, which seemed unusual in today's day and age, and I felt that the others would have been offended by that, but the fact they weren't gave me a clue to the type of people who had accosted me. My arms and legs were roped, and a thick black hood was over my head with plenty of space for air. I felt liquid on my cheek and wondered whether my nose was bleeding - it could have been tears.

We seemed to travel for about an hour, but that could have been time displacement, and it could just as easily have been ten minutes before we came to a stop, crunching gravel. I could hear the van door open at the front, then the double van doors open at the back. Two of them picked me up, rough and tumble, one of them sticking a knuckle into my ribs, saying something I didn't hear and the next minute, I was being frogmarched blind.

I knew to keep my mouth shut, and I kept my breathing even paced, conserving air. I heard a door open and a muted conversation, then a smell of horses, hay and manure, a foul, rural smell, acrid and heavy on my nostrils. A barn. They sat me down on a chair, untied my hands and tied me to the backrest. Removed my hood.

The men who had kidnapped me walked to the front of the barn, hooded themselves (one removed his just before they left the barn door, and I could see he had a tattoo of an eagle across his brawny bald neck), laughing and joking, like five men coming off a five-a-side football pitch on a Tuesday afternoon.

The barn had a high ceiling, and the chair was in the centre. Haybails stacked high, and the floor was covered in straw. It was cold and silent, and I guessed it was coming up to midnight. I tried to free myself from the binds on both my arms and my legs, but they had done their job professionally and I was locked in tight. The rope dug into my wrists and ankles, and my entire body was beginning to throb. I had no clue whatsoever why I had been abducted.

None at all, but when the door opened, and a big beefy burly man walked through it toward me, I could see that I was about to find out. I looked at him closely. It was the bloke from the pub who had been talking to Carla. He wore a black coat, jeans and green Wellington boots. A cloth cap, one of the old-fashioned rural ones. Mid fifties, ruddy, hair unkempt and over his collar, a mix of powdery grey and owl feather brown. As he got closer, I could see his eyes were bloodshot, and he'd been drinking; his nose suggested that this was a regular thing, and not real ale …Scottish real ale, more like. He stood in front of me and looked me up and down.

"So you're the bloke, are you? You're the bloke."

I didn't say anything. His voice was croaked and cavernous, like a frog emerging from a muddy pond. His hands were in his pockets, one of the many on his coat.

"You ought to know better, didn't you. You ought to know better."

I had no idea what I ought to have known better, and didn't say anything. I noticed a droplet of blood fall onto my quilted jacket and realised that my nose was bleeding after all. He didn't speak for a bit. Just stared as the temperature dropped. He reached into his inside pocket and removed a leather-covered hipflask about the size of a large chocolate bar. He unscrewed the top and took a draught. I felt for a moment he might offer me some, but after he had taken his fill, he put it back into his pocket. He was one of those controlling, domineering, bullying characters, but at least you knew it. He wasn't going to pretend to be friends. He wasn't going to bother drawing me into a false sense of security.

"Man your age. Should be at om. Wife and kids. Slippers, falling asleep in front on fire…"

"As opposed to what?" I replied, curiously.

"As opposed to trying to get in my Carla's knickers…"

Carla's dad.

Of course, I should have known. Who else could it have been?

"We're just friends."

"Should be at om, looking after nippers. You got nippers?"

"No."

"I had me first kid when I were eighteen. Our Nige. Terrific lad. Works in bank nah. Down south. Love my Nige. I were eighteen when I had him. We had our Jenny when I were twenty one. Our Vaughan when I were thetty. I've always loved me nippers, Johnnyboy. That's point of wold intit. To ey kids. Why ha'nt you had kids?"

"Never met the right woman, Mr…"

"Mr. Benedict to you. And you think my Carla is rate woman foyya?"

"I've told you. We're just friends."

He stared at me for a moment. "Don't tek me forra cunt," he said, viciously. "What you got in common wi a girl that age."

"Lots of stuff. We get on."

I could smell his breath, his seventy proof breath when he leaned into me, almost snarling, the beast within unleashed. "I mind yo trying to get in my Carla's knickers, Johnny, but I mind even more you taking me forra cunt."

"I've not laid a finger on her."

"I'll bet my farm to a five bob note you plan to," he said, unmoving.

"I'll take the bet."

He was furious, I could tell. He seemed to get bigger the more we talked, and I wished I'd not made that comment, especially when he grabbed hold of my lapel. When he spoke to me next, he sometimes slipped into a pronounced and clear Queen's English mode and then back again.

Money. Serious money.

The whole place reeked of it. I knew Carla was hiding something, and it looked like she was hiding her past. Something funny about that. Most young people from privileged backgrounds carried it on their sleeves - it was unusual to find someone who was trying to play it down. Even so, I was scared to death when he leaned into me.

I looked at his mouth, tongue and lips and to me, he started to resemble a living gargoyle, and when I saw that in him, it wasn't a step too far to see the saliva dribble onto his polo neck jumper, and to see his tongue turn into one the size of a cow, charcoal coloured, and rubbery, licking the inside of his lips when he pronounced his vowels.

A technicolour world. 3-D, Hi-Def and Blu-Ray. I could see the pores open above his mouth. Some began to weep. I could see the hair beginning to grow between his nose and top lip, wiry, fly hair. His tongue licked his top lip before he spoke, and I saw one of the thick wiry fly hairs snap forward and backward like hard rubber. I wasn't going to like what he had to say, I knew.

"Carla and I have a difficult relationship. I had her late in life, and we don't have a lot in common. I ain't spoke to her for three years now. We had a disagreement about a boyfriend of hers and she had to mek a choice between her family and the boyfriend. She chose boyfriend, and that was the end of that."

"Who was the boyfriend?" I asked.

"She not told you, Johnny?"

"No."

He snickered. "He were a black lad. From City. Met him at school. I ain't eying that, oh, no. She brought him om without telling me one night. Her mother made him dinner, and we were looking forward to meeting him, only she didn't tell us he were a black lad."

"She never mentioned that."

"How do you feel about it, son?"

"As I say, we're just friends," I replied.

"Course you are, son. Course you are. Nah, I don't know about you, but my generation don't hold wi' all that at all. Oh, of course, we pretend to. We pretend to, otherwise, they call us racists and them liberals get hold of us, and we end up in big trouble, but when you put a gun to my head, I don't like it much and neither do you, I can tell in your eyes..."

"Does it matter how I feel about it? It's hard to avoid. It's so common now it's like just wallpaper."

"Not rahnd here, it ain't," he said. "They can keep it all in City walls. Anyroad, I didn't approve and let her know when she came back later wi'out black lad. We had a massive rah and then she stormed off, presumably to black lad's ahs. I try to speak to her in that pub of 'ers, but she ain't eying any on it. She mention me?" He asked, drawing back slightly from me.

"Sometimes. Not much," I replied, truthfully.

Benedict got up. He looked incredibly sad, empty, not at all like I expected him to look. For a moment, he looked lost, and a lot younger, and you could feel the emptiness radiate from him like heat from a bar fire.

"We loved each other, Carla and I. I had more time for her than I did for me other kids. Me others don't come back and visit much because of that, Johnny. One lives in London. Another in New York, another in Monte Carlo with a bloke who is so rich he makes me look like a street corner tramp. I sent em to proper schools and I gave em the lot except…except…"

"Time?" I added.

"Time. Yes. Time." He took out his hip flask and this time he offered me some, but I declined. He seemed to finish it off, and he put it back in his pocket. Whatever was in the flask wasn't filling up that sense of emptiness inside him. In fact, it was probably making him worse. I was on my guard. I couldn't understand why he was opening up to me, and he continued to do so. It was starting to get cold. Underneath my quilted jacket, it had been warm enough for a tee-shirt, and now I was regretting that rash decision.

"I gave Carla time, you know. I gave her all the time in the world. I employed people to do me work for me and I spent all the time wi' Carla I could." He turned to me, and his eyes were bright red. Maudlin drunk, seriously emotional. "We were inseparable, inseparable, we were. Two on us did the lot together. Walking together, took her to school, picked her up from school, I sat wi her for breakfast, and I read her bedtime stories every night of the week. I bathed her, dressed her, took her shopping to City, brought her toys and watched telly wi her, all them Tellytubbies and that, all them Tweenies, I sat wi'er and…and…she were so beautiful…so…so beautiful."

He put his head in his hands, and he began to sob.

From my time in various asyla, I was used to watching grown men cry like babies, sometimes for days, sometimes for weeks. Indeed, I had given it maximum waterworks on many occasions myself, so it didn't make me feel uncomfortable like it does with many men, but it did make me feel nervous. I was in a difficult position and if he started belting me, the rage and the pain getting the better of him, escape was unlikely. I said nothing, just sat and listened. Sometimes that's the best way.

"Seeing her wi…im…after all that love and all that time. It was like, it…were like I were worthless. Know what I mean, Johnny?"

I said nothing, just listened to the newly fallen raindrops tapping on the barn frame outside.

"Course you don't, son. You ain't got kids." He walked over to me and dropped to his knees in front of me and put both of his meaty hands on my thighs. Tears flooded down, and his voice had gone from baritone to tenor. "It hurts. It hurts. She's gone from a black lad from City to an old cunt like you. Where did I go wrong, Johnny? Tell meh. Enlighten me. Where did I go wrong? Our Jenny's turned out to be the most normal lass on the planet, and I don't reckon I spent more than a month in total wi'er. Hardly spoke to her except to gi her money for dresses. See, along wi farm, I had me stables to look after."

"Stables?"

"Point-to-point. Did well in the eighties. Lots of horses on books. You like racing?"

"I do, yes. Dad's got horses."

"Thoroughbreds?"

"Yes."

"You aren't that bad after all, son." He stood up, scraped away the straw from his knees and pulled out a handkerchief to mop up the tears from his cheeks. Then he returned to the topic. "Would Carla be wi'me nah if I'd have treated her like Jenny?"

"Have you tried to make it up with her?"

Benedict shook his head. "I worra bit stupid, son."

Something occurred to me.

"What did you do to the lad?"

He turned to look at me and switched into Queen's English. "That, Johnny, is a remarkably apposite question to ask. Very perceptive. I'm afraid it all got on top of me. All of it. I were grief stricken, but Carla won't speak to me now."

"Do you want me to have a word with her?"

He walked up to me, his emotions slipping gear. "No, Johnny. I want you to fuck off." He punched me, knocked me over, the whole kit and caboodle, the chair, the ropes, me. While I was on the floor, Benedict crouched on both knees grinning.

"I'm going to give you a chance, Johnny, which is more than I gave the coon. Just one chance. I want you to fuck off from the Fields, and I never want to see you near Carla again. If you try and see her, I'll set the dogs on you. That's how they settle scores round these parts, Johnny. With dogs. You look like a well-to-do sort of bloke. I keep hounds here, and some I keep mean for the likes of people like you. Your death will be long and painful, and I'll fucking laugh all the way through. If you try and arrange to run away with her, I'll force you to eat your own meatballs. If you see her in secret, I'll bury you alive and sit on the gravetop mesen."

I said nothing, now angry and straining at the leash.

"No point being angry with me, son. I'm her dad. She's my little baby. I'm not having some bloke a bit younger than me crawling over my little girl. Put yourself in my position. How would you behave?"

"I wouldn't be killing people if that's what you mean."

"What, not even for your own kid?"

"I've never touched her. It's all in your head. I bet the other young kid didn't. She's a good girl, Carla. She's quality. You don't crawl all over Carla. She's not a crawling over kind of girl. That's all in your head. You see, you actually did a proper job, you just don't see it."

He laid down on the straw. His gargoyle head came close to mine. The angles were all wrong and I felt a bit nauseous. My cheek lay swollen and sore on the straw, and he was at ninety degrees to my own.

"That's as maybe, Johnnyboy. She's a vulnerable, shy, quiet little girl, and it's up to daddy to look after her," he said, slowly. "Keep her away from old cunts like you. When she were a kid, I swore I'd look after her, and I am doing, son. I'm looking after her now."

I watched his cow tongue lick his lips, and the barn door behind him seemed to flicker, and the light from the fluorescent above began to oscillate and fizzle.

A smirk.

I knew from experience that I was in the presence of someone who was just as mad as I was.

He would never be diagnosed because of who he was, and he'd be allowed to do his stuff to his heart's content for as long as he wanted to do it. I knew that if I went to the Police, I would be underground in 24 hours.

They would never believe me. The word of a recidivist, incurable mental patient against a farmer and respected trainer of point-to-pointers. That's a fair match. I wouldn't even get protection.

"Don't gi'me your answer nah, son. Think abaht it a little bit. I'll gi' you two wik. Then you're history. Don't ever want to see you rahnd Fields. I've got eyes all over shop, and they'll tell me. I'm also eyyin Carla followed as you might have suspected by nah! I don't care where you go, and you and I will witness hide nor hair on each other e'er, son. Am I gerrin through to you? I hope so…" With a lithe snap that belied his bulky frame, he got up and walked to the barn door. Just before he left, he turned back to me with his hands in his pockets. He gestured to one of the giant haybails. "Carla loved it in ere, Johnny. She used to jump all the way from the top bail onto bottom. Never seen a happier kid, Johnny. I'll be going to see her this week…talking to you has given me an idea…be seeing you, son. Well, back on you, anyroad."

As he left, the five men returned, tracksuited and hooded. I had no idea who they might be. Day labourers? They were a lot less rough with me than they were the first time, and they didn't even throw me out of the van when we arrived in Wheatley Fields. They even dropped me at my door, which was more a message than anything courteous.

Chapter 23: Columbus Park

I pondered long and hard about what to do about Benedict's request.

Then I decided there was nothing I could do. I was so deeply into Carla at that point that I was incapable of leaving her behind. It would be like making the decision to stop breathing. A beating wouldn't be enough to stop me, and I guessed that Benedict was just a bully. He bullied Carla's friend that time, and it worked. He couldn't threaten a man of my age. It was all like something out of a shit film, and something like this didn't happen in real life. It didn't seem real. There were times over the next two days where I believed I had undergone a psychotic episode and my meeting with Benedict hadn't actually happened at all.

Nevertheless, I didn't go to the pub the next night. I needed to think. It was the first time I'd not been to the pub while Carla was on shift since two Saturdays past.

Carla called me on her break. She asked me where I was, and I explained that I was feeling poorly. A spring chill. Didn't want to infect her or the regulars. Didn't feel like drinking.

I could tell she was only just about okay with that. Hesitation in her voice. I'd got to know her, and underneath her veneer of confidence, she was insecure and at times I noticed that she felt she was impinging on me, as if she was a burden to me.

I wondered whether she considered that I'd rejected her, strange as that may be. I couldn't understand it myself - I mean, this was a girl who could have her pick - and I was getting the impression that she deemed I was pulling away from her.

Hard to believe, huh.

Of course, nothing could be further from the truth, but I didn't want to overassure her because to do so would play my cards, and I wasn't ready, couldn't face the rejection. We'd kissed several times and held hands, and there was naturally going to come a point where, if this continued, other matters would appear on the agenda.

I'd seen the City at night. I'd seen twenty year old girls drinking. I caught a couple having sex in a skip behind a burger joint. Not even twenty, I don't think. On top of several black bin bags surrounded by burger wrappers.

I remember being twenty.

Carla was all woman with a woman's body and a woman's needs.

I have needs.

I don't talk about them much to you.

After all, I'm an ex-mental patient, and you've had your breakfast.

Nevertheless, I have needs, and I needed Carla. In my…no…

I was prepared to wait, as long as it took.

I read something the other day about over-delaying.

About men who, scared of rejection, didn't make any moves at all and thus took a dumping. It was tough being a man and being able to read those signals. I knew I was over-delaying with Carla, but I would rather take that risk than act too soon. I didn't know what we were to each other. There were times it felt like we were going out, to coin an old fashioned phrase. Other times, I allowed myself to believe we had a future together, but I rammed those feelings down tight, took each day at a time, each minute at a time.

As long as I was with her, everything was okay. I didn't need to put a label upon it. As long as she was there. There was Dino to consider. She had never mentioned him to me apart from that brief introduction. Sharna hadn't mentioned him.

What was I to think of that? Who WAS he?

I don't know why I didn't go to the pub that night. I was powerless to act because of last night. Her dad. I spent the night wrapped in a quilt on my sofa watching TV. Didn't know what to do. Something was stopping me, and I didn't know what. I needed to work it out.

Carla called me when she got home. Not e-mailed. Called. She told me about her day at college. She said she missed me (I noticed the change in her emphasis) and said she couldn't wait until Sunday. Asked whether I'd be able to go to the pub tomorrow or Saturday and I said yes, that I would go tomorrow night. She asked whether there was anything she could get for me, and I said tea and sympathy would be fine, and she said she'd have a cup of tea on my behalf, and she had sympathy for me.

Carla even sent me an e-mail to end the day as she always did.

Two smiley kisses.

Not xx

Smiley kisses.
The first time.
(Jesus…)
How could I leave this behind?
I'd not done anything stupid.
I'd not exploded.
I'd not said anything stupid.
I'd not pushed it.
I'd done nothing untoward.
I'd been the perfect gentleman.
I'd played it straight as a die.
I wasn't mad any more.

I wasn't going to leave her behind because her dad told me to. There was no way I could do it. Yet I had to tell her what happened. I had to. She wasn't safe. I didn't care about my safety, but I cared about hers. I didn't believe she was being followed. Wheatley Fields is a small place. They could have seen me with her on many occasions, purely by chance, but I was almost sure he was bullshitting about following her.

Still.

I couldn't take any chances on her getting into trouble. I loved her intensely, and if my ignorance of her father's request was going to get her into trouble, I would walk, but I wasn't going to walk until I was absolutely sure of the position.

The next night Carla called me about six.

"John?" She sounded breathless, concerned, which made me instantly breathless and concerned. I shot off the sofa.

"Carla. How are you? Okay?" I hadn't expected the call and its appearance jarred, sent my reality tilting a little.

"Can I come to your house? I've news. You need to know."

"Aren't you going to work?"

"I called Leah. She's covering. I need to see you."

"Do you want to meet? For a drink?"

"No. Can I come to yours? I'd invite you to mine, but…"

"Yeh, sure. Mine's a bit of a tip. Give me an hour."

"I'm not bothered about that! Can I see you now?" There was an urgency about her that I had never heard before in her voice, and she had never asked to come to my place before.

"Sure, that's great."

"Do you feel well enough?"

"For what?" I replied.

"Not fluey?" She said.

"No, I'm cool"

"I'll be round in ten minutes. I'll come on my bike."

"I'll wait outside for you."

Luckily, my flat was just scruffy - not dirty, not filthy, but scruffy. I took some mugs off the table, put away the Racing Post and turned off my laptop, and poured some hot water in the bowl. I turned the heating on and went into my room to change into clean jeans and a black shirt. Changed my socks. I had no idea what she wanted, and I was in a panic. I looked across the room for any evidence of my history - psychiatric appointments, medication - but it was all sealed away.

This was the first time anyone had ever visited me in my flat, and I felt like I was sixteen, introducing a new girlfriend to my parents.

Carla. Green vest top. Makeup, cherry-red lipstick. Her dangly earrings. Hair down, eye makeup. She came inside and hugged me straight away. I hugged her back, and we stayed for a while. She was in tears, and I could feel her tears spread onto my chest. "What's wrong?" I asked.

"You remember that man you saw me talking to."

(bastard)

"I do."

"That's my dad."

"Is it?" I played dumb.

"He says unless I finish with you, they're going to hurt you."

(bastard bastard bastard bastard)

"When did he say this?"

"He haunted the halls after lectures. He said horrible things about you."

"Come in...let's have a cuppa." I ushered her into the flat. I was almost certain they'd followed her, but I didn't care. He'd stepped up a gear, crossed a Rubicon. "Did he threaten you?"

"No," she sniffled. "He asked me to come home."

"What did you say?"

"I told him to leave or I'd call security. That's why he threatened you. He hates you. I told him we were friends, and you helped me with my work, and we go walking together, and he called you…he called you…you know…"

"Sticks and stones, sweetness. He's only behaving like many fathers."

"I hate him. He's horrible. I don't want anything to do with him."

"But he's your dad."

"He's not. And I'm not going to stop seeing you. I'm not going to do it. I enjoy your company, and you're not that much older than me. He said some horrible things, and you've been nothing but kind to me. You've been a complete gentleman. I tried to tell him this, but he wouldn't listen. He…just…just…wouldn't listen."

With this, she started crying, putting her head in her hands. I stopped making the tea and sat next to her on the sofa, put my arm around her, felt her warm body melt into mine. 'I had a boyfriend when I was young, a mixed-race boy named Reuben. He disliked him straight away and forced me to choose. I chose Reuben because my father was such an arse about it - and he threatened Reuben, threatened him so that Reuben never spoke to me again. He…he…scared him to death. I've never spoken to him since. Never. He's a nasty man, and I didn't know."

I didn't let on that I knew about this incident, and I just nodded. Her father had clearly not mentioned the other night, and I saw no reason now to mention it. He had intervened directly and changed the rules of the game.

"How old is your dad, Carla?" I asked.

"He's about fifty five," she replied. "Something like that."

"He looked older when I saw him."

"When?'

"Outside the pub that night."

"Yes, he does. You look young for your age," she said smiling.

"Thanks," I replied.

She sat back on the sofa and took off her boots. She wore yellow socks and tucked her legs under her thighs. "When I was young, I idolised my father. I would have done anything for him. I loved mum, but I loved dad. We did it together, but he couldn't deal with me having my own life and growing up, and we argued. I was thirteen. We never stopped arguing, and when he did what he did to Reuben, that was it. I'd had enough. I've not seen him properly for three years. I stayed with a friend's family for a year, and I've been in halls for another two. Now he wants me to go back home. I'm not doing that! I'm twenty for a start, and I hate him for another."

"Was he drunk?" I asked.

She nodded, made a drinking gesture with her hand. "I could see all his mates in the van outside. They've been in the pub. All his labourers and stable lads. They drive him around. I can't understand why he bothers with me. He loves that lot…he gets drunk in the Haywain and up in Follow Field, and he comes to see me. It's like he's compelled." She leaned forward and looked at me earnestly. "You see, I'm a Scorpio, John. You cannot cross me. Once I make up my mind, I make up my mind. And after he did what he did to Reuben, I was never going to go back."

Half of me wanted to counsel her on the merits of forgiveness. After all, I wouldn't have had a family had the concept of forgiveness not existed. The other half of me empathised with her. I didn't know what to say, so I nodded, went back into the kitchen and finished the tea, brought it into the living room.

"John?" She asked.

"Yes, dear?" I said, pushing my spectacles to the end of my nose and peering down at her, something which made her giggle.

"What are we doing?"

"Cup of tea, I think."

"No, silly. What are we doing?"

"I've no idea, Carla. Have you?"

She sat back, folded her arms. "Is it the age difference?"

"In what sense?"

"That's putting you off me. Am I too young for you? I've got a friend who has older men ringing her up, taking her off to Charlestown and that."

"Oh, okay." I was tongue-tied, felt stupid. "I'm not put off by you, by the way. Not at all."

"Well, that's something, anyway. When you didn't come to the pub, I wondered whether there was…a problem of some kind. You always come to the pub. Regular as clockwork." She moved next to me and cuddled into me. "John, I need to know where I stand."

"You're sitting at the minute," I replied.

She punched me lightly. "Be serious."

"Carla, I don't know. I don't know what to say. Can you tell me what you want? That might help?"

"You're the man...you're supposed to..."

"Come here, Carla." I put my arm around her, and she cuddled into me. "Do you like films?"

"Sometimes." I started to stroke her hair, and she let me.

"You ever seen a film called *Crazy Heart*?"

"I've never even heard of it."

"It's a love story. It's on Star in a minute. Is that masculine decision-making dominant enough for you?" I grinned.

She punched me lightly on my shoulder, awkward. "I hope it's fun. Have you got anything to drink?"

"I've got some wine." I replied.

"Pour me a glass. And we'll watch your girly love story," she said, kissing me on my cheek.

And the two of us watched *Crazy Heart* on my sofa.

Half way through, I laid down, and Carla laid down with me. My body covered the entire length of the sofa, but it was deep enough for two of us to lie on side-by-side. At first, she watched the film and I spooned her, cuddling her from behind, enjoying her body heat and her warmth. I stroked her shoulders, and stroked her hair, and before you knew it, she was asleep, and she rested her head on my chest, wrapped her arm round me and laid her thigh across my legs. I laid listening to the soundtrack and the script, but I stared at the ceiling and luxuriated in her, sensed all of it about her. I saw the patterns in the freckles on her copper-coloured shoulders.

I detected a rhythm in her breathing, her incredibly light breathing. I craned my neck forward over on occasion and smelled her neck, a freshness of rare quality. I kissed her shoulder, and the feeling of her thigh trapping and constricting my legs gave me an erection, which I tried to suppress (not altogether successfully). She didn't seem to notice. She'd been working hard. She'd had college, assignments, the pub, and all the stress with her father and with me, no doubt, and my heating was full-on, and the front room was sauna warm. I let her sleep and was content to be part of her slumbers, proud she could be so comfortable with me, and I absorbed the intimacy of it.

As I laid with Carla in my arms, I wondered about my friend Leroy. He'd sent me an e-mail earlier. On average, his e-mails arrive three times a week. I always read them, and I always reply. Usual hospital politics, and some of his obsessions, but they were always value. I wouldn't want Leroy to come visit me in Wheatley Fields - not that he's ever going to get out after what he did.

Twelve years so far. Twelve years he'd spent in various institutions, and it was only due to the intervention of a kindhearted Charitable Trust that he had been allowed to spend his time at a decent place like Cedar Forest. The Trustees paid for his stay in the hope he'll be cared for in the community one day.

Discharge and release.

Leroy is of Nigerian Jamaican extraction. He's thirty eight, a hefty six foot seven and built like half the side of a house. He's a giant and generally, a gentle one. One problem.

The Devil's Leaf, as he calls it.

Cannabis Psychosis on top of a tendency toward Schizophrenia.

Paranoia.

I never smoke much gear because it does two things to me. It makes me quiet (you'd probably order it by the shipload), and it makes me paranoid. It doesn't give me the giggles, and it doesn't make me want to eat, so I never used it much outside my undergraduate experimentation.

But Leroy.

Wow.

The guy told us that from the age of twelve, he smoked a minimum of an eighth of an ounce a day. He took to smoking grass like a baby takes to swimming straight out of his mother's womb.

He loved cannabis. However, fourteen years of high intensity cannabis smoking brought out the worst in him.

Mr. Hyde (I know that fella).

Jealousy. Conspiracy theories.

Obsessions. Suspicions.

Mostly, but not always, about the fidelity of his wife, Rosemary, some ten years younger than him and a girl of considerable independent spirit.

"Oh, the craic," Leroy said, to us. "We were at it like cat and dog. I spent many a night in the shed with me greyhounds. She spent many a night at her mothers. Boy, we fought. She did what the hell she wants, that woman! I couldn't control her. I don't know why she married me at all. I love the woman, and I never did no bad things, I never catted about, I never spread me favours, but she…she…she was an evil woman. I know twice she played around, and both times I took her back. She drove me up the wall. I come home on a Saturday night after work and she wouldn't be in. She'd be in town with her bitches, and she wouldn't come home. Then we'd fight some more and some more…we kept splitting up and getting back together. Couldn't live together, couldn't live apart, know what I mean? This went on for years, and it got real funny…real funny."

Turned out, Leroy tried to cope with his wife's independent nature by smoking more and more cannabis until the point where his moments of sobriety were vastly outnumbered by his moments of tuned-out euphoria. Permanently stoned, more or less. He worked under minimal supervision for the Council on the parks, started smoking at the beginning of his shift, stronger and stronger stuff the older he got, and he'd go home, fight, and watch his marriage explode. He'd longed suspected his wife of nefarious activities, but friends assured him it was just the blow talking until one night he returned home early from work by pure chance and caught his wife, Rosemary, underneath his elder brother, Trevor, on the marital bed. Watched by his next door neighbour, Bryn.

It transpired that the trio didn't expect him to be home for another two hours and the three of them were making a film on an early video camera, a big old Sony with a video tape rather than a DVD. Rosemary. Rosie. Mid twenties, curly haired blonde Ultra-Sound specialist in the maternity ward of the main City hospital, was dressed in her nurse's uniform, black stockings and the pristine high heel Louboutin shoes that Leroy had bought her for Christmas. A roped pillowcase protected her identity.

Brian, his neighbour, was a white man in his fifties.

Bald and wearing nothing but his socks, and according to Leroy, "armed and ready for business;" he directed activities while his brother Trevor fornicated with Rosemary, her pale legs wrapped around his back and whose wrists, on closer inspection, were tied to the headboard with cable ties.

"It were the noise, you see. She were making so much noise. She never used to make noises like that with me, know what I mean. She were always quiet wi me, special toward the end. It were the noise that sent me over the brink, man. And my bro were my bro, know what I mean? I loved him, and I never knew. I never had a Scooby fucking Do. He were giving it to my wife all the time. He knew how much I loved my Rosie, and there he was balls deep. Balls deep. Any of you white boys seen your wife, your beloved, balls deep with another man? Giving it the big one? It isn't nice. It ain't nice, specially a black man…"

We laughed, even though we shouldn't have.

Leroy smirked, clearly not the first time he'd carried out the sketch. I always remember that joke. Leroy was - and still is - a man of wit. I often wonder whether Kenny would have joined in, but he wasn't part of the group by then.

"I lost it, you know. Lost it…"

High on Beelzebub Skunk - Rotterdam, 40% THC, some of the highest strength weed known to man - with a sickening crack, Leroy snapped a petrified Bryn's neck with one twist. Then he dragged Trevor down the stairs naked and ignoring his pleas, sliced his throat with a catering-standard Kitchen Imp carving knife.

"Never seen so much blood blood. I always make that joke for you white boys. Blood blood. Get it. Get it? It scooted all over the kitchen floor. It made patterns on the cupboards, and I sat down on the floor, and I watched them patterns. I watched em for an hour. I knew that Rosie, my baby Rosie, my woman, *my woman,* was tied up upstairs, full of my brother's seed, and no one had heard anything. There were no rush. Eventually, I picked up the knife and…and…I went back upstairs…"

If he'd have left at double murder, a crime of passion, he would have been out by now. On the streets, working some bum job, with a woman, a car, a new life.

If he'd have left it, he wouldn't have been condemned to life in various mental institutions because it doesn't matter what Lord Newton Dulverford's Charitable Trust wished would happen, the promise of release, and forgiveness, and rehabilitation; keep your wife alive for three days, a pair of lacy lemon panties in her mouth while carving slices of her flesh from her body and forcing her to watch you eat it, raw, bloody, rare pork steak, you aren't ever getting out, cannabis psychosis or no cannabis psychosis.

Plunkett tried to stop him telling us the gory details, but I don't know about you, I couldn't stop listening to it. It also made Leroy feel better telling it. It gave him a sense of peace.

I don't know why I laid there thinking about that story. It's not as if the presence of Carla inspired something in me. Murder and cannibalism. It's not like that at all. Before long, I was asleep, and we remained that way until morning, the TV turning itself off, the red standby light the only evidence it was ever turned on.

In the morning, I made breakfast and Carla and I sat on the table talking like an old married couple. I made bacon, eggs, tea and cereal, and Carla ate the lot.

"I bet I look a right dog."

"You look lovely," I replied.

"Oh, I'll bet," she pulled a face and twisted her jaw unfetchingly. "I'm a right minger in the morning. I never wiped away my makeup."

"You slept like a log."

"I was…so comfortable." She reached over and squeezed my hand. "I could have slept for days. It was only your snoring woke me up,"

"I don't snore, do I?"

"Yes, Johnny. You snore a lot."

"Oh."

"An alarm call. I've got lectures in an hour," she took a big bite of sandwich and stood up. "In fact, I better go."

"Are you on your bike?"

"It's outside on the railings," she said, putting on her coat. "You coming in the pub tonight?"

"Wouldn't miss it."

"I can come tonight, if you like. We've got something I want to discuss … we…we…er, never got round to it last night."

"Sure. I'll walk you back."

She leaned over. "I'm not going to kiss you properly. My yucky breath. See you tonight, Johnnyboy," she said, kissing her fingertip and placing it on my lips, and as fast as that she was gone. I heard the door shut, looked out of the window and saw her cycle out of the forecourt.

Oh, My. Was I utterly in love at that point. Absolutely.

You ever been so in love that your mind stops working? That you cannot remember who you are. Your mind regressing to a lower state of evolution.

Amoeba'ed. You ever been amoeba'ed? I was a non-thinking being, and I sat stirring tea and staring into a bowl of cereal, my cheeks warm, beads of sweat on my forehead, my head a white hole of nothingness. That whole sense of body over mind. That sense of nothing mattering.

Not space.

Not time.

Not mind.

Not body.

Not spirit.

Not fate.

Not life.

Not past.

Not present.

Not future.

Not birth.

Not death.

Nothing.

Nirvana.

That sense of your brain liquefying, dripping out of your ears, all you have ever known, and you don't care. Nothing mattered except Carla.

Ah! You ever felt like that?

I envy you. I did.

If you've never felt like that, you've never been in love.

Honest, you haven't. I don't mean to be rude or anything.

Chapter 24: Top Hat

Like Frankenstein is the name of the Doctor, not his creation, Big Ben is the name of the bell, not the tower, and alarm bells started ringing like Big Ben in a small bedroom that night in The Saddler's. When I arrived, Dino was at the bar for a start. In a beige jacket, a gold earring, blue jeans and eco-trainers, he stood at the bar of The Snug, and he had her full attention. I'd been in this situation before, and I had handled it well - much better than I used to, perhaps because of the ambiguity in the relationship between them, the ambivalence, the confused state of it in my head, because she had never kissed him or shown him any affection in my presence, nor on the Open Day - so I let it pass, but when I arrived at the bar of The Snug, saying hello to Dino, she went to serve someone else and her greeting to me was less than enthusiastic.

I spoke to Dino for a bit about stuff - his top of the range iPad, actually, and a Green Radar app he showed me, which was charting the clearcutting of virgin rainforest in real time and comparing it to the size of the UK - and when Carla didn't come over to say hello, I went to sit down in the far corner with my pint of Hammer.

The minute I left, she came over and started talking to Dino.

(Duck Five)

(Duck Five)

(Duck Five)

I drank the pint in three gulps, went back up and ordered another. No reaction from her. She looked ashamed of me, her eyes looking away involuntarily. Guilty at her association with me.

(Duck Five)

Sick inside, the nausea began to expand and to envelop my body, and I nearly tripped on the way back to the chair (bitch), and I steadied myself on the mantelpiece of the disused fire, wondering why she was behaving like this.

Someone from the Pop Side came in and sat down on my table to talk to me, one of the first times ever that a local had shown any interest. An owner, he spoke to me about a horse he had running at Wheatley Races on Tuesday next.

Apparently, as was common, they had been saving the horse for this particular day and his form figures were 460005877-000, the horse not running at all well for nearly a year. He was part of a syndicate, and they were hoping to recoup their entire outlay on training fees in one hit. With form figures like that, he was expecting anything between 12/1 and 50/1, and he had been assured by his trainer that the horse had been working the gallops down like Dancing Brave and would be cherry ripe on Tuesday afternoon. I wondered why he was telling me this, and as I watched Carla - her jet black hair down, a Glastonbury 2008 tee-shirt and two giant silver earrings - chuckle at something Dino said, I remembered that we had talked in the library two weeks ago, and I had told him that racing was my bag. Politely, I listened, and nodded, and did all the right things, but the last thing (*kill him*) I needed to talk about was horse racing (*now*), and I wanted him to go away, but he sat with his point telling me about a double he had on Saturday, which paid out £2,500, and ordinarily (*he's taking the piss*) I'd be interested, but not tonight. Head buzzing, I visualised the ducks landing on the wall, and I tethered them so they wouldn't fly. Duck one (*Mallard*) and three (*Common*) and five (*Widgeon*) quacked loudly, but two and four were absent, and thinking calmed me down because I had destroyed places for less than this.

I remembered the Works Christmas party where it had been expected by my entire department that I would end up with a girl I worked with (Alyssa), and in the end she ended up with Buddy, rejecting me harshly and unnecessarily, despite weeks and weeks of office flirting and hammered on white wine, I lost it.

I'd only worked three months; my father had influenced the decision to recruit me, and I repaid him by...well...well....

Well.

The racehorse owner and I went to the toilet, and I did a brilliant job of disguising my pain and steadily growing anguish, and I told him that I'd be present on Tuesday, and he asked me whether I'd help him lay out some money with the track bookmakers, and I nodded, said I'd be glad to and when we came out of the toilet, he went and had a fag with all the smokers, and I went back to watch Carla flirt with Dino.

Carla came over to talk to me on her break, but she didn't look interested, and our conversation was brief. She wouldn't look at me, and I asked her if anything was wrong, whether she was tired or whether she had a crappy day at college, but she just shook her head and told me that she'd mail me later (forgetting she was supposed to be coming back), and went back behind the bar.

I didn't even bother with the third pint and left without saying goodbye.

On the way home, elaborate whorls in the bark of an oak tree resembled Dino, and I headbutted it silently, drawing blood, the impact making sure I vomited later and left me with a bruise the size of an apple. I waited diligently by the PC, Carla didn't mail me.

After fifteen minutes, I listened to *Octoberon* by Barclay James Harvest on the CD player, listening to *Suicide,* the final track on the version I owned. Distraught and angry, like Leroy was with Rosie, I started to slice the top layer of the skin of my arms until after an hour, my laminate floor was awash with my own blood.

I so wanted to write to her. I did, but I didn't.

She wrote to me the next morning and appended the mail with one kiss. She asked whether I was going to the pub and she said she would meet me at Pietro's Café on Sunday morning for our trip to Columbus Park. One kiss, no implied intimacy. I was so upset that day that I didn't even bother leaving the house. I mopped the floor from last night (my flat was like the house that dripped blood by that point), and went back to bed and took a self-pitying mental journey through my entire history, wondering if I could have done anything to change things, to stop me from feeling like this, and all the other stupid distractions and pointless deliberations that stop people from actually living their lives.

She didn't text me.

Nor did she mail me throughout that day.

Worse, Carla didn't go to work. When I arrived at the pub, Christina was on. Late cover. Big Keith was by all accounts, not happy about it. I immediately texted her and got no reply.

For the first time in our relationship, she didn't e-mail me last thing.

(No kisses this time.)

And as a consequence, I played noughts and crosses on my thigh with the model-making knife as I watched the Football League Show, watched the liquid drip slowly, like thick red rain. The cutting ensured I felt a sense of peace and made yet another mess on the laminate that I would have to clean up the next morning.

Carla e-mailed me in the morning.

"J,

I can't make today. I'm sorry. I'm not feeling well, and I have homework. I didn't go to work last night. I feel fluey, tired. Hope I haven't spoiled your day. I'll e-mail or text you later.

Cx"

I didn't bother replying to the e-mail. Went back to bed until midday. Showered, dressed and caught the 1.15 bus into the City. Drank myself into oblivion on cider and brandy and caught the last bus home, just me and six others. I don't remember getting on the bus. I don't remember the journey, and I don't know why I was turfed off the bus at Thor's Garden, meaning a three-mile hill walk home. I must have upset someone.

I hope I didn't, but I suspect I might have done.

In the City, I don't think I spoke to a single person outside bar staff all day, and I didn't think of anything. I didn't eat, and the copious drinking I engaged in didn't even begin to medicate the acidic, rotting, despairing pain in my soul.

Carla didn't text, and I was too drunk to turn on the PC. In fact, I slept half the night on the communal bench outside my flat until I was woken by the Police, called by a concerned neighbour. They didn't even take my name, and I caused no trouble.

In fact, if I remember correctly, I cracked a joke or two.

They didn't laugh.

I didn't see her Monday, (myohmy that was a terrifying day), but she texted me on Tuesday morning and asked whether we could go to Pietro's for coffee as she had something to tell me.

I texted back and agreed. Then I dressed as if for a funeral. Black shirt. Black trousers and black shoes.

A waiter's funeral. A funeral for an unhappy waiter.

In Pietro's, Carla told me that things had gone too fast for her, and she wanted to take a break.

(Dino)

Even though I felt like it, I didn't hit her or destroy the café. I sat drinking Americano in my mausoleal clothes. Sipping the hot coffee slowly and staring out of the window. A light drizzle fell on Wheatley Fields that day and few shoppers ventured out. Those who did sheltered under umbrellas of a diverse range of colours. I saw emerald green and electric blue, and two at least, as black as my shirt. I even saw a gentleman with a golf umbrella, a huge thing more like a hot air balloon, suitable for a small child to gain his first airborne experience. The umbrella was so voluminous, I couldn't see the person underneath, and as she described her feelings (I didn't listen, to be honest), I imagined the man underneath the giant umbrella, and in my head he was tall with pince-nez spectacles wearing a top hat. My family has three top hats, which my father shares on special occasions. Jubilees, Weddings, Royal Ascot. By all accounts, one of the top hats is worth just shy of four grand, which, when you think about it, is an astonishing price to pay for a hat, even a top one.

I tuned in and out of Carla's monologue, catching predictable snippets of note. She delivered it with alacrity and sincerity, and she could scarcely look at me in the eye.

I remember some of the jumbling snippets. It is said that Adam created language in the Garden of Eden just prior to Eve's temptation, but I wonder who it was who invented the perception of language and function of memory, because what language she used wasn't perceived in the correct sequential order.

Snippets here, fragments there, a mosaic, a kaleidoscope of language, and words, and spaces, and sentences, and accents, and semantics, a lexicon, a scrabble bag full of sentences on a giant board. Some of what she said came across as if I was watching a TV programme with no sound. I could see her lips move, but there were no accompanying sounds. She was deliberately, poignantly silent, white space on the page.

Other times she spoke on fast forward, animated, and frenetic. At other moments, her voice was slow and ponderous, almost as if I was a dribbling idiot or as if she was speaking underwater. Fragments, shattered, fragments, dreams ripped asunder.

College taking priority, don't know my feelings (top hat), busy with work (Glyndebourne), going too fast for her to cope with, friends, good friends (special ways to look after a top hat and they explain the continued existence of specialist British milliners, versed and trained in the ancient arts of top hat preparation and maintenance), best friends, keep coming to the pub, don't want to lose me, don't want to lose me as a friend (top hat making is a modern form of alchemy, how does one become a top hat preparation apprentice? A sorcerer's top hat apprentice in a top hat).

After she had finished, she told me that she had run out of things to say, helpfully, and a little tear in the corner of her eye appeared, like dew, and I said…I said…

"Oh…"

I said

"Oh…okay."

And she seemed nonplussed with that, almost irritated. She didn't say is that all you have to say, but her eyes said it, and that was true (four grand for a hat). I didn't have anything else to say because I already knew what she had to say before I arrived (heirlooms) in the café (all families of aristocrats should have a four grand top hat for Ascot), and I hadn't been able to think or communicate for days, and I watched her get up, ask me whether I was going to the pub on Thursday because she wanted to be friends, and I said I don't know, and she said goodbye.

Goodbye.

Took her jeans, her hooded quilted jacket and her Wellington boots back on to the road. I don't know whether I was being paranoid, but I saw the Barista stare at me as Carla left, as if I was a fool, a pitying glance. I looked at her, and I wanted to wipe the grin off her chubby face, and I remember gripping the saucer between the thumb and index finger of my right hand, like you would hold the edge of a frisbee, and I targeted her, underneath her dyed, fashionably bright raspberry-coloured hair, and I split the saucer in two. The cup spilled onto the floor and shattered, and the diners turned to look at me, tables full of Wheatley Fields leisurati sipping lattes, the independent businessman on laptops, in smart shirts and polished shoes, harvesting the café's Wi-Fi, the young mothers with the three babies on the top table, all of them, all of them ceasing their flow to watch the dumb, lanky, awkward, gawky man in the black shirt struggle to cope with the shattered pieces of both the coffee cup and the tenuous remains of his sanity. I apologised to the café owner and gave him ten pounds, which he tried to refuse. I left it on the till, zipped up my coat, put up my hood and walked out into the April shower.

(Dino)

I should have asked about Dino, but it was obvious. In my short experience with women, I knew one thing to be true.

A Good-Friend dumping like that always involves another man.

Always.

(Dino)

It took ten minutes to walk back to my flat and by the time I put the key in the door, I knew for certain she was with Dino now, and I was doomed.

Only one thing left to do.

I didn't do what I usually do, which was something.

Not what I have usually done on other occasions, and what you might expect me to do. Perhaps because I knew it was all an impossible dream and that the chances of Carla and I spending the rest of our lives together were a thousand to one from minute one, which meant that I hadn't truly got my hopes up.

Some American psychologist described what Carla and I attempted as a Construct of Original Instability. It could never have worked and subconsciously, I must have known this.

So when Carla walked away from me in Pietros, I didn't destroy the place. I didn't key cars on the way home, nor smash windscreens, or let tyres down on Steeple Street.

I didn't put windows through or scream my pain into the maw of the grey rain. Couples walked past me unmolested. A group of lads from the gym walked past me and waved, and I waved in return. When I arrived home, I didn't turn my flat into a warzone. The pyrotechnics you've probably been expecting from the moment I saw Carla didn't happen.

Maybe, just maybe, all the two decades plus of psychotherapy, medication, incarcerations, imprisonments and self-reflection had finally, finally worked and that I was developing a sense of perspective.

No one died. Police, Camera, Action camera were conspicuous by their absence.

Fully clothed, I lay on my bed for ten hours listening to music and thinking.

My emotions were on standby.

Tabula rasa. Numb, listening to the traffic on Northgate pass back and forth, trying to focus on the myriad conversations taking place between the people who passed by my window.

I didn't eat.

I didn't check my PC. I didn't move.

If you knew me, you would not have believed the way I behaved.

The reasonable way I behaved reminded me of something I read about Anti-Social Personalities. You know, the Psychopaths we talked about earlier.

No cure has been invented for psychopaths. They're just evil people, rotten to the core, but they do slow down as they get older.

That's encouraging.

It's as if they can't be bothered to be evil anymore.

Psychopaths armchair.

As in the verb To Armchair.

Instead of going out drugging and gambling, raping and pillaging, the Psychopath commandeers the most comfortable armchair in the house in front of the telly. An eight pack of lager on one side and twenty fags and an ashtray on the other - one of those stand-alone ones, the ones with the push-button top, which hides the detritus, often made of brass or onyx.

Psychopathy cured by time and a comfortable armchair, huh.

Maybe I got old.

Forty two, the answer to the meaning of life, one of the most popular lottery numbers in the country.

Forty two.

I remember lying in the darkness, a thin smile on my fizzog thinking about *that* one.

The next day, however, a Wednesday, my emotions came back. I remember laying sideways on my cold pillow dreaming about playing chess with my mother and her boyfriend, Carlos.

And it was warm in Caracas, and the sky was an incredibly vivid aquamarine, and I was losing all over the board, and I didn't mind because mum was with me, and I remembered that Carla had told me it was all over, and the dream faded, and the Goggle Eyes hit me, and dear reader, dear, dear reader, I have never in my entire life ever felt as lost as I did in the next hour. All the remorse, the broken marriages, the realisations of unavoidable imprisonments, broken friendships, lost jobs, girls, opportunities and the disintegrated respect, which litter my life narrative like unwelcome reminders, none of them felt as empty as this, and there was nothing for it.

Medicate.

Medicate.

Medicate.

I didn't shower, put on a Timberland blue shirt, my best jeans and boots. Didn't shave. Splashed on some aftershave.

A gunmetal coloured strong box about the size of a house brick called to me from the top shelf of my kitchen cupboard, and I reached for it, pulled it down, and opened it with its tiny key. Approximately two grand, rolled up twenties tied with red elastic bands. I knew that I had five grand left in my account (it was ten, but the horses and hypnotics in Charlestown had taken most of that), and made sure that I had my bankcard with me just in case. I checked the time - seven forty five, tried to chase certain images of Carla out of my head because they kept coming, and their aggregate impact made me feel like digging out my Adam's Apple with a sharpened spoon (a technique I learned about ten years ago in The Windmill, just off Salisbury Plain). I checked the weather through my living room window. It looked like I might need a jacket and so I put on my quilted blue Barbour.

Caught the bus into the City.

Chapter 25: Smash Box

Straight into The Magic Spoons, breakfast being served, the smell of bacon and sausages in the air. I approached the bar and ordered two double Woodsmoke bourbons and two pints of Thor's Hammer. In front of the barman - a young lad no older than twenty with a just out of bed haircut and eyeliner - I downed the bourbons in two hits and asked for another brace, plus the obligatory bacon sandwich, because they can be funny in The Spoons about people drinking early doors without eating. I needn't have worried. The barman took the money as if ordering a quarter of a bottle of American whisky, and a bacon sandwich at 9.30 in the morning was the most normal thing in the world. The beer, bourbon and I found a comfortable slot near the window, and I watched the early morning activity in the City's Market Square. When watching people pass by bored me, I accessed my poker site app, noticed a seat in a six handed ring game, and I loaded up with five hundred pounds.

The first hand I'm dealt 37 off suit, sitting on the dealer button with blinds at a tenner and twenty quid. When it came to my turn, I raised sixty quid hoping to pick up the blinds. The Swede next to me in the small blind re-raised me to a hundred and twenty, and the big blind threw away his hand.

I knew the small blind was sitting behind a monster of a hand (either that or he's a typical Scandinavian), but I was bereft, haunted by loss, afflicted by images, which burned from my temples to my tortured retina.

As I sat, I knew that I was slowly taking the first steps toward an entirely necessary death.

So I re-raised him to two hundred and forty.

The next thing, the Scandinavian is all in and do you know what, dear reader, so was I.

So. Was. I.

The cards on their backs.

He showed me KK, a pair of cowboys, and I was history. He left me a message on the chat box. **Thx Cunt** and I knew that was the last time I would ever, ever play internet poker because it rots the soul more effectively than anything else on planet earth.

Not that it will matter.

I drank all four of my drinks, gave my bacon sandwich to a foetid, unemployed Estonian sitting next to me with fingerless gloves and a red woolly hat, went back to the bar and ordered what I did before to the penny.

The young metrosexual man served me. I bought the timewaster a pint of Hammer, and when I got back to my window seat, I gave it to him. He was delighted, but I didn't want to talk to him, so I stared at my Berry app and opened up the Sporting Horse site.

That Thursday was Craven Day at Newmarket, one of the most significant days in the flat racing calendar. Father won the Craven Stakes with a horse called Corinthius, but it broke down on the gallops before the Guineas and was promptly retired. My father took the loss of his best chance of glory ever with the same reasoned equanimity he takes everything.

For the next half an hour, while I finished the drinks, I emptied my online bookmaker account of its remaining fifteen hundred pounds by making a series of wagers on horses at Newmarket.

Wins, accumulators, forecasts, tricasts, doubles, trebles and luckies, including a whopping seven hundred pound bet on **Adam Warlock,** the favourite for the concluding handicap at seven to two, which I was reliably informed by certain invisible friends, was considered a stone bonking certainty.

By the end of all this, it was ten thirty, and the City was beginning to bustle, and I decided to go and find another pub, preferably one without tramps who smell like old socks discovered in a shed.

Before I did, I popped into a bookies near the old cinema to waste a few hundred pounds on the morning dog card. Felix, a West Indian fella who suffers from Parkinson's Disease, someone I sometimes bet with when I come into the City, came over speak to me. He speaks in an unfathomable Caribbean brogue with traces of the rough City accent - being fifty and set in his ways. He generally wears a dark hip length coat and a baseball cap and today was no exception.

"Yo," I said. "How's you?"

"So, so," he replied. "How's your luck?"

"Dire. You?"

"Fifty quid down already, man. First race at Crayford. Fifty quid, man. Fifty quid today. Not a single winner since Monday." He looked at me with profound sorrow in his eyes, as if by betting that fifty pounds a morning loosener, he had done something naughty, something which he now bitterly regretted.

Those eyes told me there was no turning back.

"How's it going on the Blackjack?" I asked, writing out a betting slip for the second race, the fast trapping trap three.

"Poor. Seriously poor. They love me in Casino, man." The greyhound form on the board behind me came under his beaten gaze.

"Man, I know about bad luck." I attempted to empathise, but empathising with gamblers never does any good. Empathising with gamblers is one of the most pointless things you can do. It's hard to lie when the person you are talking to can see the space behind your eyes.

I felt the worst ever, and all I could see in place of horses and dogs on the screens in front of me was Carla and her new boyfriend cavorting down the secret flower garden, on the trail, or sitting outside The Saddler's holding hands and worse, the worst thing, I knew that I would never see her again, and that ripped me to pieces inside. The loss pierced my insides like a woman with red nails sharpened to points. Leaks burst and my sense of loss, emptiness and abject worthlessness grew with each minute I spent away from the fevered glasses of booze, the only balm that sometimes worked.

Slowly, Felix shook his head with an imperceptible tremor. "I'm a proper loser, mate. A proper born loser," he said fatalistically.

I needed a buzz. I needed to fill my soul, but winning money was pointless for me, so I changed tack. "So am I. Here…" I handed over five crisp purple notes. "Put that on trap three in the next at Crayford."

"No, man. No. Really?" He said, not quite believing it and having no idea how to deal with such unique largesse. This was a man used to betting in fivers and tenners, if that.

"Trap three," I assured him. "'If it pings, it wins. The Crayford smash box. The two dogs on the outside won't go with it to the first bend and his sectional is mercury. The blue jacket's a pensioner and the black takes an age to warm up. He'll finish, but by then it will be too late. Watch the white jacket go."

"Do I keep the winnings?" He asked, tentatively.

"Course you do. And the stake."

"Oh, no, man. That's..."

"Just do it, Felix. Now," I said, assertively, guiding him to the counter.

The Crayford trainers paraded their dogs in a line toward the six tin canisters. I handed the cashier my hundred pound bet and with shaking hand, Felix followed suit. The young fellow with the goatee and two gold earrings behind the counter took the bets. Some of the other punters who had been watching the money change hands, came up to the counter and backed the same dog, convinced there was a plot on. Thirty punters played the machines, the most ethnically diverse shop in the City, a rapidly developing kinship between all of us, a sense of togetherness, of being in the same doomed lifeboat adrift under a perfect storm. Felix rallied some support amongst his friends, some more bets were made, and about ten of us watched the race on the big fly's eye array in front of us.

It takes approximately twenty seven seconds to run the 380 metre circumference of Crayford greyhound track and trap three, in the white jacket, at four to one, did it faster than the others, from the front, the smash box, winning the race by three lengths.

The punters in the betting shop went wild. Underneath a torrent of back slaps and congratulations, I smiled for the last time that day.

(Lucky in cards.)

Gave Felix my winning betting ticket and walked to the door.

He tried to return it, saying it was excessive, and I winked at him, and said I wasn't going to be needing it, and he shrugged his shoulders, and I shook hands with all the local Jamaicans who'd lived in the City since the fifties, all the Moroccans, the Ugandans, the Bosnians, the Montenegrans, the Macedonians, the Poles, the Somalis, the Congolese and the Sudanese feeding their government issue food and rent vouchers into the hypnotics, because they'd all backed trap three and there wasn't a single penny left in the bookies to pay them that early on. Leaving the frantic multicultural hubbub behind, I found the Redback Bar, a cheap dive up an alleyway - one of the few remaining decadent holes in the centre of the City, the property companies wiping them out, the Pubco's drawing stumps, their spaces let to the global chain stores, turning the diverse, unique centre into a homogenous copy of Barking, of Skipton, of Chatham, of Greenwich, of Walsall, of Newcastle, and proceeded to spend the next five hours ramming straight vodka down my neck as if the Russians were about to cut off the Caspian grain fields

Two things.

One, I couldn't get drunk.

Two, the pain wasn't going away and if anything, the images were getting worse.

I could see her, and I could smell her.

The barman asked me to leave at five because he said he had no vodka left, and he didn't want the trouble I was guaranteed to bring to his bar.

He could see it in my eyes.

I asked him whether I could have one last half of bitter and he agreed on condition that I left straight afterwards.

Shaking, desperate for more spirits, loads more spirits, I sat and sipped the keg bitter.

My need for extra liquid had a reason.

From my top pocket, desperate measures needed, I removed my last half strip of Temazepam and a strip of twelve Co-Codamols. Alongside the booze, the prescription drugs would do the trick, I knew. They would quell the buzzing wasps. Expel the buzzing flies. Crush the beetles eating away at what remained of my cortex. Suppress the toxic spiders poisoning my limbic space. Eliminate the lizards gnawing at my nervous system. Insects eating my insides away; controlled, the pills would also stop the grinning Projectionist in my head from showing me any more of his insidious, frightening, X-rated films.

Paradoxically, the films he showed me became more and more X-rated the more booze I forced down, so while the pain in my body had been medicated and salved, and I didn't feel as empty as before, the pictures in my head became unbearable.

Carla and Dino's gentle, almost chaste kisses in the Secret Flower Garden.

The touch of her moisturised hand.

A passing glance.

Naked on her bed, a bed I have never seen, nor would I ever see.

Her legs spread, pale arms outstretched, Dino, above her, removing his shirt to reveal rippling muscles, taut and tensed…

Kisses…entwined…

Her voice, breathless and light…

(You have never existed)

(Just good friends)

Her ecstasy…

Her wounded, tender cries.

(Carlacarlacarlacarla)

Certain that I could not be saved, that my only peace would be a long and endless night of oblivion, I took the tablets in one go, a palmful of Dolly Mixtures and flooded them with the keg as they slipped down my throat.

The barman was pleased to see me go, it must be said.

Tall, bulky, unshowered, dishevelled, unshaven, talking to myself, I'd wiped out a litre of vodka and eight pints of Agincourt cider in just under four hours.

You do not want people like me in your pub after that amount of booze.

You want my money, but you don't want me.

I can't remember what I talked about with the Redback regulars.

Nothing much.

Most of them, if I recall correctly, were in the same state as me.

The modern world.

A world of cynicism.

A world where the naïveté between men and women had been replaced with cruel and heartless knowing.

A world of the bereft.

I will tell you one thing.

I had my phone out all afternoon.

Waiting.

Waiting for a text.

A phone call. A mail.

I don't think I took my eyes off that phone all afternoon, but she didn't call.

I waited in vain.

Did you expect her to?

I deleted her number on the bus this morning when I was sane and sober. I knew the consequences of a crazyman like me having the number of a woman he loves when he's on a suicidal drunk. When I was sane and sober in the morning, I knew that I couldn't inflict myself on Carla; four in the morning, weeping, wailing, begging, telling her that I had a knife in my hands pointed at a jugular vein, or that time in Edinburgh when I was about to do a swallow dive off the Castle battlements.

(Oh, she came. Suicidal threats usually work.)

When I was travelling down this morning, I knew I didn't want to hassle her. She deserved better than that.

Nevertheless, sitting there in the Redback, the regulars drifting away from the drunk with the staring eyes beginning to dribble on his quilted jacket, the maudlin drunk on the verge of tears, the barman ready to come out and have words, serious words, I would have sawn off a foot to be able to call her. I would.

Oh, man, that drunken compulsion to call.

Is there a more powerful, hardened compulsion than that one?

I would have given anything for that number.

I would have called her, and I am sorry to say, threatened suicide down by the walls of the City's Castle if she'd have answered.

That's what history tells me anyway.

That's what I do.

There's something scary about a man wandering about drunk in a town centre at office kicking out time. All the shoppers going home, the queues for the buses back to the suburbs. All the suits. The New Affluent sipping wine in Tapas bars, queuing up at Jim Olive's new restaurant, a place that charges eighteen quid a starter and a minimum of thirty-three quid for a main, and there's a waiting list of three months. In a recession.

The City, one of the most bipolar cities on the planet, wealth, poverty, happiness and anguish living side by side. The City's residents gave me a berth as wide as the gap in the Red Sea after Moses had finished, something a bit scary about watching a big bloke staggering about, off his head on prescription drugs mixed with nine hours' worth of top quality booze. It wasn't long before I attracted the attention of the local plod. Not wanting to be separated from booze, from my goal, I trotted off down to the rough area of the City where you can wander about to your heart's content and no Police will ever bother you. They followed me, made sure I'd left the shopping centre behind. Turned back.

It's just the shops the Police care about in the City.

Don't frighten the shoppers and don't frighten the tourists.

The drugs began to reach places the booze couldn't. Summoning up my last ounce of sobriety, I found a pub I knew by reputation to be frequented by gangsters and criminals on the border of St Martin's. At six in the evening, it was busy. Conscious of where I was (hah!) I ordered four pints of Thor's Hammer and four double bourbons and the barman served me with pleasure, taking forty pounds from me in one hit, pocketing the change.

(They want my money, but they don't want me.)

(They want my money, but they don't want me.)

He helped me to take the beer to my seat.

I was gone by then. Didn't know who I was, didn't know what I wanted, why I was in that pub. All I could feel was my coming death. I could see it coming, and I felt peaceful with the prospect, I did.

On the table next to me, I saw three black lads, no more than twenty, twenty five, enjoying the company of their girlfriends, and I envied them. I envied their freedom, their girlfriends (who were pretty), their carefree attitudes and most of all, I envied their sanity because watching those six people in that pub, that rough and tumble pub on the Southside of the City, where I had heard the price of wiping out a rival with a paving slab or a bag of fortified bleach is a ton, and the price of a machine gun is a monkey. They looked happy, and jolly, and content, and (normal), and in tune with their surroundings, and I drank the drinks in front of me, and watched the lads in their red saucepan hats, and I went back to the bar and ordered the same and the barman asked me whether I was cool, and I said to him in all dishonesty that I had never, ever felt better in my entire life, my friend He took another forty pounds from me and helped me back with the drinks, and I watched one of the lads put his hand on his girlfriend's knee and give her a fairly chaste kiss, and they looked in love, and I felt something go inside me, something like a twig cracking underfoot, and I drank the bourbon and instead of the red headed girl with the man, I saw Carla sitting there in her green vest and her denim mini skirt, and I saw her kiss the man who turned into Dino, Dino, Dino.

I saw her tongue. I saw her tongue, and I felt a jolt at the back of my head, a jolt like the crashing of gears on an old double-decker bus, and I walked over to Dino, and I told him to take his fucking hands off my woman, and I spilled his beer, and Dino stood up along with his friends, and the barman came over, and Dino punched me, and I fell to the floor, felt nothing, nothing.

The barman picked me up and threw me out of the front door into the now lamplit streets. Dino and his friends, and girlfriends, and hangers on, the entire pub, came out into the street, and several of them dragged me into an old arcade full of artists studios, and doughnut shops, and printers, and creative ironworkers. Dino, who didn't look like Dino any more, all those teeth, eyes blazing, headbutted me on the bridge of my nose, and I fell to the floor, and they picked me up and he headbutted me, called me something I don't remember, and I felt my nose go, and they picked me up, and he punched me several times, and do you know what I did? A normal man should have begged for mercy, on his knees, begged for his life, but quick as lightning, before he could react, I reached out for his saucepan cap, took it off his head and spat in it, then wiped my bleeding nose on the New York emblem. I watched his face contort. I heard a hush, and that hush was loud. Louder…

And that, dear reader, was that.

They took turns, those St Martin's gangster boys.

And for the *coup de grace*, my assailant said, "that's for me 'at. No one messes wi me 'at," and he carved a trench along the full length of my cheek with an easy to conceal decorator's knife, and I grabbed hold of his wrist as tight as I could and I looked at him, mad, crazy. The liquid from my bleeding eyes seeping on to the pavement, my fizzog of bruises. Plasma and mucus, both eye sockets, cracked, lumpy, swollen and elongated, and told him that he was doing it wrong, that the silly boy was cutting me in the wrong place hahahahahahaahhahahaha, and I laughed, and laughed, and laughed at my own joke, slightly scaring him, making him pull away, his eyes not quite so fiery any more, tasting the blood dripping from my flapping cheek as the Police came.

Chapter 26: Doctor Plunkett

I lay in the Trauma ward for two days and two nights. At one point, they told me afterwards, my heart stopped, and I had to be resuscitated. I don't believe them. One of the ambulance drivers, Mulhall, told me that he gave me the kiss of life and because of all the booze inside me, he wasn't allowed to drive for the rest of the night, but I guessed he was having me on. Surprisingly, when I woke up, I wasn't in pain. I guess I must have been in shock or they were feeding me morphine on drip. The Police came to interview me, and I tried my best, but I knew no one in that pub on the Southside of the City would talk, and they would never find my assailants. I didn't tell the Police the full story because they wouldn't believe me if I did.

Doctor Plunkett sat next to the bed, and he stared at me in that way of his. He wore a rainmac, one of those old Gannex ones, almost Khaki, and thick, black spectacles.

He seemed younger than I was; however, in our time together he had never confirmed that and if you asked me, he seemed much older than his years. He told me that psychology and human behaviour were his only interests. Not football, or horses, or women, or cards, or model making, or stamp collecting, or walking in the hills, or exploring old Mayan monuments. Just psychology. He was driven, and his face told you that. He was shorter than I was. Heavier set - the anchor on a tug of war. Creased, wrinkled from thinking, and his dark hair had receded three dimensions. One saving grace for him; his eyes were clear blue, and they didn't deviate from mine. They were interested eyes to go along with his interested ears. He never missed a trick with me, Plunkett. If you asked him, he would tell you things I said to him the first time, seven years ago, the first time we met in hospital. He was bonus like that. It nagged me. Was it me he was interested in? Or was it his job to be so? Why was he here? How did he know I was here? Who told him?

I had lost track of time, and I had no idea how long I had been there, so I asked him. Two days and one night, he said. It was now the weekend. When he said that, I thought of Carla out there, partying, Friday night. All the things they do…then I clamped down on it, scared that Plunkett would see what I was thinking, scared he could see straight through my transparent edifice as he had done so many times before. Some drug had considerably deadened any pain I might have, and I lay there dazed.

"Bad do," he finally said, after an infinity of staring, his untamed Midlands accent resting between Derby and Lichfield, some rural in it, but mostly the accent of the steam press and the screwdriver.

"I've had worse," I replied. "Don't forget that time in..."

He ignored me.

"That was nothing like this, according to notes. You stopped breathing. Why there? Why did you go there?"

"The pub?"

"That pub," he confirmed.

I shrugged my shoulders metaphorically, and I made sure I did it in such a way that he'd notice. "The local Bobbies made it clear they wanted me out of the shops, and it was the first place I came to."

He smiled thinly. I saw him bite his top lip. "Do you want to tell me what the problem is?"

"What problem?"

"Come on. You know."

"I don't. There isn't a problem."

He leaned forward a little "Why did you go into that pub?"

"I've just told you..."

"...and I don't believe you, John."

This was typical Plunkett. Typical. He never gave me an inch in hospital, and he never gave me an inch outside. I was never sure whether Plunkett liked me or not, whether he had me penciled in as a stuck up over-privileged Southerner wasting his time. I guessed that was the case because he always seemed to assume the worst of me. I don't think I was a project for him. I don't think he was like the shrink assessing Rorschach in *The Watchmen,* Issue 6, who saw his brilliant cure of the crazed vigilante as a badge of honour. I don't think he was like that with me, and I don't know why he was giving me a hard time.

"Well it's true, Doctor Plunkett."

"Are you involved with someone?"

"In what sense," I replied. "We're all involved with someone or other."

"No need to be evasive. Are you involved with a woman?" He said.

"Of course, I am."

"How involved?"

"How involved do you think?"

"What about her? Hang on…let me answer that question for you," he said.

"No need to rub it in, Doctor."

"When?"

"When what?"

"When did you argue?"

"The other night."

"And you went into town to get rid of it all…."

"I went into town for a drink," I replied coyly.

If I had been attached to a monitor for my blood pressure, it would have been beeping, and the graph on the screen at the front would have been green and rising fast. "I had a few bets and a few drinks with friends."

"And then you tried to kill yourself."

"That's not what happened," I lied.

"Hundreds of pubs and you chose a pub frequented by some of the most violent young men in the City."

"As I say, it was the first I…"

"I'm going to recommend you come back to us, John. For your own safety," he said, somewhat climatically. "You'll be under Section so my actions will be reinforced by law. You must remain here until I can get you escorted back up to us."

I raised myself off the mattress. "You can't do that," I said. "You just can't do it."

"You know I can. You're under our supervision. Your father's explicit instructions were to keep you supervised for a year. If at any time you show signs of receding, we can get a court order, and your father will sign it. If your father doesn't sign it, I'll get someone in authority that will. I'm worried about your safety, John. Your father encouraged us to release you the last time. I strongly objected."

"Thanks," I said, getting angry at the slight.

"It's my opinion as a professional that you're a danger to yourself and to others. Recent events are ample evidence."

"It was an accident."

"You're drunk, John. You reek of it. You must have drunk enough to sink a tanker."

"I was having a day out, as I said."

"Do you remember when you lived in Reading, John?"

See! He never misses a trick. He never misses a single thing. "I explained that at the time."

"They found you in an alley behind the Woolworths in a skip. It took them a week to bleed you of the alcohol. You'd wet yourself and defecated. You couldn't speak. Your heart rate was virtually non-existent, your blood pressure at its minimum. It took you a fortnight to regain your use of speech."

"Some Stag night, huh."

"You'd been drinking - like two days ago - for about twenty four hours solid. From what we can gather, you'd been drinking three pints and three chasers an hour for most of that time. We don't think you had eaten. Your build saved you. It's only because you're tall and relatively fit that you survived."

"She didn't treat me well," I said, quietly, thinking about Kerry from Reading, who I worked with, and who I fell in love within a couple of days of her giving me the green light, and who dumped me after three weeks because I was just too much for her. She supposed she was getting that nice rowing man from the telly, and she told me so. She got something else instead, and she wasn't happy about it. Like mum, I burned her out. I liked her. I had marriage plans. Kids. The house in the country. The dumping hurt. I had to get rid of the pain. Paracetamol doesn't work - not on its own. I tried to justify my behaviour.

"What do you expect? I was upset."

"Relationships you develop at an accelerated level fail - quite naturally - and you do one of two things. You destroy things or you try to destroy yourself. You've been doing this since you were fifteen, and you're showing no signs of stopping. Nothing we seem to do helps." He shook his head and sat back in his chair. "It would be on my conscience if I let you go."

"I'll get a second opinion."

"Do that," he took off his glasses and started to clean one of the lenses. He squinted. "I could use one, but now, I'm the proxy Power of Attorney on behalf of your father. It's all here, look." He raised his Vellum folder, and I didn't need to check it to know that he was telling the truth. "At least Cedar Forest is like a hotel. There are other places you could be going after the other night."

"As if I care," I said. "It's all one big prison."

My pillow was cold when I laid back down on it, and I suddenly felt deflated.

Did it matter? Did another incarceration matter to me? Carla had gone. Off with a lad her age. I should have been pleased for her, but the hole in my heart was like a chasm. My head throbbed with the hangover and the pain of losing her. It was hard work to speak. I felt on the verge of tears. Parts of my body started to hurt. It was another day in paradise, and as I watched the fluorescent bulb flicker above my bed, the strong smell of piss and disinfectant in my nostrils, I decided that it was probably a plan, going back. Women had pretty much destroyed me, my mind, my peace of mind, my health, my mental health, my self-respect, my family. Encountering them led to the same Hell.

At least inside, I wouldn't have to encounter them, and at least I'd survive.

I grinned.

Remembered Janine Peaches. The most successful relationship I'd ever had.

'Is Janine still there?'

Doctor Plunkett chuckled. "Funny. You ought to have been on stage, Johnny."

In a moment of dry, ironic perspective, I wondered whether Carla would come and visit me.

(Hah! I am indeed damned!)

I knew her home. Wheatley Fields Agricultural College Halls of Residence. I'd drop a letter to her, ten thousand words strong, and it would be so emotive and so fulsome in my praise for her that she would come and see me, and we would walk the grounds, and I would feel the gentle pressure of her arm on my coat as we walked through the hospital's grounds.

I'd even send her the travel expenses.

The idea of Carla visiting me in hospital filled me with an ethereal calm, and it was the most peaceful I'd felt for a while.

Doctor Plunkett wrote something down and said he had to go and make a phone call. I asked him what my mug looked like, and he gave me that thin, almost imperceptible smile before he left the room. I parked the feeling of contentment and began to assess my condition. Most of the damage was to my head, and when I first regained consciousness, a nurse from Iran held a mirror up to it.

I was no oil painting before, but now, I was like something Picasso would have painted. My right cheek was patched and bandaged. Forty-two stitches made, she said, to repair the skin folds, and it would be necessary to have plastic surgery. Both eye sockets were black, and my eyes were slits. A Panda has lighter eyes. Three of my teeth were missing, only one visible. I could move my arms, and despite pain, I could move the rest of my body. Stiff and bruised, but apparently, nothing was broken. They were in such a rage they went for my head. They wore trainers. They can't kill you.

Old-fashioned hobnail boots, and my sweetbreads would probably have liquefied.

What Doctor Plunkett and the rest of them haven't realised yet, is that they are dealing with someone with an incredible constitution. It seems that I cannot be killed by conventional weapons and lord knows I've tried.

English Public School, you see.

We may sound like dandies, but they build us tough.

The entire hierarchy is designed to create Supermen.

All the better to administer the colonies, don't you know.

Thanks to my father's busy life and my beloved mother abandoning me at the age of twelve, I was dispatched to Public School, one of the best in the country.

I was slapped, chinned, belted, paddled, caned, slippered, kneed, knuckled, batted, battered, beaten, whipped, stabbed, humiliated, wounded, impaired, damaged, embarrassed, shamed, excoriated and generally ruined.

I was forced to perform oral sex on an older boy in his rooms when I was just twelve years old while his friends - MP's now, barristers, surgeons, racecourse administrators and the rest - looked on and hurrahed.

Hurrah! Hurrah!

After the horror was over, I've done all the things to myself that you've read about, dear reader, during our short time together.

All the suicide attempts. All the cutting, wounding, ingestation, poisoning, the oblivion seeking toxic attacks, all the incarcerations, the imprisonments, the drugs - oh, the drugs - the experimental medication and the relentless, *relentless*, self hatred (which is much harder to deal with than a beating), and do you know what?

I'm still here, Doctor Plunkett.

I'm still here, Father.

I'm still here, Mother.

Hah!

I'm still here.

John Dexter cannot be killed by conventional weapons.

I'm still here, Plunkett, my friend and sparring partner.

And you're not putting me away this time, matey.

I'm going to see my Carla one last time.

And then we'll see what I do next.

If Carla and I can run away together into the sunset, arm-in-arm, on our horses, into an environmental Shangri-la where all the trees remain standing, the grass is green, the water is clear, the animals wander freely, the birds sing, the little fish are sweet, and the flowers are all the colours of the rainbow, all fine and dandy.

If not - and if you're a betting reader, you'd be giving me no more than 1/10 on this prospect - I've got enough money to get to Brazil.

Those granite cliffs.

Those hardwood trees, the sound of parakeets and the rainwater brooks, so clear and cold.

The waterfalls.

Yes.

The falls.

Fighting off the pillow of contentment, I swung my legs out of bed. I winced. Movement inflicted nausea, and I was nearly sick. In the corner of my room stood a plain pine chest of drawers. Inside, my folded clothes; becalmed Berry and my wallet. I checked it. Still full - the boys hadn't robbed me. That wasn't what they wanted.

I walked out into the corridor. Surprisingly, there was hardly anyone and in my hospital gown, I found my way to the visitor toilets and dressed as fast as I could. My coat was ripped along the side and the innards spilled. It had been slashed - so someone had gone for my body after all! My jeans were bloodstained, but the blood had dried, and from a distance, the patches looked like oil.

I looked a mess, but hey, I was in a hospital and everyone looks a mess. I looked out the toilet door, and it was quiet. When I reached the door to the ward, it was locked, and I needed the intercom to get the door opened remotely. I pressed the button. "Doctor Plunkett," I said, replicating his voice as well as I could. The buzzer buzzed, and I was out on the corridor. Before long - passing doctors and nurses and hordes of visitors walking down the stairs, avoiding lifts - I was on the concourse. It was bright outside, and the puddles told me the rains had come, and recently. I had no idea of the time and strangely, I wasn't bothered at all by that. What I was about to do was timeless, subject to the laws of serendipity and Kismet.

If it was meant to be, it was meant to be, whatever Kismet pathway stretched out before me.

I watched a taxi come, a green Hackney cab, and I flagged it. The driver shook his head imperceptibly, but the next one along saw my signal and pulled up.

Wheatley Fields, I said to the Sikh driver, giving him fifty pounds in advance. He told me it might be more on the meter, and I told him not to worry. Plenty more where that came from. On the journey home, on my Berry, I checked my bookmaker accounts to see whether I'd won any money from the other day. I checked my bank account. I checked my poker account. I checked my wallet.

Overall, in all media, I had four thousand pounds remaining.

Was that enough for Carla and I?

Was that enough?

God would provide.

God always provides for young lovers.

On my doormat was a note in a purple envelope, almost lilac, addressed to me.

From Carla.

I could smell her perfume and who else would send me such a feminine note.

Sore and unsteady, I closed the door. Siege conditions. Plunkett would be coming for me, and I had little time to waste. I didn't think Plunkett would call the Police. I wasn't sure about that - he was more likely to come himself - so I felt that the house was safe for another three or four hours. If the Police came to the door, they would have to enact a warrant to enter, and that takes time. My cunning plan involved running away, and I needed to find Carla.

I looked at myself in the bathroom mirror. My face was bandaged, particularly on the cheek. That wasn't going to be pretty when I removed the bandage, I knew. I could see father's wallet coming in handy. I took off my top and trousers.

I was bruised along the entire surface of my skin, a mixture of grey, black and yellow, islands in a pale sea.

For some reason, these didn't hurt that much. My iron constitution. I sat on the toilet naked, ready for a shower, and read Carla's note, taking in her fragrance one last time, running its full length under my nostrils. I could sense her and see her face. I opened it and read the note.

Her handwriting was ornate and neat, and she wrote in blue on lilac paper identical to the envelope.

"J,

I've tried to contact you, but you're not answering your phone or replying to my texts. I'm sorry if I've upset you. I clearly have, and that wasn't my intention. With this note, I just want to let you know that I care deeply about you, and I'm thinking about you. I panicked on Sunday. I do with relationships. I'm scared of them, I'm scared of what they end up meaning, Do you know what I mean? You asked me what I want, and I didn't have an answer. Do you remember? You did. You held me all night, and I slept in your arms. You seemed so contented, so at peace, and so was I. The next morning, I have never panicked so much in my whole life. You never tried to have sex with me. You didn't try to kiss me. You just wanted to look after me and to hold me. No one I've met has ever done that, John. It scared me. It was the peace, how deep that peace was. The comfort and the rightness of it, do you know what I mean? I hope you do. I couldn't think about anything else, but how right that felt. I could have laid there forever, in your arms.

Can we speak again, John? Can we? Please come to the pub tonight. I just want to say how sorry I am.

Love,

Cxxx

PS: I'm going to try and sort things with dad. I'm going over there tomorrow. I'll be back later tomorrow night. Please talk to me on Pony, just like we used to."

Hah!

(You total idiot.)

Hah!

All that for nothing.

You must be insane.

(She cares about you. You'd done it. You WON.)

(So close.)

(You've ruined it...your mug. How do you explain your mug?)

(I don't know.)

(You're going inside. The only chance you have is to run.)

(I know.)

(Idiot.)

(I can persuade Plunkett.)

(Fat chance.)

(I can go to court.)

(They won't listen. Crazy man. They won't let you near Carla so you can't use her as a bargaining chip or even use her as a pity excuse. You're going down and this time, like Sable, Leroy, and Felicity, they're going to keep you, and you'll never feel Carla's breath on your cheek.)

(Stop it.)

(You'll never feel her weight on your chest. The softness of her lips. That pink lip gloss she uses. You'll never smell her perfume or feel her thigh draped over your cock like that night as she held you. You got hard, do you remember, as she slept. You'll never hear that Little Fluffy Clouds voice.)

(I can't let that happen.)

(You've got no choice. Plunkett's Law.)

I reached for my Berry.

Realised that I'd deleted her number. Went over to the desk and found my diary, which contained my backup copies of important numbers. Her number - Thank God! – was in red pen. I re-entered the number in my contacts and texted her. I showered, trying my best to keep the sliced cheek away from the jet, and trying to keep my murderous, cancerous negative dialogue at bay. My inner voice was beating me up, and I was being left bleeding by the side of the road. I knew I had overreacted. It's what I do.

Women change their mind all the time, and my self-esteem is poor. I didn't think that law would apply to me, and I was going to pay for it. I was going to pay for it with unimaginable suffering. I turned on the shower heat and felt the jets crucify my body, and I began to enjoy the pain.

This led me to think about another alternative ending, but I wasn't going to end anything until I'd seen Carla.

After about twenty minutes of being scorched and pummelled by the jets, I left the shower, reaching for the phone to see if she'd replied. She hadn't. I texted her. Then, panicking, feeling the irritation and worry rising, called her.

Her phone was off.

Carla's phone was never off.

Carla.

(Phone off.)

(Never off.)

I dried myself quickly, unconcerned at the sporadic pain I experienced on certain sensitive spots on my body. I dressed. Clean jeans, thick socks, Timbo's, a black shirt, wallet, Berry, and putting on another quilted Barbour, this one black, a back up, I ran out of the door into the evening, and I ran all the way down to The Saddler's in record time.

She wasn't working. Leah was behind the bar.

I saw Big Keith sitting on the bar stool supping. He nodded.

"What happened to your boat?" He said

"Car crash."

"Looks more like a bus crash. You look rough," he said, the City accent strong and reliable, working class to the core.

"Is Carla coming in?"

He looked at me strangely. “She won't be coming in, more’s the pity. Packed it in last night.”

(I don't believe this.)

“Said it were getting in the way of her course.”

“That’s not right. She loved this job.”

“How do you know?”

“She told me.”

“Everyone said you two were getting friendly. I must have missed it. She was a tidy girl, her. I’m a bit peed off to be honest.”

“Something's wrong, Keith. Her phone’s off.”

“By the way, a bloke came looking for you last night.”

“Who?”

“Old boy, cap.”

(Nelson.)

“No one knew your whereabouts.”

(No one knows WHO I am.)

“Okay”, I said.

Suddenly, I knew where she was and why.

It came from nowhere, a bolt from the blue. I ordered a double vodka from shy Leah and excused myself to the bathroom. On my phone, from that night two weeks ago, I happened to have Sharna’s number and I called it. She answered almost straight away, the phone addict that she is.

“John, what can I do for you?”

“I’m looking for Carla. Have you seen her?”

“Not for a couple of days, mate. Said she was going over to visit her plonker dad to smooth things over.”

“Has she texted or been in touch?”

“Not a word.”

“Sharna, do you know where her dad lives?”

“Gallows Farm on the other side of Follow Field. Can’t miss it.”

“Where are you now?”

“College.”

“Okay.”

“Why?”

“No reason.”

"Did you want a lift? Give me an hour and I'll take you. My mum uses his livery yard. I've never been inside, but I know where it is. I can drop you off."

"That's considerate of you, Sharna."

"Be a bonus to know she's safe. Her dad's a cunt, not a nice person."

I would have laughed in any other circumstance. "I'm at The Saddler's."

"See you in an hour."

I went back to the bar and sank the vodka in one hit. Ordered two more doubles and a pint of Thor's Hammer. I did this for three reasons.

One, I needed the Dutch courage.

Two, I needed to reduce the soreness and the pain emanating from my body and three, I had an hour to kill. Keith looked at me strangely, an indecipherable glance. The regulars started to arrive, and his attention was soon diverted. I retreated to The Snug with my drinks and sat down, waited for Sharna.

She arrived, walked in the pub. "Do you mind if I have a quick pint before we...what the hell has happened to your face?" She said, visibly shocked.

"Car crash. I'll get you one."

"'I'll have a Crimson Parrot. I'm told that's a tasty pint."

Keith interrupted. "Best I've had on for weeks."

"Absolutely, a Parrot for me. . ." she said.

Leah gave me a smirk. I pointed to the top shelf for another double and I topped up with a Hammer. I put one behind for Keith as well and tipped Leah. The Crimson Parrot, brewed outside Skipton in a converted barn by two ex-heavy metal guitarists, was so called, apparently, because of its reddish colour when perfectly poured, and because it's so potent, the drinker, largely befuddled, often repeats himself in conversation. Keith is a mine of information. There are few people in Wheatley Fields who know as much as Keith about real ale and micro brewing. He's obsessed with it. He saluted me and Sharna, and the two of us took our drinks and went to sit down. I looked out of the window as Sharna sat. Outside, despite a sunny start to the day, it had begun to rain, and the sky was now all the possible permutations of grey you could have. Slate. Military. Pallid. The clouds overlaid each other five, six times and the sky had a weird density about it, as if something was coming.

Sharna wore a thick blue polo neck, Wellies and jeans. A huge lemon pile of Texan hair piled high, scatty, unkempt, falling forward, falling backwards. Her hair was a wonder of the world. She was a handsome-looking woman, but she liked her ale, and she liked her food, and I knew that one day she was going to be a big girl, indeed. She didn't look like the type of girl who cared all that much.

"So. Your mush. That's no car crash."

"I got into bother. City."

"Upset about Sunday?"

I nodded. "She tell you?"

"In tears. I managed to pull her around. She wasn't able to get hold of you. You scared her."

"I know."

"I wish you'd have tried to bonk her now. She said you were a real gentleman."

"I didn't want to push things," I replied, surprised at her candour.

"All that niceness scared the shit out of her. It would me. Mind you, no bloke would have got this far without giving me a shag," she said, drinking half a pint in one go. "Are you gay or something?"

"No, I'm not gay."

We stayed silent for a bit. Sharna texted someone and took another call. Finished her pint, picked up her keys. I drank my drink and did as I was told. The implication of what she said had me kicking myself. If I'd have been my usual manic self, she would have known how to deal with it, and she wouldn't have struggled with the uncertainty and all the pain.

She'd have just finished with me. Yet my gentleman act had confused her - and Sharna. I remember lying on that sofa as she laid on my chest, wanting to touch her, to take her to bed with me, but I just couldn't do it. It was enough, what we did. I loved it. Loved the feel of her next to me. I was satisfied with that. Maybe if I'd have taken her to bed, we'd have been together now.

Maybe, maybe.

When the air hit me, I felt the vodka for the first time. I almost heard the vodka crunch in my ears, felt it swill. Sharna was on the phone when she jumped into her Ka. I struggled to fit in. Simultaneously, Sharna put on her seat belt, flirted with her boyfriend on the phone, put her key in the ignition and lit a cigarette with the dashboard lighter, the fumes filling the car. She said something obscene to her boyfriend and put the phone down, sped off down the road.

"She's well into you, you know. Honest, John. She is so into you."

"She wasn't on Sunday."

She looked at me, nearly missed the turning to Hampton and had to brake a little. "You ought to know what we girls are like."

"Carla doesn't know what men are like. I was bereft."

"And you're the older one! I can't believe it. You get into difficulties, and you go out, get pissed and get yourself cut up."

"As I say, I was upset."

"If I were you, I'd get her out of her dad's place and make it real."

"Do you think she's in danger?"

"I don't think she is. I think you might be," Sharna said. "Do you want me to wait for you?"

"No. I'll find my own way back. I'm going to try and reason with him."

"Best of luck with that project."

"What else can I do?"

"Call the Police," she said.

I didn't say anything. The last thing I needed was the Police involved with my history, but there was something more plausible and non-contentious I could say, and I did. "Domestic. Don't get involved. If it gets heavy, I will do."

"As I say, I'll keep my phone on."

I looked at my manic driver, window down, hair suspended by the draught, stunning; cigarette suspended from her mouth and wondered whether she would ever switch her phone off.

I doubted it.

"I'm going to get her back home. Her father is pestering her to go and live with him. He's drunk all the time and not thinking. Grief."

"It's his fault. Men and drink! Pointless..."

She sped up Hampton Hill and down, sixty, seventy miles an hour and I gripped the car seat.

"Keep your phone on and I'll hang around for a bit. My boyfriend lives in Follow Field, and we're going for a pint in the Archer. He's driving. I'll keep him out if you need me. Her dad's a bit of a headbanger, and I'm positive you're going to have problems, but you know what you're doing, I'm sure."

"I've got no idea, Sharna. No idea at all."

I liked Sharna on quite a few dimensions, and her presence calmed me. She nattered about stuff while she drove, and I was happy to listen and think. I've been known in the past to hit on married women. I've been known to hit on women with boyfriends present when drunk, and I've been kicked around a few times by said boyfriends, and I probably would have tried it on with Sharna ten years ago, and she would have rejected me, and I would have been upset, and I would have blamed her, and I would have started to cut when I got home, woeful, rejected, self-pitying, angry with her, blaming, blaming, whore, slag, slapper, evil, evil, evil, and I would have drunk myself into a form of extinction, a form of oblivion, rejected so badly by Sharna that I would need a whole new soul, but since Carla, I'd changed.

I genuinely had.

She'd done something to me.

I'd tried to destroy myself two days ago, but it wasn't over her.

It was a habit.

It was something I did.

I had disconnected Carla from it entirely.

I didn't hate her. I didn't fear her. I didn't resent her.

I understood. Yes, I got hammered and sliced because of that. Yes, I ended up in hospital, but she wasn't the reason.

Carla.

Something had happened.

My emotions were under control for the first time in my whole life. My self-image had changed. The way I viewed myself.

I was in control of the demons inside me. I had caged them.

I was tall.

Proper tall, rather than gawky, and lanky, and awkward.

Tall.

With a capital T.

I was Lantern Jawed.

My face was in place.

Geometric. Symmetrical. Coordinated. Mathematical.

A formula which if not perfect, came up with the right answer more often than not.

Chaos into Order.

You may have noticed that I am something of a film buff.

All through my life, I have seen myself as a Frankenstein's Monster.

Until I discovered that Frankenstein was the doctor's name, I called myself Frankenstein in my self-talk.

Or Frank.

My self-image shattered and fragmented to the point where I have just the one mirror in my house and even now, it's just for shaving and emergencies.

I was so ugly I could scarcely think about myself as me. I was an abstract painting. I was a Picasso, a cubist masterpiece.

I hated myself.

After all, my own mother rejected me.

(Ugly boy.)

and left me because

(Monster.)

she couldn't bear to look at me

(Begone, fiend!)

so how can I bear

(You are repulsive, Jonathan. Hideous. Begone, ugly boy!)

to look at myself.

(I hope you DIE!)

Women, replicates of my mother, rejected me, and left me to die on countless streets when all I wanted…all I wanted…

(How we howled.)

And yet, since Carla, I was Clint Eastwood in *High Plains Drifter.*

Mel Gibson in *Payback.*

Jason Statham in *Crank.*

I was all the Bonds.

Tall.

Lantern Jawed.

In control.

Therefore, as I sat I watching Sharna smoke and drive like a mad woman, the idea of Carla's dad pummelling the shit out of me was of no concern.

None at all.

He couldn't kill me - Sharna knew where I was, and I'd let him know that.

He could hurt me, but hey...he couldn't kill me.

Carla would be there, too. A brake.

I was thinking for the first time in my life. Thinking over feeling.

Carla. She'd done this.

Thank you, Carla, my love.

"There it is, look."

About half a mile down a path, I could see the huge barn I was detained in the last time. "You can drop me here, Sharna. Thanks, darlin."

She pulled over. "Mate, no worries. You take care. I've got my phone on. Love to C for me."

"Definitely. Thanks Sharna."

She dropped me off, and I jumped over the wall. I walked with some trepidation down the wooded bank and made my way to the pathway leading to the farmhouse. I considered what I was going to say, but nothing came to mind, and I decided just to let it happen. What could I do? I saw the white van come up the road toward me. They must have seen me jump the wall. I didn't know how. I let it all happen. Besides, I wanted to see Benedict and the van would take me to the place I wanted to go. It pulled up alongside. The Straw Dogs rural meatheads from before jumped out of the van. Started hitting me straight away and threw me in the back. They all got a punch in, and all of them in that rustic, farmyard accent of theirs, had their say about me, and I can tell you it wasn't flattering.

Chapter 27: Straw Dogs

Meathead One and Meathead Two held me by the arms. I was in Benedict's living room, I guessed. The TV, the mirror, the fireplace, the three piece. They forced me down onto a wooden chair and held me, They tied my arms to the back of the chair with rope. I saw Carla standing in the window in tears. Someone had hit her. Red weals on her cheeks. Probably her dad. She wasn't restrained - that would have been too much even for him, to restrain his own daughter.

The four men who had assaulted me on the way down separated. Two - big ugly beasts with undeveloped stares and big thick necks - walked over and stood on either side of her. I was surprised he let them into his living room - their boots were muddy and their jeans stained with manure. Yet the room was hardly Terry Conran: His living room was a mixture of tobacco smoke and old seventies furniture. Lots of browns and beiges. Carla's mum was absent. He'd probably locked her up. Meathead One, who had been giving me the hardest time, had worked out that I had sore ribs, and he kept kicking me and calling me names

"Bet you regret coming now, wanker," he said.

Meathead Two joined in. It was obvious that both of them had enjoyed an afternoon on the grog, and it emanated. It was a wonder any actual farm work got done. "We're going to have some fun with you, mate. Some rate fun..."

"You'll love what we've got planned for you, " Meathead One said, kicking me in the ribs. I'd had worse, a lot worse and I held on to that comfort.

That time after Sports Day, when I was fourteen, where I unexpectedly lost in the 1500 metres, and the head boy and his assistants who had backed me, kicked seven barrels out of me in the cellars after the event. I was sick for a week, and the head boy was sent home by the head, but he was soon back. Money and politics. He didn't let up on me. I know he works for one of the big nine publishing companies now, and by all accounts, he's not a nice person.

I could have told them that for nothing. A psychopath.

A corporate psychopath.

I've never met a more sadistic person. He relished pain. He lived for inflicting pain. In that sense, he was a brother to these two rural lumps kicking and punching me. Nevertheless, it's the same thing. The same concept: Rich man. Poor man. No feelings. No empathy. No morals. No consideration. No understanding.

This was what they did. This was their nature.

Rich man hiring and firing. Getting off on his own power.

Poor man kicking and punching. Getting off on his own power.

My old head boy's sadism was a lot worse than this. He was unrelenting, attempting to break both the body and the spirit. Why?

Because I allowed him to. The kicks and punches coming from Meatheads One and Two from either side of me were like the tender caresses of teddy bears compared to him.

"What's that, mate? Tea and crumpets by the fire," I said.

"You wish." Meathead One said. "You wish."

"Leave him. I said LEAVE HIM," Carla shouted.

Over by the far wall, against the huge windows, the velvet curtains pulled back, she looked genuinely distressed, and this made me angry. I noticed a photograph of her and her father on the mantelpiece. Carla was a lot younger. She wore a pony helmet, a red fleece and her eyes shone, her coming beauty signalled in advance. Next to her, Benedict had the same kind of vacant yet imperious eyes, but there was none of the damage done to his nose and cheeks by the grog, the impact of the booze over the past three years. The three years of Carla's absence.

Since she left him.

(I know loss, mate.)

If his warty minions weren't jabbing at me and twisting my arms, I'd feel sorry for him.

"We can't leave him, miss," Meathead Two said. "He's been a bad lad. Your dad's not 'appy wi im. He has to be 'it."

"No, he doesn't. I'll scream if you don't let him go..."

"Scream, Miss. We don't mind. You know how far we are away from any neighbours. No bugger will give a monkey's about your old pally here. When your dad tells you what he found aht, I tell you, you won't give a monkey's about him, Miss, so wait for him to get back. You've got Archie and Banksy for company, ain't that right lads. We'll all ey a drink tomorrah, together, down your pub. Your dad's buying..."

They roared. A throaty communal horselaugh. My blood ran cold.

(*When your dad tells you what he's got to tell you, you won't give a monkey's about him.*)

It was obvious what her dad had found out about me, and I was doomed.

(But how? Data protection? Non-criminal medical notes. How. How?)

Carla quietened. I listened to the banter of the Meatheads. One of them would kick me, punch me, or whisper doom into my ear.

If he knew…

If he knew…there was no way I would ever kiss Carla. No way. No way would we ever do what we did on the sofa the other night. No way would we ever hold hands under the stars on the way back to her dorm.

None of that would happen.

It was all over.

Hopelessness overwhelmed my anger. Panic also. The potential humiliation was worse than the pain, and the soreness, and the constant prods and kicks from my two guards.

There was no way she could ever find out.

I knew what I had to do when Benedict returned.

There was no way my Carla could ever find out.

I looked at her in her Inuit hat and combat jacket, and she looked like a big kid with tears in HER eyes and a look of confusion as she stood by the window. Her own personal dynamic duo of Meatheads would never touch her - Carla's dad would kill them, but they could restrain her, hurt her.

Someone had hit her.

(I'll bet it was Benedict.)

(He's out of control with love.)

(Bastard.)

I didn't want Carla to find out about me.

All the dark stuff.

I've got enough money in the bank to do a runner, and in many ways I was cured.

I treated her well.

I looked after her.

I treated her like a gentleman.

I did myself and my family proud.

I would have liked to go to bed with her just once, but hey, it wasn't to be. I would have loved that, loved it. I laid in bed thinking about it for long, long nights, but the knowledge that it would never happen for me didn't hurt me, didn't send me into a rage because Carla looked after me, unlike many of the other women I'd met, for whom I took the blame - women like Nina, who seduced me before deciding to skip off somewhere else with someone else.

Did she ever go to prison or to a mental health unit? A psychopath?

Yvonne and her texts? Did she? Mad as a hatter inside. I mean thirty seven texts in one day. Where did she get the time?

Did she ever go to see a Therapist?

I may not be fully cured, but do you know what?

Carla helped me.

Carla helped me love myself after all the women of the past had left me crippled and madder than I actually was.

(Including your own mother.)

All I wanted was love.

All I wanted was a woman to hold me tight and kiss me and be there for me, and all I ever got was something else entirely.

Patience.

I learned patience.

Carla taught me patience.

I looked over at her, and she smiled briefly, and I could tell she cared.

I don't know whether she ever loved me, but I didn't seem to need that from her.

Her presence was enough.

Just being near her, walking across the trail, in Columbus Park, and our wonderful day at the Secret Flower Garden smelling the spring flowers.

When he saw me glance at her, Meathead Two punched me on the nose.

Meathead One took a step back and kicked me in the ribs.

I squealed involuntarily. The pain travelled up and down my body and I winced, tears forming. On top of the kicking I received the other night, their blows had started to hurt. I looked down at the floor. The four Meatheads chortled. Carried on bantering in that unique, coded, agricultural language.

As long as Carla was okay, I didn't care what happened to me.

When the pain subsided, a strange feeling of euphoria descended upon me like a warm blanket in winter, accompanied by a bright light, an equally warm light, like the strange emanations coming from a bubble lamp when you cup your palms around it.

I knew she was going to be okay.

It was her father for God's sake.

He'd never hurt her. He wanted her back. He wanted redemption and her forgiveness.

These stinking labourers were just minions, and they'd never hurt her. I knew they wouldn't kill me, not without killing Carla.

They'd hurt me, but they wouldn't kill me.

And pain isn't the worst that can happen.

I've lived with it for nearly three decades.

I'd never had a happy day in my life before I met Carla, a whole life spent in just short of two months, a biography that began and ended in Wheatley Fields.

A life in just over ten weeks.

Carla, darling, you showed me I can live once more.

You showed me I'm not the mental case they all think I am.

They say all this BPD stuff is curable, and I know they're right.

You never changed, Carla.

You never deviated.

You sent a mail every night for two months. It wasn't a circular. Not a ring note.

You typed it individually, and you always sent two kisses.

You were always where you said you were going to be and with one exception, you were always pleased to see me.

You cared, Carla.

You considered me intelligent, and you didn't care about my awkward, dislocated, asymmetric looks.

It didn't bother you at all, did it, Carla?

I don't care if you were looking for a dad, the Elektra Complex personified, or whether you wanted me for more than that.

I don't think you knew yourself, Carla.

I think there was a love between us, a wholesome, fresh, unprocessed, natural love, embedded as it was in a vile world of exploitation, desperation, illness, cynicism, greed, selfishness, insularity, ultra violence; of narcissism, of sick porn, bad death, sadism, chasmic loss and never-ending pain.

A world where childhood ends early, a world where Indian six year olds sharpen knives and forks on grinders for the Pound Goblin, a world where an area the size of the UK is deforested every week for margarine and memorandi; a world with no fish, no tigers, no elephants, or rhinos, a world where bears commit suicide to stop Chinese bile harvesters inflicting more pain; a world where young girls are sold and traded, and a world, which, thank God, has only a hundred and fifty years to go before the systems, which sustain the parasite, which is the human being begin to collapse.

Thus, in its hospice state, its final years, it is a world, which needs love more than at any time in its 4.5 billion year history.

It needs love like the one between Carla and I in its ether, in its spirit, in its soil.

Our love transcended all that.

The love we had.

I look at you Carla, and I see the future.

I see wonder. I hear glory. Your essence will stay with me forever, Carla, for however long I shall live, and I only hope your father doesn't tell you what I think he's going to tell you because that will destroy all we shared and all we believed in our short time together.

I cannot let him do that to the essence we shared, my love.

He cannot do it.

(It cannot happen.)

I looked at her one more time before Meathead Two punched me again.

I love you Carla, and I will always love you, I said, just before a blow came, so hard it dislodged a tooth, caused my mouth to bleed, and nearly ripped the bandaged from my stitched and charred cheek.

Carla screamed. The impact of the blow was so vicious, his meaty friend started to get nervous. "Be careful, Den. Don't kill him," Meathead Two said.

"Bastard won't take his mince pies off her - STOP STARING AT HER…" Den shouted, spitting and dribbling, his drunken bloated rural boat crimson, contorted with anger. He would kill me given the chance. I looked him in the eye. Our beings synchronized just for a second, and in that brief moment, I could see that his hatred for me burrowed like a maggot into his core. He flinched a little when I grinned at him. I looked at Carla, and I knew why he hated me so much.

It was obvious.

I winked as the blood spilled from my lips. Grinned.

I knew what he wanted.

"Here..." Den passed over the snooker ball bag. "Put this on the cunt's head."

The nameless Meathead Two with piggy, tiny eyes forced the bag over my head.

"He's much better looking now, hey, Nutty," Den said, giving my second assailant a name, an opposite name.

"He's a fucking ugly big bastard, Can't see what she saw in him. Miss could have her pick."

"Leave him alone, you animals." I could hear her muffled under the hood.

"Oh, that int nice, Miss. I've known you since you were this high..." Nutty said.

I guessed he gave Carla a gesture like he was patting an invisible hound. Carla didn't respond.

(*Keep out of the way, Carla. Don't rattle the cages. Wait for your father. Wait. I've got a plan for us.*)

Living room door opened. I could hear laughter and footsteps.

Then Carla.

"LET HIM GO, DAD. RIGHT THIS MINUTE OR I WILL NEVER, EVER TALK TO YOU EVER!"

"You don't talk to meh nah, lass. It wunt mek no difference," Benedict slurred. He was drunk, and I could imagine him swaying though I couldn't see him. His six rural acolytes responded to his entrance with throaty, avuncular horse laughs.

"What's bag on for?" He asked someone.

"Gleggin at Missy, pervy cunt," Den said.

"He won't be doing much on that when..."

"Take me hood off, Benedict," I shouted. "I've got a proposition for you."

I heard him walk over. Through the air gap, I smelled his boots.

Then his breath.

"Had your chance, Johnny," he slurred. "Had your chance to negotiate. Now I want you to listen to sumut. Something you've not been telling our Carla. You, sir, have been remiss with your biography, sir."

Another set of footsteps, the door shutting.

I sensed Benedict pull away. "Seems Johnny's not bin telling you truth about himsen, our Carla."

"I don't CARE," she said. "Let him GO, dad."

"Tek his 'ood off, Den. I want him to watch this," the drunk said.

Roughly, they extracted my hood.

I saw the man standing alongside Benedict, and I saw him grin.

Willie Nelson.

Willie Nelson.

My old acquaintance from Group Therapy.

"How do, Johnny. Bin up to them old tricks again," he winked, a little old bloke in a cap, no more than five four, a jockey, fat and in a crombie, which must have been a child's size.

"Don't do this, Willie," I said.

"Got to mek a living, Johnny. Mr. Benedict has kindly offered me job. In his stables. He'll look after me."

(Bastard.)

"I never liked you, Willie."

"Feeling's mutual, fella."

"Mr. Nelson ere has got a tale to tell to my errant daughter," Benedict said. "But first, I'm going to open a bottle of my favourite champagne. No. I'm going to open two on em. You can ey a drink, Johnny, celebrate my daughter returning to hearth and fireplace…she's coming om…"

"That's kidnapping," I said.

"She's already agreed, hey, Carla."

"He says he's going to hurt mum if I don't, John. He's drunk...and mad..."

She started to sob, and I could feel it rising inside me, I could feel it, Benedict, and Willie Nelson, and Den, and Archie, and Nutty, and all the yokels not fit to lick Carla's boots.

As it always did, my mind began to empty.

Filled with something else.

Something.

Imagine a locked room. Black. Dark. No windows. The only access point is a keyhole the size of an old half pence piece.

Imagine a gas canister filled with gas. A special type of chemical where the osmosis is reversed and jumbled.

The nozzle placed in the keyhole.

Someone turns the canister's dial.

The room begins to fill.

Cold bright light.

Tiny irritating fragments struggling to form in the ether.

Ripping me.

An empty light.

Benedict slipped partially into his Queen's English. I watched him take a bottle of champagne from a bucket. "I didn't say anything about hurting her, our Carla. You're exaggerating, love."

He walked over to me.

Lined up the neck of the bottle with my head as if he was pointing a gun.

Fingered the cork. Aimed it at my forehead.

This was going to hurt.

I shut my eyes and lowered my head as far as it would go.

Heard the pop.

Craaaaaaaaaaaaaaaaaaaaaaaaaack

Felt the cork hit the top of my head at the speed of a bullet.

(Cold bright light.)

Heard the Meathead's bray.

Sickness, nausea, head spinning.

Unimaginable pain, concentrated.

Willie.

Benedict.

The meatheads.

(Ripping me.)
Heard Carla sob.
(Mum)
As it always did, always at moments like this, it came to me.

(Mum)
The packed bags below the stairs. Mum, red, rumbling tresses, like a waterfall spilling blood over a rocky outcrop.
Bright-red lipstick.
The taxi outside.
A light-blue blouse.
Utterly beautiful.
My brother crying on the bottom step, my father motionless, hands behind his back, Stewart Grainger.
Me on the top step.
My head in my hands.
(Cold bright light.)
My mother's face. Cold.
(I need a new life, Peter.)
(Away from him.)
(He will be fine. You'll find someone else. He will adjust.)
(Cold bright light.)
My brother pleading. My father motionless, a rabbit in headlights.
(She never looked at you, Johnny.)
Waterfall.
Her hair shone like Mercury exploding.
(You'll all adjust.)
(I'll write.)
(Cold white light, crystals forming, cutting me, cutting me.)
(Bye, Peter.)
(Bye, Anthony.)
My brother's screams. The chauffeur, the peaked cap and sunglasses, the black suit.
The sound of her heels tapping like a drumstick on the marble.
(Cold white light, crystals forming, drawing blood, revealing.)
And then...
...she was gone.

Head throbbing. Trapped in a vice. Nauseous and sick, blacking out.

The laughing of goaty men.

The sound of Carla's sobbing.

"Oh, stop bleating you fucking little bitch," Benedict said. "You're crying over a fucking nutter. Ain't that right, Mr. Nelson."

He started to pour the champagne into a variety of mugs, and cups, and glasses.

No class. No gentleman.

"He certainly is, Mr. Benedict," Nelson said, oily, grinning at me.

Carla looked confused and hurt. She didn't know what to think, and I lowered my gaze, watched something wonderful die before me.

She whimpered and sobbed for something.

Carla, I love you.

Then, Benedict made a mistake.

A big mistake.

When Carla wouldn't stop crying, wouldn't stop sobbing, he walked over to her, drunk and maddened.

"You fucking little tart. I'll bet you've been fucking for England. I'll bet if it moves, you've fucked it. Coons. Them at college. Old men. You slag...don't cry for a nutter like *him.*"

"He's a gentleman...I don't care what he's done. he's like...like..."

He stood over her, but Carla was made of stronger stuff. She looked into his eyes defiantly.

"He's like you were when I was a kid, dad. He's like you were. . . before. . . before. . . ."

Benedict was blind drunk and couldn't see the implied compliment.

It fazed me,

I felt the sincerity of it, felt the pain behind it, felt every word of the sentence hit me like a brick because it was true. Benedict staggered, gulped his champagne and slapped her round the face, threw his mug against the wall.

"Well you shouldn't have fucked off, should you, little bitch."

"Touch her again, Benedict and I'll kill you and everyone in this room," I said coldly, feeling it rise within me, the thing, the exploding thing, the emptiness being replaced by something hot, my head burning.

He grabbed hold of Carla's hair.

"What, like this..." and backhanded her until she hit the floor, her head bouncing off the foot of a metal table.

I watched her fall. I saw her.

Her beautiful face.

Her beautiful face.

I saw Benedict, confused and angry, dumb and drunk.

Nelson looked stunned.

The six labourers looked at each other and mentally shrugged their shoulders.

I watched her fall and heard her head strike the metal.

(bastard)

I saw her.

(bastard)

Her beautiful face.

(cold white light, filling, filling, yes, yes, yes, cold, cold and bright)

(cold white light emptying)

(there is nothing)

(dissipation)

(void)

(nothing)

And time stood still

and then…

… a ping

a whoosh in my head

something snapped

Carla...

My love.

Cold white light.

I twisted both my arms suddenly.

The rope ties were loose and inadequate, and I flexed. Out.

Den, transfixed by Benedict's brutality, didn't notice. I jumped up, headbutted him on his cheek, and he fell back. Turned to Nutty and jabbed him in an eye.

Too hard - his eye popped, and he started to scream. He grabbed at his face, blood pouring between two fingers.

Pulled his hand away. Kicked him hard. The impact of the kick snapped his neck, and he sagged like a sack to the floor.

One down.

Raging, Den came at me. I nutted him instantly on his nose, breaking it. While he was still stunned, I picked up the chair and smashed the seat pan onto his head three times in arc-like savage swoops. The impact was severe. I heard the front of his skull crack like the sound of a saucer snapping. He went limp.

Two little piggies.

The two labourers who arrived with Benedict were drunk and slow, but they came at me. I pushed one of them away. Crouched down by the fireplace and picked up the black metal poker. With both hands, I stabbed one in the eye, sending him crying to the floor. Then I swung the poker from over my head like an axe, and cracked his skull like I did with his goat herd pal a second ago. His forehead dented, and the sound echoed.

Three down.

The other didn't expect this carnage, didn't expect what he was seeing and momentarily, he stood confused. Taking advantage of his sloth, I butted him with the heel of the poker, grabbed him by the hair and leaned into his back, tripped him, forcing his head into the roaring fire. Despite his best efforts to escape, I was too strong for him: I put my shoulder in his back and forced him down, watched his skin melt.

His screams could be heard on the road as the flames scorched him.

Four of spades.

Carla's guards ran over. Picking up the poker once more, I stabbed one hard in the belly with such force that it burst, and the end of the poker emerged from the other side.

Five Easy Pieces.

I threw away my makeshift weapon, and it fell to the floor with a clatter. I grabbed the head of the final stunned Meathead as if I was mounting a trophy on the mantelpiece. With both my thumbs, I forced both his eyes back into his head, and they disappeared into the emptiness of his skull with a satisfying plop.

He fell to his knees, started to scream and beg, but I was in no mood for mercy. Spotting an antique letter opener on the desk, I walked over, picked it up, grinned, came back and stabbed him in the left side of the neck, his arterial blood spraying like a burst pipe all over drunken Benedict.

Six men down.

Fifty five seconds.

A new Olympic record.

Hubba. Hubba. Hubba.

Nelson ran to the door and opened it, but like a cat, I pounced.

Turned him round.

Looked into his eyes.

Saw his fear. Saw his sickness.

I knew him.

I knew what he was, and what he had done.

A coward's eyes.

A paedophile's eyes.

Eyes now full of fear.

I bit into his face like a lion.

A big lion.

Tore his nose off. Watched the blood drip onto the carpet.

Heard his screams.

Face.

A hole in it the size of a tennis ball. Brains oozing from the crevice.

He fell to the floor.

To make sure of Nelson's certain death, I stamped on him three times, and crushed his skull like cardboard boxes in a skip. He expired with scarcely a breath.

Seven.

Seven Dead Samurai.

Just over a minute.

T9C.

This left Benedict.

Carla's dad.

I picked up the poker and walked over to him.

Benedict, stunned and disbelieving at the carnage he saw in the room, stared.

I stood in front of him.

Over him.

"I've got a particular form of madness, Benedict. You should have left me. I'd have treated your daughter like a saint. I never laid a finger on her. I never touched her, you silly, silly man. It was all in your head. Reuben never touched her either, silly man. She's special, Carla. You need to be a special man to understand her. And she loved you, too, silly, silly man."

He stared at me, eyes full of fear. I saw him begin to tremble as he realised what he'd done.

"I'm no danger to her, Benedict. I'm no danger to women at all. You should have checked a bit further." I pointed to Nelson, bleeding on the floor and very deceased. "You took his word. He knew nothing. He's a psychopath, Benedict. He's worse than that. You're just a pisshead, silly, silly man. You took the word of someone like him against a man who worshipped your beloved daughter. I loved her so much, I couldn't even begin to think about touching her, you silly, silly man. You never asked, did you? All this could have been avoided. All this. And now, you've ruined it. Silly man. You've destroyed your life. You've destroyed mine. Let's hope that Carla forgets all this.'

"Are you going to kill me?" He asked, perfect English.

"I ought to, but no. You're my love's father and blood, sadly, is thicker than water. You ought to die. This was all your fault," I said, making a sweeping gesture.

He went back to being dumb.

"I'm no danger to women, Benedict. That's not my madness. When I meet women, I'm a danger to myself. You never bothered to check, did you? You imagined the worst of me."

He said nothing.

"I'm a danger to men. I'll give you that. I hate men, Benedict. As you can see."

Still nothing.

"Big danger to men like you. That's my madness, Benedict. They call it Displacement. I'll let you work it out, silly man."

He stared at me dumbstruck.

"I love Carla."

Nothing. His nose was running, and his eyes were red and rimmed, like lava pools.

He was going to cry.

"I would have looked after her. I would have cared for her. I would have encouraged her to make friends with you. I'd started down that road. Despite the fact you're a bully, Benedict, and a drunk."

He nodded, slightly.

Carla, behind him, was out cold. I was glad she didn't witness any of the horror I inflicted, and I was glad that her dad did. Hopefully, he would never forget it.

I was close enough to smell the booze on his breath, the wine, the champagne.

"Here's what we're going to do to correct this tragic business. We're going to get mum. Then we're going to put Carla to bed. I'm sure she's got her own room. Then I'm going to help you bury these bodies, Benedict. Somewhere on the estate. There's just you, me and Carla left. We'll use your JCB, the one behind the barn. How you explain where your staff have gone is up to you. If you grass me, I'll kill you. I'm going away, Benedict. Neither you nor Carla will ever see me again, sir."

Still the blank stare.

"I found love, sir. For the first time in my life, I found love. I'd relish the chance to be with your daughter, but you ruined that, Benedict. You win the game between us. Daddy Knows Best."

He was listening, but he said nothing. Nothing at all.

"I'm going to have a look at Carla now."

I bent down. She was unconscious but breathing. I felt her head - a swelling the size of an egg was beginning to grow, but there was no bleeding and no contusions. She would be fine.

I picked her up and laid her on the sofa.

Benedict was in shock, so I found an airing cupboard outside full of blankets and took two, placed them on Carla's unconscious body. She looked peaceful in her unconsciousness, and I made sure a cushion supported her neck.

"Now let's move, Benedict," I said, tugging at him. "You can drive the tractor. Where's the most secluded part of the farm?"

He pointed out of the window. "Near brook. No one visits…."

"Help me with these bodies."

"You killed them all..." he said.

"Yes, I did, didn't I."

Benedict started to cry. "They were me friends. Me only friends."

"You don't need friends in today's day and age," I said. "Now let's move."

It took us the rest of the evening to carry out the corpses and bury them.

They were hefty men, burly and built to last, and we struggled bigtime. Some of them were more fat than muscle, but they were all fifteen stone plus, and it took us an age to get them onto the tractor trolley. It took us a long time to dig the hole, partly because Benedict was sobbing most of the way through, but in the end, it was done.

"I'll let you say a few words, Benedict," I said unnecessarily as we both stood over the burial site. "After all, they were your friends."

Benedict had locked Carla's mother in a store cupboard, and when he released her, she slapped him, apopleptic with rage.

Some choice words followed, along with a divorce request. She said she would clean him out. He cried, got to his knees, and begged forgiveness.

I don't think I've ever seen anyone cry as much as Benedict did that night. Not in the outside world.

A maudlin drunk.

I told Carla's mum what had happened, and she gave me a look of abject fear when she saw all the blood on the carpet.

She forgot that and ran to Carla, checked her.

I looked at the scene like an out-of-body experience. I had no emotions left. They were all gone. All my life I had struggled with emotions, those horrible beasts inside me imploring me to disaster after disaster, but I had none left, I was empty of them, but at peace nonetheless.

I should have started killing bad people a lot earlier.

I should have been like The Punisher or something, if this was how it made a man feel, all that death.

First, I found love.

Now I had found peace.

I could end up at the place I was going content.

"I'm going now, mum," I said.

"You're a murderer!" She shouted, pointing her finger. "I'm calling the Police."

"Do that and I'll kill you and your husband. Sorry about that."

"But why? He was only going to frighten you..."

So mum was in on it, huh. She was part of it. I didn't expect that.

Boy, did I misjudge that situation. Fat lot of good my first in Physics did here…

"It got out of hand, mum," I replied,

"I'm Mrs. Benedict to you. And you were too old for our Carla," she said.

"I know, Mrs. Benedict. I know. I'm going now. Give Carla my love. Tell her to keep an eye on her PC. I'll send mail."

"The hell I will," she said, fire and rage in her rustic eyes. She must have been fine-looking, but the outdoor life, her bitterness and the rage within her had aged her, and her eyes were pinched and her wrinkles deep. It couldn't have been easy living with Benedict.

"I'll see you dead. I hope you DIE," she shouted.

"We all die, Mrs. Benedict. It's just a question of when and how. Look after her for me."

I walked over to my Carla.

Sleeping.

I looked at her one last time.

I felt emotion for the second last time in my life.

I kissed her on her cheek, her petal soft cheeks.

Bye, Carla, I said.

And I was gone, past the sobbing, broken body of Mr. Benedict lying on the carpet outside.

Of course, I knew they'd tell the cops about me. There was no way they could explain the disappearance of their six workers. I should have killed Benedict and his wife, escaped with Carla, leaving an unexplained mystery behind and a manhunt, which would never have succeeded. But this way, she gets to live her life, a normal life.

They would wait until late morning to concoct a plausible story and to call the Police, and I had about twelve hours to get out of England. I had to hurry. In other countries, I would be executed for what I had done, history of mental illness notwithstanding.

I knew there would be no Cedar Forest for me this time.

More like Rampton. Maybe Broadmoor.

I was a multiple murderer now, and no amount of father's money could compensate for that. My life in England was over, and I had to get out.

The keys were already in the van's ignition, and I sat down in the driver's seat. The van reeked of cigarettes and labourer's feet, but it was full of petrol and it allowed me to get to Wheatley Fields. I dumped it about a mile away from my flat, and I walked the rest of the way.

When I arrived home, I did certain things. It was 3am, so I didn't think there'd be a stakeout from Plunkett. I e-mailed my father and asked him to put ten grand in my account as I was going abroad on holiday. It was a long shot but worth a try. I had my four grand but fourteen is a lot better. I picked up my passport, wallet, cards and medication - can't be too careful - and packed my clothes into a travel bag. Left my parka behind and decided on my quilted Barbour. Where I was going was always warm, but you never know. Secreted my iPod and Blackberry in the zip pocket. I left everything else behind - even my Airfix knife - and locked the door; put the key in Heather's letterbox. I had already called a cab from Charlestown and told the operator I wanted to go to the City.

When the cab arrived, I asked him how much to Manchester Airport, and he ummed and ahhed, didn't want to play, but I offered him £250 and a drink, and he changed his mind, money being tight in all industries. I purchased a standby to Madrid. Sat in my window seat, listened to my iPod and watched the morning sky, all the time thinking of Carla as I will always do, for the rest of my life, however long that might be.

Epilogue: Four months later

Dear J,

It's been four months, and I don't know what's happened to you. I hope this e-mail finds you happy and contented and most of all, safe.

I miss you each day. I hope you don't mind me telling you that.

You had an impact on my life, and changed the way I looked at the world. I've never met anyone as intelligent as you or as caring.

You are such a gentleman.

Amazonas. Brazil.

The cliffs are white, almost pure white. Bushes sprout asymmetrically, red leaf bushes, green leaf bushes. I can see the water below, a thousand feet below me, passing through the ravine heading toward the Amazon itself. A million birds sing.

A million insects buzz around my head.

All life is here.

In the distance, a canopy of black and green trees stretches into the distance.

I am the only one on this cliff top today.

College is going well. I passed all my mock exams! The things I learned from you came in useful, and I was able to add depth and colour to my answers. Listening to you talk was much better than learning it from a book! I think I'm going to be okay.

I sit down and dangle my feet below me. I look down and feel a brief burst of nausea when I contemplate the vast drop. I have a parachute with me, but it isn't on yet, and it nestles next to me, and next to the manuscript I typed in the hotel in Caracas over two months. It is the best I can do, but I know it is an unedited mess, and I have been carrying it with me for the past month, unsure as to what to do with it.

Should I send it to Carla?

Should I send it to an agent?

On the other hand, should I just throw it over the ledge? After all, she never contacted me all that time I was searching for my mother.

What would she need it for?

I'm working at the pub, but not for much longer. I'm going on a secondment with the Woodlander Trust for a year, and I'm moving to Grantwood. Four of us are going, and we're going to be carrying out loads and loads of woodland restorations. You told me how big the Boreal forest used to be. Now I'll get the chance to help regenerate it. Even a tiny part of it. Christina asks about whether I've heard from you. I said no. I think she fancied you a bit, you know! But she's married, so you could never indulge, luckily for me.

Up above me, a Condor circles in the bright sunshine. I can hear its wooden, earthy squawk. Only a single cloud in the sky, and I've never seen a sky so astonishingly wonderful, like an upside ocean at peace. Cobalt blue, a distant sun hovering. I am covered in perspiration and my yellow vest sticks to me, and my hair is matted.

Someone will find it eventually. They will know what to do with it. I don't. I take the envelope out of the bag, remove the manuscript and look at it. Fingerprints and one of the opening pages are stained with booze from an editing session in Lima. Tequila. It smells now.

I never did find my mother.

After a while, I couldn't be bothered to look. Oilmen. All of them seemed to be called Carlos. I e-mailed my brother for the address, but I never received a reply.

Goodbye, mother.

My father is on remand. He blamed himself and said you acted in self defence. You could come home. He showed the Police the burial site. Mum tried to blame you, but the Police called that an expedient. Like moratorium! LOL. I never said anything when they spoke to me.

I no longer speak to mum. I didn't know she was part of it all.

Families are a pain, aren't they, Johnny?

To be honest, I don't miss them. I miss my father the way he used to be, but that man died, I don't know when.

I don't miss them the way I miss you, and I wish you were over here to guide me and teach me things the way you used to.

You're not mentally ill. I know that. I know that my dad was trying to stitch you up! I asked him later what he meant, and he didn't say anything. He doesn't speak much now anyway, but I know he was just making that up to hurt you and to hurt me.

You were brave and strong. With Angus and those horrible men.

You saved my life, and I'll be forever grateful.

The Condor perches on a bush about twenty feet below me. If he notices me, my presence doesn't bother him. He's imperious and a master of the entire valley. I've never seen a more magnificent bird. As I watch, I remember the Sparrowhawk on the trail. The memory is majestic, its impact is cushioned because Carla isn't with me. In that sense, the memory of Sparrowhawk, irrespective of the Condor's magisterial, regal beauty, becomes a pale copy.

Do you remember my friend, Dino? Well he and I are together now. We've been together since June. I know you won't mind me telling you that. You won't get jealous or anything. You don't hate me for telling you that, do you? I know you could never hate me, Johnny. You know how I felt about you and Dino is a different man altogether. He's a gentleman like you. He looks after me. He liked you. We all did, Johnny.

You were special. You were so important to me. I'm sorry our friendship/relationship ended the way it ended, but as you taught me, Kismet has many paths and there is nothing anyone can do about the one mapped out. Anyway, Dino is coming to Grantwood with me. I know you'll wish me the best wherever you are. I hope you've met someone and found love like the one I have. I couldn't have experienced this without you. You gave me confidence, and maturity, and you took away my fear.

Thank you, Johnny.

For the second last time, I think of Carla.

She brought me peace, and she brought me love, but it was never going to last. I could feel it beginning to crumble the minute I left for Madrid. My edifice. Like a vampire, I needed her to survive, and the moment I started killing was the moment I could never see her. Too late now. I'm a murderer and a killer. I can never go home.

And she's gone.

If you get this, Johnny, I hope you are happy, and I just want you to know that I love you, and will always love you in a special way, and I will always treasure the time we spent together. Do you remember the walk in the flower garden? Dino and I take a walk there, and I think of you and that wonderful March morning.

However, don't tell him, will you! Please write to me. I can't bear the idea of never seeing you again. But if you don't, know always that I'm thinking of you, and I'm sending a flower of love into the ether for you to pick up wherever you are.

Goodbye, Johnny.

Love,

Cxx

I stand on the edge of the cliff. I pick up the parachute. With resignation, I throw the bag into the air and watch it fall for an age, spiralling, swirling, hitting the cliffs, bouncing off, bouncing on, landing in the water, a pinprick of dazzling white foam. I pick up the manuscript one more time. I kiss it. I think of Carla for the last time. My stomach rumbles and my mouth goes dry. I place the manuscript back in the bag and leave it under a protruding bush replete with giant, ornate and crystalline purple leaves. Someone will find it. Someone will know what to do with it.

Carla.

Green vest.

Chestnut pools.

Her voice.

Little.

Fluffy.

Clouds.

Outstretched, my arms guide me into the cobalt void.

He is not a lover who does not love forever…
(Euripides)

About the Author

Mark Barry, author of *Hollywood Shakedown,* the highly acclaimed *Carla* and the top selling *Ultra-Violence,* is a writer and publisher based in Nottingham and Southwell. He writes extensively on a variety of topics including, horseracing, football, personality disorders and human relationships, but most recently, he writes about life in Nottingham and monitors closely its ever changing face.

Mark has been interviewed on several Radio chat shows where he has given readings of his work. His writing has been featured in the national press, and he has also been interviewed on television.

Mark resides in Southwell, Nottinghamshire and has one son, Matthew.

Printed in Great Britain
by Amazon.co.uk, Ltd.,
Marston Gate.